HUSKER ROAD

A Jake Caldwell Thriller

D0879722

JAMES L. WEAVER

WOLFPACK
PUBLISHING
— EST 2013 —

WOLFPACK
PUBLISHING
— EST 2013 —

Wolfpack Publishing
5130 S. Fort Apache Road, 215-380
Las Vegas, NV 89148

Paperback ISBN: 978-1-64734-099-5
Ebook ISBN: 978-1-64734-065-0

HUSKER ROAD

DEDICATION

To all the fine people in Kearney, Nebraska. I
love the time I've spent there over the years and I
appreciate you letting me borrow your home for the
setting of this book. I hope I did the setting justice.
Please forgive me for any errors on businesses,
streets and any other local information. Maybe we
can share a beer next time I'm in town.

CHAPTER ONE

The cold pistol barrel pressed against the back of Jake Caldwell's muscular neck. The force shoved Jake against the side of the home where Franco Lunetti hid, the pale stucco digging into the leather palms of his gloves. As a former leg breaker for the Kansas City mob, Jake was used to getting the jump on people instead of being on the receiving end. Now as a private investigator, he made far less money, didn't have the clout that came with working for the mob, and dealt with assholes jamming guns into his neck. He had to admit it sucked. The frigid cold and quarter-sized snowflakes pelting the window and Jake's face didn't help. Jake raised his hands, his thick arm upper arms parallel to the ground.

Light from a nearby street lamp cast a shadow of the person behind Jake onto the wood slats of the wrap-around porch. Jake didn't know who got the drop on him, just that it wasn't Franco. Through the window, Lunetti's eyes remained locked on the television screen as he lounged on the couch, already three deep into a six pack and a bowl of mini pretzels.

"Who the fuck are you?" the smoky, husky voice asked. The hammer of a pistol clicked back. "Better start talkin', big guy."

Where did this guy come from? Jake's thoughts flashed to his new bride and her swelling belly. He cursed himself for being careless as the bitter January gusts kicked up from the south.

An hour ago, Jake had spotted Franco Lunetti with three crew members in tow outside a liquor store and only one of them was sizable enough to raise Jake's eyebrows. Given the position of shadow, the way the gun pressed upward into his neck and the fact he called Jake "big guy" led Jake to the conclusion this wasn't the sizable man. Whoever he was, he was the low man on the totem pole for drawing guard duty in this Siberian weather.

"I'm a private investigator. I need to talk to Franco," Jake said, his elbow ready to lash back and decimate whomever was behind the gun trained on him. His thoughts swirled with thoughts of his wife and the promise he'd made—avoid risks.

"Franco who?"

Jake cranked his head a few degrees toward the gunman. "Come on, man. I'm looking at him through the window. I'm not an idiot."

The gun pressed harder. "You are if you think that's Franco Lunetti. You got the wrong house."

Jake sighed. "If I have the wrong house, how do you know his last name?"

"Shit." The gun pressure lessened a bit. "So cold out here my brain ain't workin' right."

His admission settled things. This guy was of sufficiently low rank to be stuck on guard duty on one of the coldest nights ever recorded in Kansas

City's history which was good for Jake. The lowest of the rank and file proved susceptible to a better deal. And if that didn't work, he still had his cocked elbow insurance policy. Cold people moved slow. Jake was bundled up and warm. Still, a few ounces of trigger pressure would end Jake's night pretty quick no matter how fast he moved.

"I bet your brain's working better than Franco's," Jake said.

"Huh?"

"Your boss skipped bail with a warrant out for his arrest, and he decides to hide out at his girlfriend's home, in plain sight through the front bay window?"

"How'd you find him?"

This was the third clue Jake wasn't dealing with a criminal mastermind. "This is the address he put on his bail application. Bet you told him it was stupid to hide out here, didn't you?"

The gun pressure let up a bit more. "No, but I thought it."

"That's because you have more than two brain cells to rub together. But there he is lounging around in a heated living room while you're out here. How long you been freezin' your nuts off?"

"Like three hours."

Jake cranked his chin over his shoulder, moving slow. "Wait. Three goddamn hours while he's snuggled up warm and cozy pounding beers and watching football? That's jacked up, man. He even give you a thermos of coffee?"

Jake could almost hear the man chewing his thoughts, pouring over the thankless shit Franco made him do. Jake knew from experience that loyalty among the lower ranks was exponentially related to the misery of the conditions you put them through. The colder, wetter, or smellier the condition, the more likely the organizational peon would bail to a better offer. When Jake ran one of Keats's crews, he made sure he took his turn doing the grunt work. Guys respected that. They know you're still in charge, but you don't consider yourself better than them. Get dirty, earn trust.

Jake snuck a peek back to Franco, the thug's hooded eyes drooping on the couch. He cranked his head back to the low man. Two beady eyes peered through a facemask and hood. "What happens to your rank in the crew if Franco goes away?"

"Fuck you. I ain't no rat."

"I'm not talking about snitching. I'm askin' what happens to you. Do you move up or go down?"

"I don't know."

Jake blew out a breath. "You ever watch Star Trek? The original series?"

"You mean with like Yoda?"

Jesus, this guy is galactically stupid.

"Like Captain Kirk and Mr. Spock."

The eyes narrowed. "How old do you think I am? I ain't seen Star Trek."

Jake kept talking. As long as the conversation continued, the man wasn't going to pull the trigger.

"Sorry, it's hard to tell with all the layers. There's this episode called *Mirror Mirror* where the crew goes to this alternate universe and there's evil clones of the Enterprise crew. These clones move up the ranks by assassinating the ones above them."

The gun pressed hard again. "If you expect me to kill Lunetti—"

"Dude, he doesn't have to die. All you have to do is

step aside and let me take Franco back to jail. There's enough on him already that he won't get out again for a long, long time. Now, what happens to you when I do that?"

The man was silent for a beat. "I move up."

"So, here's what we do. You call Franco out to the porch and I take him down. I collect my fee, he goes back to prison, you move up the chain and out of this cold, and nobody has to know."

The guy let the concept churn for a couple of breaths. "Franco would know."

Jake had the guy like a fish on the line. Time to give the man the option that Jake wanted him to take before he had too long to think about it. "Only if it's not believable. You give me your gun. I act like I'm holding you hostage. Franco will see and you'll be off the hook. Then you can go warm up by the fire. Win-win. Deal?"

The man's beady eyes probed Jake's face. "So, are you like a bounty hunter, like Dog on TV?"

"Something along those lines."

"I always thought I'd be good at that."

Jake gave an exaggerated nod. "You would. You got the drop on me and that's no small feat. Where the hell did you come from anyway?"

"Window well. Down out of the wind, I could still see everything."

That explained it. *Still sloppy, Caldwell.* "Pretty smart. Tell you what, after I take Franco in, we'll grab a beer and talk about it. I have more cases than I know what to do with and could use a partner."

The hammer on the gun clicked closed, and the pressure on Jake's neck disappeared. "No shit? Cool."

Jake turned. At six foot three and two hundred

thirty pounds, Jake towered over the little man. The man tucked the gun into his waistband and pulled down the face mask, revealing a mouthful of jagged, stained teeth.

"Who's with Franco?" Jake asked, ticking his head to the house.

"Just him and his girl. The rest of the crew went across town to grab Franco some Q39 barbecue. They ain't gonna be back for a while."

God, his teeth were messed up. "What's your name?"

"Dale. Friends call me Hound Dog."

"Why?"

Dale shrugged. "Franco said it was cuz I ain't never caught a rabbit, whatever that means."

"Did he also say you ain't no friend of mine?"

"Whoa, how'd you know?"

Jake sighed. "It's an Elvis Presley song."

"Oh. Ain't heard it, but I'm more of a rap guy."

Of course you are.

"Outstanding, partner." Jake reached his right hand forward in a handshake offering. He'd promised Maggie to use his brain more than his brawn but couldn't shake the feeling of a gun crammed against his neck. Vulnerability pissed him off. Dale gripped Jake's right hand to seal the deal and Jake unleashed an anvil with his left fist to Dale's bony chin knocking him out cold. He sagged and Jake eased him to the snow-dusted deck. Jake pulled the .38 Special from Dale's waistband, dumped the rounds into his hands, and threw them into the front yard. He tossed the gun into the bushes.

Pulling his stainless-steel Sig Sauer from his waist holster, Jake snuck across the porch and tried the doorknob. Locked. That would have been too easy. He peered through the window again. Franco's head tilted back, his mouth open, the pretzel bowl rising and falling on his chest. No sign of baby mama.

Jake dropped back a step then threw his full weight into the cheap front door. It splintered at the top where his brawny shoulder smacked it but held at the deadbolt. Through the crack, he saw Franco jerk from the couch, pretzels spilling to the floor. Jake reached around the opening to turn the deadbolt but couldn't reach it. Franco's hands darted around the couch, probing. Jake reared back and kicked above the door handle and the lock assembly collapsed. He swept into the living room, bringing up the barrel of his Sig Sauer as Franco pointed a black object in Jake's direction. Jake's finger tightened on the trigger, a half-ounce from plugging Franco before realizing what Lunetti held in his hand. The TV remote.

In another room a baby wailed. Lunetti's chest heaved, eyes flicking to the coffee table.

"What are you gonna do, Lunetti? Mute me?"

Lunetti threw the remote at Jake and twisted toward the coffee table, a Glock resting on top of a pile of magazines. As Lunetti's hand touched the butt of the Glock, Jake lunged and cracked him on the side of the head with the Sig. The Glock flew across the room. Lunetti crashed to the floor and rolled to his back, probing his head and drawing spots of blood.

"You're dead," Lunetti hissed. "Whoever you are."

"That's smart. Threaten a stranger. I could be a cop for all you know. That's a felony and another four years in the State of Missouri."

"You ain't no cop. You're a piece of sh—"

"Yeah, yeah. Roll over and spread your hands and

legs nice and wide."

Lunetti propped himself on his elbows. "I got a better idea. You let me up and put away the gun and we fight like men."

Jake pulled handcuffs from his pocket. "Don't threaten me with a good time, Franco. Roll over before I plant my boot up your ass."

Jake felt movement to his left. He kept the Sig trained on Lunetti but turned his head, ready to move. The baby mama stood in front of an open door, thin blue robe over flannel pajamas and an Alter Bridge t-shirt. In one hand she held a whimpering baby sucking on a pacifier plastered to her hip and in the other Lunetti's Glock 19, barrel pointed to the hardwoods. She was young, late teens, pretty in a trashy kind of way with caked-on makeup that failed to hide the dark bags under her tired eyes. She seemed unsurprised at the situation in her living room. Jake wasn't worried about her using the gun. If left alone, she would probably fall asleep standing up like a horse.

Lunetti grinned. "Deidre, shoot this asshole."

The baby threw the pacifier in Jake's direction and wailed again.

"Who're you and waddya want?" Deidre asked, treating Jake like a Jehovah's witness who knocked on her door and woke her up from a nap.

Jake picked up the pacifier, holding it out to Deidre. Lunetti scrambled halfway up and Jake knocked him back to the floor with his boot. "I'm here to help your boyfriend find his way back to jail."

She cast a disgusted squint to Lunetti, like he was a pile of dog shit she found in the middle of her living room.

The grin fell from Lunetti's face. "Did you hear what

I said, you dumb bitch? Shoot this motherfucker."

Deidre dropped the Glock in the pocket of her robe and took the pacifier, silencing the infant. "Told you it was stupid to stay here, Franco. Have fun in prison."

Jake handcuffed a stunned Lunetti who hurled expletives at the woman. Jake hauled him from the floor toward the broken front door, the icy wind blowing in powder.

He shoved Lunetti in the back seat of his truck, secured his cuffs, and slammed the door shut. When he turned, a groggy Dale staggered toward him down the walkway.

Dale spread his hands out for balance, eyes unfocused, legs wobbly. "What the hell, man? Thought we were gonna be partners."

Jake took two steps forward. "We are, but I had to make it good for Lunetti. Otherwise he'd kill you."

Dale peered over Jake's shoulder. "He's lookin' right at me. Fuck me, I'm dead."

"Hit me."

"What?"

Jake cocked his fist. "Try and hit me. Then he knows you tried to stop me. I'll call you later to set up something."

Dale squared up and his face crunched. "But you ain't got my number."

"Don't worry, I'll find you. Now quit screwing around and hit me before he gets suspicious."

Dale threw a lazy roundhouse. Jake blocked it easily and clocked Dale on the chin again. Dale thumped back onto the snow-covered sidewalk, arms spread wide like he was about to make a snow angel.

He raised his bloody head, "What the...thought I was gonna hit you."

"I said try and hit me. No way Lunetti would believe you took me out. I'll call you later."

Dale's head dropped to the sidewalk, his eyes slamming shut. Jake turned and strutted back to the truck.

Deidre called out over Jake's shoulder, "Hey, whose gonna fix my goddamn door?"

Jake pointed to the unconscious body on the lawn. "Ask Hound Dog here. Think he's gonna need a new job."

Jake grinned as he hopped in the driver's seat. Maggie would be proud. He took down his bad guy with no shots fired and only three punches thrown. He just wouldn't tell Maggie about the last one.

CHAPTER TWO

Juan Hidalgo wondered what would kill him first. The bullwhip shredding his back, the shotgun at his face, or the frigid wind howling unabated across the snow-kissed Nebraska field. Powder from the previous night's blizzard danced and swirled in the headlights of the ring of trucks surrounding his broken body, the halogen lamps blasting back the darkness.

Nobody ever warned Juan about the Nebraska wind when he left California. He knew the terrain would be flat. He knew the summer would bake the earth until it cracked, and the winter would turn his marrow to ice. But nobody said a word about the punishing wind slicing through him like a knife as he knelt on bared knees with sheared cornstalk stubs biting his skin. Nothing about the sleet whipping down from the light starved evening sky, abrading his face like sandpaper. And certainly nothing about the prospect of being tortured and murdered by the locals.

He screamed as the bullwhip cracked against his skin again, the tattered remnants of his flannel shirt flapping against the angry crimson tracks carved across his back. With a wind chill of twenty below, he would freeze to death soon if the men forming the half-circle around Juan didn't finish him first. Especially not Darius Frost who leveled a twelve-gauge shotgun at Juan's bloodied face.

"Last chance," Frost said, his breath a smoke screen backlit by the headlights of the trucks. "Where is it?"

Juan spat a bloodied wad to the frozen cornfield, tears freezing in his eyes. "I don't have it."

Despair tugged at his limbs, regret stabbing him like a knife at the things he wouldn't see or touch again. The beautiful face of his Maria, the way her limbs wrapped around his like they were one. His mother and father who begged him to stay in California and work the family-owned hardware store with his father. Learn the business and work his way up the chain. But Juan knew he'd never get rich on a quarter of a cent margin on washers and penny nails.

Frost thumped Juan on the head with the shotgun barrel. "Try again. Where is it?"

Juan's voice cracked. "Jesus, I don't know. Please stop."

Frost stepped back and turned to one of his men. "Hit him again."

Juan flinched, waiting for the whip to strike. Instead, a voice behind him sounded. Maybe Stumpy? It was hard to tell as the world swam in and out of focus. "Darius, man. What're we doin'? He can't take much more."

"Fuck him. We've been scouring the Earth for his scrawny ass for two weeks, and you wanna take it easy? Hit him again."

"Maybe he really doesn't know."

Another voice creaked to his right. Parker. "He knows. Bet your ass he knows."

Stumpy stammered. "M-m-man, I don't know if I can—"

Frost's voice boomed. "Hit him again or you can join him. Christ."

The lash came, the leather biting into Juan's raw flesh. Then another. And another. Waves of pain blurred his vision, black dots dancing as he prayed for it to end.

As his vision cleared, Frost squatted and pulled the face mask below his chin, letting the wind rustle through his thick cinnamon beard. "I get it, man. You saw an opportunity to score big, but you fucked up. Just remember, I gave you a chance. Showed you how our system worked and even let you get your hands dirty."

Juan longed to prove his parents wrong. They had smuggled themselves to the United States from Honduras and made something of themselves by scratching and clawing their way out of poverty. They wanted more for their children, for them to realize the glorious American dream. Juan wanted the dream, too; he just took a dangerous shortcut to get it—a path that led him to this blood-soaked cornfield.

Something smacked Juan's face. He pried his eyes open, focusing on Frost's gloved hand hovering for another strike. "You still with us, amigo?"

Juan stared at his frozen hands, the cold turning them as red as they were the night everything went wrong. "The blood won't wash away. No matter how hard I try."

"You get used to it. You don't even notice it after a

while. Last chance. Where is it?"

Juan's teeth rattled and his thin body trembled. The muzzle flashes from two weeks ago danced across his vision, along with images of the blood-stained snow and the vacant dead eyes. Thank God his father couldn't see him now. "It is not the man who has too little, but the man who craves more, that is poor."

Frost scowled. "What?"

"Something my father said that I never understood 'til now."

"The money, Juan?"

Juan raised his dark eyes, the resignation to his fate pulling him down into the snow. "What difference does it make? You're gonna kill me whether I tell you or not."

"Not if you tell me where it is. We'll let you go back to California."

Juan locked in on Frost's blue eyes—empty, the coldness matching the Nebraska wind chill. "No, you won't. But, it's a mistake. You don't know who you're dealing with."

"What the hell are you talkin' about?"

Juan blinked away the darkness crowding his vision. "My people will come looking for you."

Frost bared his oversized teeth. "You work for me, you little asshole. And yeah, I'm gonna kill you. It's up to you if I shoot you in the head and end it quick, or let you freeze to death nice and slow. Tell me where the money is and I'll make it easy on you."

Parker grabbed Frost's arm. "Hang on, man. Who is he talkin' about?"

Frost shook Parker's hand away. "Shut up. He's delirious. What's it gonna be, Juan? Fast or slow?"

Juan knew where the money was, but he wasn't

telling Frost. He also knew he couldn't take any more of this torture. Time to escalate things and hope Maria followed their plan. He knew the right buttons to push with Frost.

"Your *daddy* know what you're doing?" Juan asked.

Frost jammed the barrel of the shotgun against Juan's forehead. "He's got nothing to do with this."

Juan laughed. Somehow, staring death in the face as the bitter cold whipped through him and raked at his raw skin, he managed to laugh. "Seriously? You're nothing but his puppet. With the shit you've been up to, my people will skin you alive."

Boots crunched the snow to his right. Closer. "Frost, whatever you're thinking—"

Frost waved the shotgun barrel in front of Juan. "Last chance, man."

Juan spit from a mouthful of bloody, broken teeth. "You won't find the money. And when daddy finds out what you've been doing—"

Frost swung the butt of the shotgun, cracking Juan across the face. He wobbled and dumped to the ground, rolling to his back and groaning as the cornstalk stubs raked his open wounds. Frost pressed to his feet. Eyes wide, nostrils flared, rage seeping from his pores. He leveled the shotgun at Juan's face, his finger tightening on the trigger.

"Estás muerto y ni siquiera lo sabes," Juan said, chin raised to the night.

"What the hell does that mean?" Parker asked, his voice edged with tension.

Frost brought the barrel of the shotgun within kissing distance of Juan's head. "Like it matters."

Juan squeezed his swollen eyes closed, his tears battling the Nebraska wind as they snaked down his cheeks. There was always the wind. Then there was nothing.

CHAPTER THREE

Lunetti yanked at the cuffs binding his hands behind him. He was secured to an inch-thick steel ring Jake had installed in the back of his truck. Two months earlier, Jake forgot to engage the child locks and a bail jumper managed to get the door open and take off down the street of a sketchy neighborhood at two in the morning. Though he'd cuffed the man behind his back, he ran like a deer, and it took Jake a block and a half to catch him. Jake hated to jog, much less run and he took out his frustration by kicking the guy in the ass all the way back to his truck.

Lunetti abandoned any semblance of diplomacy and resorted to threats, insults and insinuations listing things Jake could do to himself. Some were physically impossible, though he gave Lunetti an "A" for creativity. Jake responded by veering around corners like he was an Indy car racer, sending Lunetti tumbling around the backseat.

"You're gonna break my fuckin' wrists," Lunetti spat.

"Shut up and I'll take the turns slower."

Lunetti pulled himself upright. "You should slow the hell down anyway in this weather."

"You worry about you and I'll worry about the roads."

"I am worried about my hands getting ripped off when you drive this piece-of-shit truck into a goddamn ditch."

Jake swung into an empty parking lot. He cranked the wheel, floored the truck and did donuts in the accumulated snow.

"Say you're sorry about my truck," he yelled over the roar of the engine.

Lunetti howled in the back, slamming face first into the seat. "I'm fuckin' sorry. Stop for Christ's sake."

Jake slammed the accelerator to the floor for one last donut and headed back out to the street, a smile creeping across his face. He hadn't done donuts in a parking lot since he was a teenager.

"Jesus," Lunetti panted, working himself to a seated position again. "You know, I was just gonna have some of my guys kick the shit outta you. But since you separated both my shoulders, it's gonna be worse."

"You think threatening me is going to make me drive any better?"

"You have no idea who you're messin' with, man."

Jake glanced over his shoulder. "You know how many people tell me that?"

Lunetti bared bloodied teeth. "I'm connected."

Jake rolled his eyes. "Ah, yes. The great Franco Lunetti, lackey for Teddy Garrett."

"I ain't no fuckin' lackey."

"Teddy *was* once a big deal in town but ain't much anymore. I heard he's bringing in anyone who can fog a mirror, which would explain how you got in. You've spent more time in jail in the last decade than you've spent breathing free air. You were busted for running drugs out of a bunch of storage units you supposedly own and probably stood a good chance of getting the book thrown at you when you went to court, given your record."

"Which is why I was tryin' to get outta town."

Jake cut his eyes to the rearview mirror. "I had no beef with you, Franco, until you tried to shoot me and insulted my truck. She's sensitive. You're nothing but an easy payday for me."

"I can pay you a hell of a lot more than the chump change you're gonna make off taking me to jail."

"That isn't how I roll."

"I can give you an interest in Enterprise Transition Management. A steady income stream."

Jake glanced in the rearview mirror. "Your storage unit company? I think your steady income stream is about to get seized by the Feds. No thanks. I'll have to be satisfied hauling your ass in."

A sneer curled Lunetti's lip. "Actions got consequences."

"Tell me something I don't know. Listening to you is giving me a headache." Jake turned on the radio and cranked up the volume.

Ten minutes later, Jake rolled into the Kansas City Police Department parking lot. He unhooked Lunetti from the backseat and hauled him inside, glad the snowfall had dissipated. The thought of driving home for an hour and a half to Warsaw in a blizzard was less than appealing.

A squat desk sergeant clad in powder blue peered over a pair of wire-rimmed glasses as Jake approached. "Evening, Jake. What'd you bring me?"

Jake shoved Lunetti against the counter. "Hey, Madsen. I offer you Franco Lunetti. Missed his court date a couple weeks ago. I need my check, a shower, and my bed in that order."

Madsen ticked his thinning red head, and a uniformed officer emerged through a secured door. He took custody of Lunetti and dragged him toward the inner sanctum of the building.

"How's the wife?"

Madsen returned to his paperwork. "She keeps watching those true crime dramas. Think she's plotting to kill me."

"Well, if I don't see you next time, I'll be sure to point the detectives in her direction. Have a good night."

Twenty minutes later, Jake had his check in hand and was out the door. The thought of snuggling Maggie's warm body sounded mighty appealing.

***

As the cop hauled Franco Lunetti toward central booking, a routine Lunetti was all too familiar with, he turned to the cop. "You just said goodbye to a dead man."

"Caldwell?" the cop laughed. "Ah, Lunetti. Caldwell isn't a guy to mess with. Judging by the look of your face, you already know that."

Jake Caldwell. Lunetti had heard of him. Used to work for Jason Keats and somehow managed to get out of the mob, a feat few ever accomplished. Something of an underground legend around Kansas City as an all-around badass. Still, he didn't work for

Keats anymore and wasn't untouchable. Lunetti had plans to touch him.

"I want my phone call," Lunetti said.

He knew who to call and it wasn't his attorney. Caldwell might be tough, but he wasn't bullet proof.

CHAPTER FOUR

Jake winced at the squeal of his brakes as he pulled to a stop in front of his house. Lunetti wasn't far off; the truck would turn into a piece of shit soon if he didn't make repairs. He needed a few more jobs to pay for them.

Jake slipped through the front door of his Warsaw home as the grandfather clock in the darkened living room bonged a single tone, still thinking about the interesting voicemail he'd listened to multiple times during the ride from Kansas City to Warsaw. But, he was too damn tired to think about the proposition now.

He peeled off his boots and set them by the door in the mudroom off the kitchen, then creeped along the hallway. With Maggie at the end of her second trimester and sleeping erratically, he didn't want to wake her. He hoped the rain pattering against the roof covered the sounds of his steps.

Cat-stepping along the hallway, he pushed Halle's door open, catching a glimpse of his teenage daughter's blonde head poking out from a mound of blankets. He ignored the clothes scattered on the floor, like a bomb went off in her closet. Her messiness was the one thing he wouldn't miss when she went off to college. Across the hall, his wife's soft snores slipped through the dark, and he eased both doors shut.

The plink of water from the next room caught his ear, and he stuck his head through the doorway to the soon-to-be nursery. The smell of fresh paint hung heavy in the darkness. Plink. Jake flipped the light switch and spotted the metal pail in the middle of the floor, an inch of water in the bottom. He groaned as he spotted the water-stained ceiling. His wallet tightened as dollars they didn't have to spend on a new roof tried to slip from the leather. Add it to the cost of the new brakes for his truck and a hot water heater on its last legs.

He set the check for Lunetti's bounty on the kitchen counter so Maggie would see it first thing in the morning and grabbed a beer from the refrigerator. Sleep pulled at his eyes, but he deserved a beer after listening to Franco bitch and moan the entire way back to the police station. He settled onto the couch and sunk deep into the worn cushions, turning on EPSN and muting the volume. But, Jake's attention was drawn to the pile of baby clothes stacked on the floor. His sister Janey must have dropped by.

A baby. Though he was a father already, Jake hadn't been around for the first sixteen years of his daughter's life. Hadn't even known Halle existed until he ventured back home on a mission from his ex-mafia boss to rub out a rival drug kingpin a couple of years ago. Halle was a fully formed spitfire when he arrived on scene and there was not a lot Jake could do over the last couple of years to mold, shape and guide her.

A baby was a whole other ballgame. Jake wasn't a man who scared easily, but the responsibilities of a baby terrified him. *What if I screw the kid up? What if I'm no better a father than Stony?* He batted the thought away. He could be in a coma and be a better dad than his own father was.

It was a surreal thing to think about, especially considering Halle was a senior in high school preparing to embark on college visits. Colleges who had them questioning how they would come up with the money. Student loans were a last resort. Jake had no credit history, he'd always preferred paying cash, and Maggie didn't believe in operating on credit to anyone. They had some money saved, but not enough. Jake drifted, the voicemail and the easy money it promised pulling him into a deep sleep.

***

A tap on the shoulder jolted him awake. The sun streaming through the front window backlit Maggie in an angelic glow. She bent over and kissed him, her sleep-mussed hair brushing his face.

"Hey, you. When did you get home?"

Jake kissed her again and yawned, stretching his muscular arms wide. "Around one. Didn't want to wake you."

"You should've. It was colder than Alaska in the bedroom, and I could've used your body heat. You get your guy?"

Jake slid off the couch and followed her into the kitchen, rolling the stiffness from his shoulders, and started a pot of coffee. "Wasn't hard. Idiot holed up with his girlfriend. Guess he thought nobody would look in such an obvious place. And, you'd be proud of me."

She tucked in her chin and peered at him. "How so?"

After Jake's encounters over the last couple of years taking down kingpins, terrorists, Russian spies and bikers, he and Maggie had a serious discussion about his sometimes-reckless mode of operation. With a baby on the way, she'd persuaded him that his bull-in-a-china shop approach would be better if replaced by a safer, more sophisticated and intellectual tactic.

Jake grabbed cups from the cabinet. "Had a guy come up on me with a gun and I totally could have taken him out with an elbow. Instead, I used my head."

Her eyes grew wide. "You butted him with your head?"

"No, I used my head and talked him into handing over his gun."

Maggie's eyebrows shot up. "Check you out. Nice work, babe. Then what?"

Jake's lips disappeared. "Ummm...I gave him a straight jab to the chin and knocked him out cold."

"Jake Caldwell!"

"Well, he jammed a gun in the back of my neck. The point you're missing is I used my head. Check's on the counter."

She patted him on the shoulder as she poured the coffee and picked up the check. "Baby steps. Another college fund deposit. Cha-ching."

The fund wasn't big enough. Business better pick up.

"The ceiling in the nursery is dripping water," she continued.

"I noticed last night."

"Unless we want the baby to undergo Chinese water torture, we need to get the roof fixed."

Jake groaned. "The roof, my truck, Halle's college..."

"We'll figure it out." She took a sip, scrutinizing him. Between her wages at Hospice House and him trying to get his private investigation business off the ground, they were fine. But college? "You have any other jobs coming up?"

"A couple of surveillance gigs. Not a huge payday. Maybe a more lucrative one brewing. Some guy left me a message last night."

Her eyebrows shot to the ceiling. "Some guy? Who?"

He didn't like to lie to her, but in this case he didn't have a choice. It would ruin her whole day for no reason since he wasn't going to take the job.

"Don't know who. They left a vague voicemail and a number. You working today?"

"At nine. I need to get in the shower. You and Bear set for the trip with the girls?"

Jake huffed. "Nebraska in January. Sounds awesome."

"And you'll get to do a nice, long campus tour. Maybe the cold will help Halle decide to stay closer to home. In state."

"Can't imagine it's any colder there than here."

"It'd be cheaper if she stayed in-state. Plus, I don't know if I can handle having her too far home. Especially with what's happened in the last year."

Halle already looked at the schools closer to home like Missouri and University of Central Missouri. Jake even hauled her out to Kansas and Kansas State, but one of her best friends went to the University of Nebraska last year and inundated Halle's social media feeds with pictures of football games and parties. The hook was set deep. She even enlisted Bear's daughter to agree to go on the tours.

"I don't know," Jake said. "Looks to me like she has her sights set on being a Husker. Bear said Landry wants to look at the University of Nebraska in Kearney, too. The soccer coach there is looking at her. I think we'll be gone an extra night."

Maggie's brow furrowed. "Where's Kearney?"

"Couple hours west of Lincoln. Decent sized town. Spent a couple of nights there a decade ago doing an errand for Keats."

She jabbed a finger at him. "Put ten bucks in the K-jar."

Jake grabbed his wallet. After all of Jake's run-ins over the last couple of years with his ex-boss, who happened to run the mafia in Kansas City, Maggie made Jake swear he wouldn't do any business with Keats. Any mention of his name was ten bucks in Halle's college fund jar which now boasted a little over a hundred dollars, enough to pay for a few dozen pages of one text book.

He dropped an Alexander Hamilton in the jar. "My bad."

She sauntered up to him. "You're not getting off that easy. Now you also have to come in the shower with me and wash my back."

He kissed her softly, her tongue electric as it slipped across his lip. "You're gonna be late for work."

Her hand slid down low and pressed. "What are they going to do, fire the pregnant nurse?" She grabbed him by the belt and pulled him down the hall toward the bedroom, an extra sway in her hips.

"If this is my punishment, I might drop his name more often."

"Don't push your luck, Caldwell."

Jake thought it would be an inopportune time to mention the source of the voicemail and the easy money job was, in fact, Keats. He'd have been showering alone for sure.

CHAPTER FIVE

Retired Detective Marc Conover of Los Angeles's Robbery and Homicide Division slumped in the front seat of his rental car staring through semi-fogged windows at snow, slush, and a bleak array of mobile home trailers.

"Why didn't you take your pension and retire to Florida instead of this blizzard bullshit?" he muttered. Then he remembered his ex-wife took half his assets in the divorce settlement along with demands of a healthy alimony check due the fifth day of each month. He should've hired a better lawyer.

Like Kearney, Nebraska, Conover's leads were ice cold. Juan Hidalgo's girlfriend, Maria Almodavar, wasn't home, and Juan never specified in the letters to his parents which hotel she worked. The people he needed to talk to at the grain elevator where Juan worked weren't there when he stopped by. They told him to try back first thing in the morning. Aside from a high school photo, Juan's family gave him little else to go on to find their missing son.

Knocks on the doors of the surrounding trailers

most often went unanswered. The rest were quick invitations for him to go fuck himself. A rail thin Hispanic lady claimed she didn't speak English despite the fact the television in the background was on an English station. When he switched his questions to Spanish, she slammed the door in his face. If he had a dollar for each time someone had that unhelpful reaction to him, he could have retired five years earlier, something he should've done anyway.

A light flicked on in the trailer across the street from Juan's. He climbed from the rental car, bracing against the bitter wind. A sagging chain link fence bordered the trailer lot and chocolate colored deposits marred the snow, but no sign of the little dog who made them. He tried the latch on the fence. Frozen shut. Placing his hands on the icy top rail of the fence, he swung his legs up and over. His back foot clipped the rail and he spilled to the ground. Brushing himself off, he spotted a set of eyes peering through the blinds from the trailer.

Conover looked frailer than he was—a good thing in his line of work. More than one thug in L.A. found out the hard way he could scrap. Still, this fence debacle was another sign the years were taking their toll. Five years ago, he would've cleared it easy. His body's check engine light displayed its ugly face more than it used to and he seemed to meet his medical deductible earlier each year. Getting old sucked.

An elderly lady with paper thin skin named Mabel answered the door, a bemused smile adorning her lined face. She reeked of menthol ointment and loneliness and invited Conover in from the cold. A brown and black Yorkshire Terrier yipped and jumped at Conover.

"Pepper, get down. He likes you," Mabel said. "That means you have a good soul."

Conover explained why he was there while nursing a cup of luke warm coffee. When he was done, she put a hot top on his coffee and doled out a few clues.

Her high-pitched voice cracked with age. "Maria drives a blue Honda Accord. I don't know what year. I was never good at that."

"Anything special about it?"

She spoke slow, like it took extra time for her brain to fire the synapses required for each word. "The driver's side rear window was covered with plastic and duct tape after someone broke into it last month."

Conover jotted notes on a pad he produced from his pocket. "Juan's parents said she was a housekeeper at a hotel. Any idea which one?"

Mabel scratched her cheek. "She used to work at the Ramada but switched to somewhere else a couple months ago. Would you like a cookie, Detective?"

"No, thank you, ma'am."

Mabel waved her bony hand and cackled. "Don't you call me ma'am. Makes me feel old. Are you single, Detective?"

"Divorced. Eight months ago. But, I have started seeing someone."

"Oh, shoot. All the handsome young men are taken."

"I'm not that young."

She winked. "You're young to me."

She labored to her feet and brought over a plate of chocolate chip cookies and set them on the table before lowering herself back to her chair. "Juan drove a red Chevy pickup—an older model, but I don't know what kind."

"When's the last time you saw either of their cars?"

Mabel pushed the plate of cookies toward him. "Eat one. You're too thin."

Conover took one and bit into it, almost breaking his front tooth. The cookie was like chewing gravel. Tasted like it, too. Mabel was sweet, but she was no baker.

Mabel twisted the rod to open the blinds, pointing across the street. "The Accord was here this morning. I haven't seen Juan's truck for a few weeks. I wondered if those two broke up. Would be a shame. He really is a sweet, sweet boy. He used to take Pepper here for walks for me. I don't get around as well as I used to."

Additional questions produced no fruit. Conover left Mabel his card and asked if she'd call him if she saw Maria come home.

"Only if you promise to come back. I'll thaw out the Sara Lee cake I've been saving for a special occasion."

He thanked her, patted Pepper on the head, and made his way back to the gate. Rather than repeat his fence hopping disaster, he tugged at the gate latch until it gave way. Sliding the rental Taurus in drive, he roamed the streets around the trailer park. He bounced around the gas stations and fast food places nearby, flashing Juan's picture to the staff. A couple of people recognized him but hadn't seen him in a while.

He bought another coffee and camped out back at Maria's trailer. After two hours of no lights and no blue Honda Accord, his mind began to wander, turning to dark, self-reflecting thoughts. If Patricia hadn't left him, maybe he wouldn't need to do this. Of course, if he hadn't been such a complete asshole, maybe she wouldn't have kicked him out. If he hadn't worked eighty hours a week, maybe he wouldn't have been an asshole at all. If he hadn't shot the cartel guy in the LA alley because he was tired of working those eighty hours...shit. It was a maddening circle of maybes.

One thing Mabel said stuck in the back of his brain as he'd opened the door to leave her place. "They were so in love. You could tell by the way he looked at her. I don't think I saw them together when they weren't somehow touching. It was very sweet. Then he was gone."

Then he was gone.

Juan's letters back home were happy. Before they stopped.

He had the love of a good woman.

He liked his job and co-workers, though his boss scared him.

He was making more and more money. More than he should have, which led Conover to question what he was doing to earn the extra cash.

Life was good for Juan Hidalgo.

Then he was gone.

After thirty years in law enforcement, Conover's gut was finely attuned. Today, it told him Juan Hidalgo was still in Kearney, but he was no longer in the land of the living. He'd have to kick over some rocks to be sure.

As he pulled out of the trailer park, he glanced to the rearview mirror, spotting the truck two cars back. The same truck from the grain elevator earlier in the day. He was being followed. The question was, by whom?

CHAPTER SIX

Jake's cell vibrated as Maggie finished dressing. He cringed at the name on the screen and ignored the call. After slipping on a pair of boots, he headed toward the kitchen to top off his coffee when the phone vibrated again. Same name. *Son of a bitch.* This time, he answered.

"No." Jake kept his tone even but firm, determined to keep this call cordial but quick.

Jason Keats chuckled. "Well hello to you too, asshole. I'm doing great. Thanks for asking."

Jake sucked his lips tight against his teeth and strode to the front porch, wincing at the cold. *I should've let this go to voicemail again.* He peeked at Maggie through the window as she crossed into the kitchen. He didn't want to think about what picking up a phone call from Keats would cost him. If she found out.

"You still there, Caldwell? Hello?" Keats asked.

"I'm here. What do you want? I'm under orders to not even talk to you."

"By who? The cops? Feds?"

Jake leaned on the railing. The brisk morning breeze blew through his shirt. He couldn't go inside and wouldn't last long out there without a coat. "Someone far more important. My wife."

"Maggie? Jesus Christ. You scared me for a second. You can't even talk to me? Who wears the pants in the family?"

"She does and she'll have my balls in a vice for even answering your call."

Keats paused. "So why did you?"

"I'm bored."

"Bullshit. You're curious."

"What do you want, Jason?"

"I've got a job for you, though I should send a crew to Warsaw and beat you with a bag of doorknobs. Hell, I might do both. I haven't decided."

Jake stiffened. "What for?"

"Franco Lunetti."

"How do you know about Lunetti?"

"One, this is my town, and I know everything happening here. Two, he called me from the precinct. You know he works for me, right?"

Jake spit over the rail and ran his hand over the stubble on his cheeks. He'd done everything in his power to stay out of Keats's crosshairs, though it seemed to be futile given the amount of things Keats had a vested interest in. "I didn't. If I did, I wouldn't have taken the job. Sorry."

"Sorry isn't gonna replace my lost income with Lunetti out of commission."

"You should've taught him how to play hide and seek. Helen Keller could've caught him."

"I'll let you make it up to me with a simple job of—"

"I don't want it." Jake's head throbbed. This was

taking too long. Keats had a way of wearing you down.

"You act like I'm giving you a choice."

"If Maggie would put my balls in a vice for answering your call, imagine what she'd do to them if I take another job from you."

Keats laughed. "Sounds like she already cut them off and keeps 'em in her purse. Better start getting persuasive. It's low-risk and lucrative."

"If it's so easy, have one of your goons do it."

"I didn't say it was easy, and I hate it when you call them that. Makes people think all I bring on is a bunch of low-brow Neanderthals."

"Don't you?"

"I hired you, didn't I?"

Jake glimpsed Maggie through the window as she waltzed back toward the bedroom, blowing him a kiss. He made the cheesy gesture of catching it. His standing outside for this call was going to draw suspicion and beg questions. Who could he say he talked to when she asked? Guilt rippled through him at the thought of lying to her. But, he wasn't going to take the job no matter what strong-arm tactics Keats employed. There was no need to spike her blood pressure and dodge whatever she would throw at him by telling her the truth. The road to a peaceful marriage was paved with little white lies.

Jake dropped to the driveway, a slight limp from the bad knee his father shattered with a lead pipe when he was a teen. The cold always made it worse. He walked away from the house as if the increased distance from Maggie would weaken her ability to read his guilty face. This call was taking longer than he wanted, and the fact he hadn't hung up on Keats signaled to both men an arrangement was still possible. "Can we get to the point?"

"Fine. Vinny V got taken out in transit a couple of weeks ago and lost his cargo along with most of his grey matter."

Vincent Varano was a bagman. He collected from the various illegal operations Keats ran. After Keats paid off his expenses, Vinny transported the money train to a launderer. Jake thought Vinny was a dick, so his death meant nothing to him.

"How much?"

Keats let loose a guttural groan. "One point five."

Jake stopped walking. "Jesus Christ. In one load?"

"Had a guy handling a portion of it in your neck of the woods, but things got jacked up with him. I sent Vinny with the whole load to Omaha."

"You're getting sloppy in your old age, Jason."

Keats growled. "This one's going to hurt, unless you can—"

"Sorry for your loss and for busting Lunetti, but—"

"You know how inconvenient you made my life… again?

Jake scratched his chin. Why was Keats working with Lunetti in the first place? "Wait, I thought Lunetti worked for Garrett."

"He does."

"You have a side deal with him?"

"It's part of a plan that's none of your fucking business."

Jake's brain worked the jigsaw puzzle. Keats dwarfed Garrett with his operations, but Garrett held some lucrative territory in the Kansas City Metro area. "You're making a move on Garrett, aren't you?"

"What part of none of your fu—"

Jake batted the line of thought away. He had bigger

things to worry about. "Forget it. I don't wanna know. Sorry, but I have zero interest in helping you find your money train."

"I'm offering you ten percent. And again, I'm not asking."

Jake turned back toward the house. His brain jumping to their savings account statement with the inadequate balance on the desk in the den.

"I like that pause, Caldwell," Keats said.

A hundred and fifty thousand dollars. Jake gnawed on the inside of his cheek. Could he do it after what he'd put Maggie and Halle through in the last couple of years?

"Look," Keats continued. "You just gotta point me in the right direction and my guys take care of the rest. You won't even have to draw your shiny little gun out of its holster."

"There's other guys who could do this for less."

"Not with your skillset. I want someone discreet and someone I can trust. You're the best and by a wide margin. I know it and you know it. No drama, no violence, if that's what floats your boat. Just finger the guys who took my money and I'll handle the rest. Me and my low-browed Neanderthals."

"You have any leads?" *Goddamn it. That sounded like an acceptance.*

"A five second grainy video clip of guys in hoods. They took Vinny down at a rest stop and shot him twice in the head. Picked his truck clean, dumped him in the bathroom and put up closed signs. Nobody found him for hours."

"That's it?"

"One of the guys had a tattoo of a stag with big ass antlers on the back of his left hand. From the first knuckle to his wrist."

Jake paced the driveway, kicking the gravel. A hundred fifty thousand for a little detective work? It would pay for Halle's undergrad college degree. He could rationalize time in the dog house for that kind of cash. He just didn't want it to be the Caldwell Memorial Scholarship Fund.

Keats broke the silence. "It's easy money for a guy like you, Caldwell. Tell the wife I'm just an anonymous client who hired your little PI firm to do surveillance."

Jake turned to face his house. Omaha. The Lincoln college visit trip was perfect cover as the two cities were an hour apart. If he could squeeze some time away from Bear and the girls. That'd be tricky. Keats was right, though. He'd only have to find the guys.

Overhead, charcoal clouds beat a path north on the winter wind. The acrid odor of burning wood from a nearby fireplace floated in as his feet crunched over the driveway. The smart thing was to say no, if that was even an option, but a hundred and fifty thousand reasons to say yes weighed heavy on one side of the scale.

The words slipped from Jake's lips like greased shit from a goose. "Send me the surveillance footage and let me see."

"I'll send it shortly." Keats's voice dropped an octave, to that growling level which made your hair stand on end. "And Jake? I know you don't work for me anymore, but you've interfered with my livelihood by taking down Lunetti. You owe me. I'm being very, very generous by even offering you a cut of the recovery. You may consider finding the guys who robbed me as optional, but you're wrong."

Keats ended the call without waiting for a response.

Jake ground his teeth, glad he wasn't near a wall or he'd put his fist through it. He jammed the cell phone in his pocket. He was fucked.

CHAPTER SEVEN

The Warsaw sunrise backlit the skeletal fingers of the trees off Poor Boy Road. Jake sipped coffee, bare elbows clenched to his sides, as frigid morning air nipped his skin. He needed the zero-degree air to wake him up after a restless day and a sleepless night weighing what Keats's money could offer his family against the hell he'd pay if they found out. There was also the risk of what Keats would do to him if he didn't find the guys who'd stolen his money.

Sheriff Bear Parley's black Expedition rolled up the driveway, the brakes squealing as he stopped. Jake motioned toward the house and headed inside to motivate Halle to be less than fifteen minutes late. She was busy putting the finishing touches to her long, blonde hair with an implement Jake wasn't sure the name of.

"Let's go, Halle. Your hair's curled enough."

She held up the implement. "It's a crimper, Dad. Maybe by the time I graduate you'll get it straight."

He shucked his eyebrows. "You want me to get the curling straight?"

If her eyes rolled any harder, they'd detach and plop to the floor. "Good Lord. That's bad even for you."

Jake tapped the door. "Hustle up. Bear's here."

"You and Mom still going to Kansas City next weekend to see your favorite geriatric band? What are they called again?"

"Perpetual Change and they're not geriatric. They rock. You'd like them."

"Can I stay here by myself when you're gone?"

"And drink all my beer? Zero chance. Let's go."

She batted doe eyes. "What if I scored my own alcohol?"

"Dream on, little girl."

A minute later, his best friend Bear and his daughter Landry shivered through the front door. Bear's six-foot-five inch, three-hundred-pound frame dwarfed his daughter. Landry slapped Jake's outstretched palm as she passed him in the hall on the way to Halle's room.

Jake took in the scowl on Bear's face. "What's wrong with you?"

Bear growled. "It's too fucking cold and early to be outside."

Jake entered the kitchen and grabbed a coffee mug, pouring Bear a cup. "Don't be a pussy. It's not that bad."

"It's zero, Jake. Which means there are literally no degrees of heat. Too damn cold for my old bones."

Jake handed him the mug. "We're not even forty yet."

"It's not the age, it's the mileage. And stress like dealing with Carla Daniels."

"Uh oh. What'd she do?"

When Jake first arrived back to Warsaw to track

down drug lord Shane Langston, Randy "Sad Dog" Daniels, one of Bear's deputies, was on Langston's payroll and kidnapped Maggie to get to Jake. Jake tracked them down and put three rounds in Sad Dog's chest, killing him on the spot. It made for awkward encounters when Jake ran into Carla in town.

"I'm guessing she blew through the life insurance money and is threatening to sue the department for wrongful death."

"I'm the one who shot him," Jake said. "Should I get a lawyer?"

"Think she's fishing, but it might not hurt to talk to one. You nab that Lunetti dude? What'd he do, again?"

"Skipped bail after getting busted running a chain of storage units across the country he used to store meth. Idiot was holed up at his girlfriend's."

Bear winked. "Told ya he'd go there. How much is my cut?"

"I believe you said, and I quote, 'no goddamn way the dumbass goes to his baby mama's house.' End quote. So yeah, you're not getting a dime."

Bear's jaw craned open to protest when the girls entered the kitchen. Halle poured coffee into a travel mug, the latest adult habit which made Jake sad. Another sign she was growing up and wouldn't be around as much. She added enough milk and sugar to ensure she wouldn't be able to taste the coffee, which gave him hope she wasn't quite as grown up as he feared. She hoisted her backpack over her shoulder as Landry grabbed a water bottle from the fridge.

"You bring your county vehicle, Bear?" Halle asked.
"Why?"
"With lights and sirens, we can cut the travel time

to Lincoln to three and a half hours."

Bear huffed. "As if I need lights and sirens for that."

Jake turned to Halle. "You sure you're interested in being a Husker?"

Halle's eyes narrowed. "Can we afford it, even with my partial scholarship?"

"It's not the money, it's the distance."

"You saying you're going to miss me?"

"Every minute."

Halle wrapped her arms around him. "Don't get all sappy on me, Dad. Hey, if it's not about the money, can we check out Stanford?"

"Don't press your luck, sweetheart."

***

They drove toward Kansas City, planning a quick stop there to gas up and get road snacks. The morning sun budded behind them, blinding off the snow-crusted landscape on either side of the highway. Music whispered from the classic rock station on satellite radio, nobody quite awake enough to stand anything louder. Landry sacked out in the back, head sunk into a pillow against her door. Halle scrolled through her phone, earbuds in place. Jake worried the skin around her ears would absorb the ever-present devices. Maybe it was Apple's evil scheme. He scratched the thought when he realized they wouldn't be able to sell a new version every twelve months.

Jake's phone vibrated with a text message from Keats. Jake leaned against the window and double clicked the attachment and a video sprang to life. The footage was shot from a dash cam with a green, night cam hue. Four guys jumped from a white panel van, dressed head to toe in black with face masks. The only exposed body parts were their eyes, mouths and hands.

The men stormed the front of Vinny's money train van, brandishing pistols and AR-15s. Jake backed the video up a few frames when the right hand of one of the pistol men turned. He zoomed in and out, getting as close as he could before the picture blurred. It appeared to indeed be a stag with giant antlers.

No license plate was visible on the back of the van. The guys were around the same size, except for one who stood a head taller than the other three. Judging from his position against the van, maybe six foot three. A big guy. Jake knew the guy to call about the tattoo but couldn't do it with Bear and the girls around.

As Bear drove, Jake gazed out the passenger window, watching the bleak winter landscape blur past with Keats's six-figure offer weighing on his mind. Maggie would kill him, but would full payment of Halle's tuition for her entire college career change her mind? After running through scenarios of him telling her the news, he was pretty sure the money wouldn't help his cause. Maybe Keats putting him in intensive care, or worse, might.

Jake's mind rolled with the bad memories, risky decisions and dangerous outcomes when he dealt with Keats. Maggie saw nothing but blood and violence when Keats's name was spoken. Plus, there was no guarantee Keats would stop with Jake pointing out the guy who ripped off Keats's money laundering deposit. Chances were good Keats would up the ante once he had Jake on the hook. Besides, his lone lead was a tattoo on a random guy's hand. He wouldn't offer a hundred and fifty thousand for just pointing a finger.

Jake's cell rang. It was a woman with a Jersey accent who wanted to meet with him today to track her cheating husband. Roughly half of Jake's cases were cheating spouses. It was a sufficient volume to make anyone question the viability of marriage in general.

Jake said, "I'm sorry but I'm heading out of town and won't be back for a few days. Next week is the best I can do."

"Hope you're going somewhere warm."

"No such luck. College visits in Nebraska. Lincoln and Kearney."

The woman thanked him and promised to call later.

"This trip costing you a job?" Bear said.

Jake waved him off. "I could use the break from providing ammo to warring spouses."

"A job's a job, my man. Something else on your mind?"

Bear had been caught in some of the collateral damage over the years due to Keats. Including getting shot twice. Telling him about Keats's offer would be worse than telling Maggie, because Bear would likely make it physical. "It's okay. Got a call from a potential client, and I'm debating if I should take it."

"Since when are you in the position to turn down jobs?"

"I don't know if I can pull it off," Jake said.

"Now *that* I can believe. What's the gig?"

Jake turned to the backseat and said Halle's name. She kept her gaze locked on her phone, her head bobbing to whatever song was permanently damaging her hearing. "Has to do with money laundering. Not in my wheelhouse. This guy had some cash he tried to keep off the books and was ripped off. Asked if I'd help track it down for a percentage."

Bear's lips disappeared and his narrowed eyes cut to Jake. "What guy?"

Bear's question dripped with venom. He was already suspicious. Jake didn't want to lie to his best friend, but figured since he hadn't accepted the job, they were still talking hypotheticals.

"Some investment banker in KC."

"Did he earn it or steal it?"

"I didn't ask. What do you know about money laundering?"

Bear scratched his head. "Not much. They take dirty money, run it through legit businesses until it comes out clean."

Halle snorted from the backseat. "That's pretty simplistic, Bear."

Bear's eyes shot to the rearview mirror, and Jake craned his neck to the back. "Thought you were jammin' to your tunes."

Her face crunched in teenage disgust. "Nobody calls them tunes anymore, Dad. Or jammin'. I was between songs."

"How do you know about money laundering?"

"My boyfriend does it all the time," Halle said.

The vertebrae in Jake's back cracked as he twisted his torso to face the backseat.

Halle rolled her eyes. "I'm kidding. Geez. From *Breaking Bad*, mostly. And, Mom and I watched this special on 20/20 or something."

"Explain it to me, Al Capone," Jake said. "Why couldn't he drop the cash into a bank account?"

She pulled her earbuds free. "Because banks have to report anything over ten thousand dollars to the

IRS. You could deposit smaller amounts over different banks, but it's pretty easy to track by the good guys. That's why Walter White buys the car wash in the show."

Jake loved she knew this kind of stuff. She was so freaking smart.

She angled forward. "People run money through cash businesses like car washes and laundromats. But, the problem with those is taxes. If you have a hundred thousand dollars from your drug deals or whatever and run it through your pizzeria, you have to report the hundred thousand as income and you lose a huge chunk of it to taxes. A lot of people hide money using real estate. Flipping properties. I didn't totally understand the tax stuff, but supposedly you could take your hundred thousand, buy some dumpy house, flip it and sell it and you keep the profits."

Bear snorted. "That's pretty much exactly what I said."

"She said it better."

Halle slipped a satisfied smile on her face, donned her earbuds, and sank back into the seat. A few seconds later, her head bobbed again.

How would Keats launder one point five million dollars? How many houses could you flip or how many cash businesses could you buy without drawing attention from someone? And who would be insane enough to rip him off? To start pulling the thread on this story, Jake would have to agree to help Keats, which he wasn't sure he wanted to do.

Bear slipped a pinch of tobacco between his bottom lip and gums. "You going to help this banker find his money?"

Since Jake didn't want to lie to his best friend, he

told a truth. "Sounds like more trouble than its worth."

Bear settled back in his seat as the Kansas City skyline rose in the distance. A familiar unease grew in the pit of Jake's stomach. He said he wasn't going to take the job, but he knew that wasn't the case.

CHAPTER EIGHT

Darius Frost dragged on a cigarette in the bed of Twila Meadows, watching the tendrils of smoke float toward the water-stained popcorn ceiling before being swept away by the slow blades of the ceiling fan. The ceiling stain looked like a brown Smurf fucking a cat. He cut his eyes to Twila, a twenty-two-year-old dancer at the Fuzzy Clam, a shady strip club south of Kearney, Nebraska. Wrapped in a sheet and snoring softly, his stripper with benefits, who went by the unimaginative stage name of Chastity, poked her g-stringed ass through an opening in the faux satin. Some dickhead at the Clam pawed at it last night while she danced on center stage and, unfortunately for him, Darius reached him before the bouncer.

Darius studied his bloodied knuckles, pondering if there was a way to hide them or avoid the inevitable ass chewing from his father. Darius thought for a futile moment about wearing gloves. He took another drag, resigning himself to the fact his father already knew about the fight. Nothing happened in Kearney that Xavier Frost didn't know about. Especially when it came to his only child.

Twila mumbled. "Goddamn it, D. Told ya I don't like it when you smoke in here."

"I made your ass smoke last night," he said, offering her the cigarette.

She raised her head and squinted against the morning light creeping through the plastic bedroom blinds. She took a drag and handed it back to him. "I'm serious. I smell enough of that shit at The Clam. Put it out."

Darius dropped the cigarette in an empty beer bottled on the nightstand. "You workin' again tonight?"

She worked herself to a seated position, leaning back against the headboard. "Yeah. Iola got whacked in the face last night, and Kenny won't let her dance with a shiner, not that anybody would care. They ain't starin' at her face."

Darius sat up and swung his feet to the floor, spots filling his vision, his head thumping from the shots of Jäger last night. How many did he have? Too many if he couldn't remember. Seems the more he stressed over the missing money, the more he drank. "Serves the dumb bitch right. You take some scumbag to the trailer out back and bad shit's gonna happen."

Twila slapped him on the back. "Hey, she's my friend."

"She's an idiot. And a slut."

"Didn't stop you from hittin' it."

"That was before I met you, sweetheart." He slipped on his stained blue jeans balled up on the floor and held up his t-shirt. Was that blood? He'd have to go back to his place and change clothes before he went to Husker Road.

"You coming to the club tonight, baby?" she asked.

The Club. The Fuzzy Clam was a concrete floor, corrugated steel shell dumped in a field serving canned beer. "Can't. Xavier's going to have my ass for last night as it is. 'Sides, got shit to do."

After slipping on his work boots, he sensed her pouty silence and turned.

Her bottom lip jutted out, baby blue eyes wide and pleading. "I don't know what's worse. My dead old man or your live one. Think you could get me some more coke?"

Darius bent and smoothed her wild red hair, kissing her on the forehead. "I'll see what I can do. No promises. Gotta go."

"Love ya," she called in her whiny, pleading tone as he left the bedroom.

Darius loathed the neediness. Still, he turned and gave her the wink she loved. "Love ya too, babe."

The frigid morning air bit his lungs and slapped at the exposed skin on his face. What would be colder? The Nebraska temperature or the reception Xavier would give him when Darius set foot in his office? Twenty-five years old and an ex-college defensive lineman, and Darius was as afraid of his old man now as when he was a scrawny ten-year-old.

Darius climbed into his truck and headed to his house. After a quick shower and change of clothes, he cruised north on 2nd Avenue, past the shops, gas stations, and restaurants.

He called Randall Parker, his number one guy. "Any leads on the money?"

Parker groaned. "What time is it?"

Darius turned east on Highway 10. "Time for you to get up and start earning your paycheck."

A lighter clicked and Parker's exhalation rattled the

speaker. "Maybe if you hadn't blown the head off the one person who knew where the money is, we'd be sittin' on a beach in Mexico. People are gonna start putting pieces together eventually leading to us, and I don't wanna be anywhere in the U.S. of A. when the puzzle gets finished. You wanna find the money, I could use a little help."

"I gotta meet with Xavier first," Frost said.

"Triad business or about last night?"

"I assume both."

"Ain't you the lucky one."

Frost sniffed. "Get me some more coke while you're out. For Twila."

Parker hesitated. "Thought you were done with that."

"I said it's for Twila. Call me when you're done."

Darius clicked off the call. The Triad ran their operations from his father's ranch atop four hundred acres of some of the most fertile soil in the county. Darius turned north on Antelope Avenue, and a few minutes later spotted the house sprawled across the horizon, a dark shadow framed by the morning sun. He slipped on sunglasses to cut back the glare of the snow and paused at the mouth of Xavier's two-hundred-yard driveway, the ranch in the distance. He glanced to his bloody knuckles, heartrate increasing, palms damp. He wished they hadn't snorted all the coke last night. He could use a line, because this wasn't going to be good.

CHAPTER NINE

The University of Nebraska campus sat on the north side of the city of Lincoln and south of I-80. Lincoln was home to three hundred thousand people, a charming town if you could get past, through, or around the horrendous traffic on Highway 2.

Even in the winter with remnants of snow clinging to the ground, the mass of trees and sweeping sidewalks connecting the red-bricked structures of higher learning were enough for the green jealousy monster to nibble at Jake. His desire to go to college dropped to nil once Stony erased his football dream with a steel pipe to Jake's kneecap, but he sensed what he missed within seconds of eyeing the football stadium in the distance. He envisioned Halle walking these very sidewalks going to class, and his smile matched his daughter's, who appeared to be floating on cloud nine.

After a long, icy walk through the campus, their bubbly tour guide stopped in front of some memorial fountain by the union. Bear yawned, his feet dragging along the sidewalk.

"You gonna make it?" Jake asked. "You look like you're about to keel over."

"How long is this tour? I'm used to drivin', not walkin'. Should've worn better shoes because my dogs are howlin'."

"Maybe we can get you a couple of those motorized scooters," Jake offered. "Strap 'em together to haul your out-of-shape ass around."

"My out-of-shape ass is heading to the john. At least I'll be able to sit for a while. I'll find you when I'm done, that is if Bambi over there finishes talking before I'm back."

Jake patted him on the shoulder. "I'll send up a flare."

He took advantage of the girls' engagement with the sparkly tour guide and Bear disappearing to the bathroom to call Cat Topher, his go-to computer hacker who Jake could always rely on for hard-to-find information.

Cat answered on the third ring. "I'm not sure why I'm even bothering answering any calls from you."

"Because I pay you well."

"Not that well. What's up? I'm slammed at the moment."

"I know this might be a long shot, but can you track down a person based on a tattoo?"

"Depends on if they're in the system or not," Cat said. "There's this organization called NIST, don't ask me what it stands for. But they've been working with the FBI, encouraging police to snap tattoo photos of inmates and tagging the photos with metadata about the tattoo."

Jake perked up. This sounded like it had potential. "What exactly is metadata?"

"Jesus, Caldwell. What are you? A caveman? Metadata is data providing information about other data."

"Didn't your teachers ever tell you not to use a word you're defining in the definition itself? Pretend I'm computer illiterate."

"Pretend? That shouldn't be hard. If you have a book, it would have metadata associated with it like the title, the author's name, the publisher, etcetera. Law enforcement tags tattoos with metadata codes like position on the body, ink color, and the type of image. Instead of a binder with thousands of tattoo photos you have to look through, it's all digitized and you could search for a particular image using the metadata."

"How do you know so much about this?"

Cat crunched something, probably a Cheeto. He had an addiction to them. "Because I have a ton of tattoos. I got picked up eighteen months ago and they snapped a bunch of pics. It made me curious what they were doing, so I did a little research. They have this thing called Google. It's amazing. You should try it."

Jake ignored the jab. "So, if I send you a pic of a tat, you could tell me who it belongs to?"

Silence hummed on the other end for a beat. "Theoretically, but the owner of the tattoo would have to be in the system in the first place. Plus, I'd have to hack into the FBI's system, which I wouldn't do if you put a gun to my head. I'd have to bounce the signal all over the place and, say what you want, they take their cybersecurity very seriously."

"I'll make it worth your while."

Cat snorted. "Heard that before and you don't have

enough money."

"I'm serious. You find the guy I'm looking for, it'd be worth thousands to you."

"How many?"

Keats's angry face popped up in Jake's mind. "Enough to keep you in Cheetos for the rest of your life."

Cat crunched some more. "That's a lot of cheese puffs, but not enough to screw with the FBI. Happy hunting. Call me if you need something that isn't going to land me in federal prison for life."

Cat ended the call. Bear hadn't come out of the bathroom, which meant he would be perched on the porcelain throne for a bit. Cat said the FBI had the database. Good thing he had contacts there. He scrolled through his directory and found the number for Victoria Snell, an FBI agent out of the Kansas City office who worked with Jake to take down bioweapon terrorists and the Blackbird spies. Since Jake also helped rescue her kidnapped daughter, the two remained in regular communication. Though, Jake now realized months had passed since he'd last talked to her.

He punched her cell number, and the call went straight to voicemail. He left a message for her to call him as Bear emerged from the bathroom.

Their next stop was a tour of Memorial Stadium, home to Husker football. An amazing site. Over 86,000 available seats, and each game was a sellout dating back to 1962. The ring below the press box listed the school's string of national championships. Two in the 1970s and three more in four years in the mid-90s. He would have played on this very field against the Huskers if things had turned out differently. Rotating in a full circle, the phantom roar of the crowd echoed.

A few minutes after noon, Jake tried Snell's number again. Straight to voicemail. He scrolled through his directory and found the contact information for Foster, Snell's friend and co-worker at the FBI. As the tour group headed to the student union, Jake tapped Halle on the shoulder and held up his phone. She nodded and Jake slid to a quiet place in the Union.

"What's up, lady? Haven't talked to you in a while."

Foster blew a sigh into the phone. "Ready to get off this stakeout."

"Who're you staking out?"

"Nobody exciting, I can tell you that. What's up?"

"Have you talked to Snell recently?"

Foster jumped on the question. "What's wrong?"

"Nothing, just trying to get ahold of her."

"When's the last time you talked to her?"

"I don't know. Maybe four or five months."

Foster was quiet for a beat. "She hasn't been in a good place. I think she's supposed to be on vacation, which may be why she didn't answer."

Jake stopped pacing. "Not in a good place?"

"She couldn't keep her nose out of Keats's business, and when it started affecting the cases she was supposed to work on, the brass finally had enough. The boss told her to pack up and reassigned her to Nebraska."

"When was this?"

"Three months ago. The two weeks off didn't sound voluntary. I'm a little worried myself, because she's not answering my calls, either."

Jake dropped to a bench near a staircase leading down to the bookstore. Students passed as he hung his head low. Keats was the one arrest Snell craved going all the way back to her task force days with Bear. Just when she thought she had Keats reeled in, he'd squirm from her grasp. He'd become her White Whale, and it appeared her obsession caught up with her.

"What about her daughter?" Jake asked.

"Beth said her mom told her she was taking a couple of weeks of vacation and was going away to clear her head. Didn't say where but told her not to worry. She was due back in the office yesterday. As soon as I'm done with this case, I'm heading to Omaha to see what I can find. Jake, I'm really worried. This isn't like her."

"Keep me posted," Jake said.

"You need something else?"

"You guys have software that can track a tattoo to a person?"

"Yeah," she replied. "Database coordinated with a group called NIST. Don't ask me what it stands for."

"If I send you a picture, could you look it up?"

"I can't. I don't have access, but I know the guy who does. The problem is he's a prick who's been harassing me."

Nothing was ever easy when it came to Foster's love life. "You break his heart?"

"One tragic date that was over within five minutes of meeting him. He thought we had a great time. I'd rather swallow my tongue and choke to death than go out with him again."

"Think you could sweet talk him for me? Say it's for one of your cases."

She let a few seconds of silence pass. "You'd owe me big time."

"Put it on my tab. I'm good for it. Keep me posted

on Snell. I'll help any way I can."

"I'll be in touch."

A nasty thought rolled through his head. "Hey, did she stop chasing Keats when she was assigned to Omaha?"

Foster paused. "What do you think?"

"That's what I thought. I'll talk to you later."

Jake clicked off, studying the polished white floor at his feet before sending Foster the image of the tattoo. He ran the timeline through his head. Snell tracking Keats's movements. She takes vacation the same time the money train gets taken down. Now she was missing. The cops found the body of Keats's bagman, but what if there was another one?

Jake wanted to think Snell was on a beach somewhere to clear her head. But missing work and no contact with the daughter she worshiped was a major red flag.

CHAPTER TEN

The next morning, Jake dug his fingers into the armrests during the ass-clenching ninety-minute ride from Lincoln to Kearney as Bear cursed his way west. Between the thirty mile an hour winds rocking semi-trailers across the snow-swept lanes of I-80 and Bear's insistence the Expedition could defy the laws of physics, Jake would consider them fortunate to arrive in once piece.

"Did you happen to notice the half dozen cars in the ditches since we left Lincoln?" Jake asked.

Bear huffed. "I hate inexperienced drivers."

"I'd hate to die in Nebraska. Considering our daughters are in the back, could you drop it under the speed of sound?"

The speedometer crept to closer to something reasonable as they passed the multi-colored water tower at the town of York.

Bear asked, "You worried about Snell?"

"A little. She and her daughter are tight. If Beth hasn't heard from her, that's worrisome. Foster's going to call when she finds out more info."

Jake kept his thoughts concerning Keats, Snell, and the money train to himself for now. It would make for a more peaceful ride.

The girls engaged in an animated discussion about the potential college experience, freedom, the dorms, sororities, and the cute guys in their tour group, becoming fixated on two of them.

Halle leaned forward. "Dad, which one did you think was hotter? Zack or Christian?"

Jake scowled. "Are you seriously asking me that question?"

"Come on. If you were me or Landry, which one would you choose?"

"Zack," Bear piped up. "He was going to be an engineering major while Christian was going for general studies or some shit."

"What's that got to do with their hotness?" Landry asked.

"Trust me. Christian isn't going to look as hot when he graduates and is living in his parents' basement because he can't get a job."

"And I almost poked Christian's eyes out," Jake said. "He spent more time watching you walk than paying attention to the tour."

Halle laughed. "Is that why you bumped him off the sidewalk into the bushes?"

Jake grinned. "It was an accident."

Before the girls could counter, Bear's cell rang and he became engrossed in a conversation with Deputy Klages back in Warsaw. Someone tried to torch the Rusty Skillet last night with a half-assed drive-by Molotov cocktail.

They hit Kearney a little over an hour later. They passed under the Archway, a fifteen-hundred-ton historical exhibit spanning I-80 that was built to resemble a covered bridge. Jake thought it might make for an interesting tour if they had time, but assumed he'd have a teenage mutiny on his hands if he even suggested it. They wheeled off Exit 272 and turned north up 2nd Avenue.

"Hell, they have all kinds of businesses here," Bear said. "Not what I imagined at all."

"What were you expecting?"

"Something more like Warsaw, I guess."

"It's a college town, man. There's like thirty thousand people here."

They hit a stoplight. A strip of hotels and restaurants walled them in on either side of 2nd Avenue as it flew arrow straight to the north, shrinking to a point in the distance.

Bear craned over his shoulder. "Landry, what time is your first meeting?"

Landry popped her earbuds out. "Ten o'clock. Some players from the soccer team are supposed to take me around for a behind-the-scenes tour. They said Halle can come."

Bear scowled. "Girl players, right?"

Landry dug through her backpack and passed up the parking permit they'd sent her. "They said we should look for the oiled up, shirtless, single guys who are giving us piggyback rides from the parking lot to the locker room."

Bear shot his daughter a look that would have burned through steel.

"Yes, girl players," she said. "You're going to have to loosen the reins, Dad."

Bear punched the address into his Google maps. They hung a left on 25th Street, and a half mile later the campus sprung up on their right in a series of red-bricked buildings sitting flat and low. An electronic sign flashed "University of Nebraska Kearney – Be Gold, Be Bold." They looped through narrow drives to three-story flat-roofed residence halls lying east to west. Further down, the fraternity and sorority housing were of the same construction, but differentiated by peaked, shingled roofs with green gutters.

Bear whistled. "Jesus, big fan of red bricks, aren't they?"

"Brick-layers union must have paid off somebody," Jake said, scanning the campus.

"I think it's charming," Landry said.

They parked and the girls led the way inside. The University of Nebraska at Kearney had six thousand students and was ranked one of the top ten public regional universities in the Midwest. But, it was nowhere near the size of the University of Nebraska at Lincoln. What would Halle think of it? He hoped she hated it as it would put her another two hours farther from home.

Jake's cell rang as they climbed out of the Expedition. Foster. He stepped away and answered. "You have something?"

"Jesus, you owe me. O'Roarke wanted pictures in exchange for the tattoo information."

"Pictures of what?"

"Use your imagination, Caldwell. The guy is a total perv. I said in exchange for the tattoo info, I wouldn't report him up the chain for sexual harassment."

"Sorry about that. You got something?"

"Maybe," Foster said. "Two potential hits. A Delores Updyke in California and a Randall Parker in Buffalo County, Nebraska. I'll go out on a limb and assume the Parker right there in Nebraska looks more likely than the California girl."

Considering they were in Buffalo County, it was a stroke of good luck. It also made sense if Parker was involved in the robbery. "Any chance you have an address for this Parker guy?"

"No. He was popped for misdemeanor assault fourteen months ago, but they dropped the charges. Address is blank which is odd. Garbage in, garbage out, I guess. I'll send you a picture."

"Thanks. Would you mind checking if you can find an address on this guy?" Jake held up a finger to Halle to let her know it would be another minute. "One more thing. Did you check Snell's credit cards and phone records?"

"Doing that next," she said. "I've got a request in to track her phone."

"Big Brother at its best."

"We're the government, Jake. We have eyes on everything."

After filling out forms, the UNK soccer girls showed up to give Landry and Halle the tour and take them out for dinner. Jake and Bear were free to do whatever they wanted as long as it wasn't there.

"Pick us up at eight, Dad," Landry said over her shoulder before she and Halle disappeared down a hallway without a wave.

Jake watched Halle go, tears stinging his eyes as he realized in a matter of months this would be the real deal.

Bear cleared his throat. "Jesus, this is going to be a hell of lot harder than I thought."

"You ain't kidding. I need a drink."

Bear yawned. "How about a freaking nap first? All

the walking and driving over the last couple days has kicked my ass. Think we could check into the hotel for a siesta?"

"Sure, if I can borrow your wheels. I'd like to check out the town while you're snoozing. You need me to tuck you in and read you a story?"

Bear showed Jake his longest finger as Jake's cell dinged. A message from Foster. *No credit or debit card activity for last twenty days. Waiting on cell phone records and location.*

Nothing for three weeks. That wasn't good news. Snell saved his ass from a bullet between the eyes. He hoped she wasn't in any position where he'd have to return the favor.

CHAPTER ELEVEN

Darius Frost perched on the end of a thousand-dollar high back chair in front of the crackling fireplace in his father's study, beads of sweat dotting his forehead. Not from the heat of the flames, but the familiar heat he knew was coming from his father. His legs jackhammered up and down as the afternoon sun filtered through the bay windows. The earthy odor of his father's Cuban cigar lingered in the air, the smoldering stub resting in an ornate hand-blown glass ashtray on the tidy desk across the room. He ogled the wet bar on the bookshelf on the other side of the room, tempted to grab a quick drink to nip the hangover thumping his skull. But drinking with light lingering in the sky was a sign of weakness and Darius saw no reason to give Xavier Frost any more ammunition.

The iron ball in his gut hardened as the click of familiar boot heels on the hardwood floors approached the study at a deliberate pace, as if each step was intended as a menacing message. Darius caught himself gnawing on his fingernails like he did when he was five and about to be spanked.

Xavier clipped into the study, rolling the cuffs of his starched white oxford sleeves to his pointy elbows as if preparing for a brawl. Darius considered slitting his wrists on the sharp creases of his father's pressed khakis and sparing himself what was to come. Instead, Darius jumped to his feet and stood at attention.

Xavier's thick, white eyebrows knitted together as he studied a piece of paper from his desk, the light from the overhead ceiling fan glinting off his liver-spotted bald head. Darius swore he could connect those brown dots to form a perfect pentagram.

Xavier grabbed the wrought iron poker, jabbing the burning logs in the fireplace and placing two more split pieces of wood. He spent the next sixty seconds lining up the edges of the logs until they were perfectly aligned. "Thank you for being prompt for once, Darius."

"What's going on?"

Xavier turned, wielding the poker like a sword and aiming the smoldering tip at his son. Darius was sure his old man would club him or stab him yet again. His old man's eyes held the same steely disappointment as when Darius informed him he'd been kicked off the vaunted Nebraska Cornhusker football team for fighting, despite repeated warnings. Darius had put a kid in the hospital with a half-dozen broken ribs and a fractured skull. Xavier's pull saved him from jail time, but wasn't enough to keep his son on the team. Husker football was everything in the State of Nebraska, and the fact his son was a starter on the Blackshirt defense was a source of great pride for the elder Frost. Darius knew his father would never forgive him.

Xavier raised the poker to Darius's face, the heat radiating from the steel tip. "How many times are we going to do this?"

"Do what?"

The poker drew closer, an inch from searing flesh. "I think you know."

A bead of sweat rolled down Darius's cheek, worried he'd end up with a scar on his face to match the one Xavier gave him on his arm.

Xavier raked his upper lip with his capped teeth and blew his frustration through his nose. "The whore and the strip club, you idiot. The man whose nose you broke over that two-dollar piece of ass works for Representative Howe, who called me this morning."

"So what? Howe isn't going to win re-election anyway."

Xavier's eyes narrowed and he leaned in close. "That's not the point. We still need him."

"For what?"

"That's my business, boy. I told you to stay the hell away from there, because you seem to lack the ability to go to that cesspool of humanity without causing trouble."

"The guy was—"

The blue vein in Xavier's temple pulsed as he cracked Darius in the thigh with the poker. Darius fell back into the chair clutching his leg. Xavier poked his son in the chest with the warm poker end. "I don't give a good goddamn what the other guy did. Stay out of that place or I'll burn the fucking thing to the ground with your little coke-head bitch inside. Understand?"

Xavier rarely cursed, but when he did, it punctuated a real and dangerous point.

"Sorry, Dad."

"You are sorry. A sorry excuse for a Frost. I'm getting tired of hearing the word. Stop presenting yourself with the opportunity to say it."

"Sor...I mean, yes, sir."

Xavier paced to the fireplace and set the poker in the rack. He dropped to a chair opposite his son, crossed his legs, and let the blood in his face settle. "Now, head over to Elevator B. There's a shipment coming in around six o'clock."

Xavier's enterprise, The Triad, ran their operations through three different grain elevators under the umbrella of the ETC Elevator Company. Ninety-eight percent of the shipments to these three elevators came from legitimate local farmers. The elevators took harvested crops via truck to the grain elevator where it was either stored or shipped out. Elevator A was located in Lexington, forty miles west of Kearney. Elevator B was in Kearney itself near downtown, and Elevator C was forty miles east of Kearney in Grand Island. Darius was happy he didn't have to drive far to oversee the other two percent of the shipments where the real money came from.

"Can't Nate handle this?"

Xavier grabbed the stub of his cigar. "It's the shipment from La Familia through Lansdale. Nate's out doing an errand for me."

Darius met a couple of the cartel thugs from La Familia once. He'd seen corpses livelier than those guys. "That it?"

Xavier flicked a lighter and twirled the cigar under his thin lips, puffing until the tobacco took fire. "No. Who is Juan Hidalgo?"

Darius's asshole puckered shut like a time lock vault at a bank. Luckily, he played enough poker to keep a straight face. "Juan worked at Elevator B. Haven't seen him for a while."

"Define a while."

Darius shot his eyes to the ceiling, thinking. He pictured Juan's head exploding like a melon from the shotgun blast, peppering the white snow in red. "Maybe three weeks. Possibly four. Haven't seen him since he grabbed his last paycheck."

"Something happen to him?"

Darius pumped his broad shoulders. "Not that I know of. Got his pay that Monday, and I ain't seen him since. Assumed he hauled his illegal ass back to Mexico."

Xavier's eyes narrowed. "He's from California and he's not illegal."

"How do you know that?"

Xavier handed him the paper he'd been holding. It was a security camera picture from Elevator B. A man, average height, fit with close cropped white hair, late fifties standing beside a white Taurus.

"That's not Juan," Darius said.

Xavier blew a stream of smoke to the ceiling. "No, worse. This guy came looking for Juan. PI named Conover from California. Apparently, Juan's family hasn't heard from him in some time and is very concerned. Should they be?"

Darius focused on the picture to avoid looking at his father, willing the tremor in his hand to still. "Beats me. Last time I saw Juan he was driving down the road with a wad of cash in his pocket. He never showed back up to work."

Xavier stood. "What did Juan know about The Triad?"

It didn't matter what Juan knew about The Triad or

anything else. He was deader than fried chicken and buried in a field far from Elevator B. But, he couldn't tell his father, because it would open up questions about why Darius killed him. If the truth came out, it would be disastrous.

"He didn't know anything. Just had him doing grunt work."

Xavier appraised him, face pinched in the condescending glare he threw on when he knew Darius lied. "I don't need anyone sniffing around our operations. If you see this Conover fellow, make sure he knows that. And if something did happen to Juan, it better not lead back to you or me. La Familia is sending a crew our way to check things out. I don't need to remind you of the repercussions to both of us if things aren't buttoned up."

La Familia? Here? Darius's balls crept up. "When they gonna be here?"

"Soon. They don't put things on my calendar. Just get it done."

Xavier turned and left the study without another word. Darius let out the breath he held and picked up the picture again, the tension in his hands threatening to tear the paper. The cartel sending a crew their way would be a death sentence with all the cash missing. Xavier didn't seem to know about the missing money yet. If he had, the fireplace poker would've been buried in Darius's skull. He still had time to find the money train cash and replace what he'd stolen from his father.

As he walked back to his truck, he knew he had very limited choices now. Make Conover lose interest in finding Juan Hidalgo or make it his last act on this earth.

CHAPTER TWELVE

With Bear hibernating, Jake took advantage of the alone time to check out the town and do some digging on Randall Parker. Despite Google showing Kearney as the most populated town in Buffalo County, he figured he had a decent chance of finding Parker. He stared through the windshield at the dirty gray clouds, pondering his next move. He might as well get a lay of the land while Foster hunted for an address.

Jake cruised south on 2nd Avenue crossing over the bridge spanning I-80. On his right was a large red, wood-paneled building with a Skeeter Barnes BBQ sign decorated with a mosquito dressed like a cowboy. Behind it, a Holiday Inn Express. Across the road, a massive warehouse building amid a sea of semi-trucks with a white and grey sign announcing Monster Logistics.

Why would Keats ship one point five million in one load? That kind of sloppiness wasn't like him.

He cruised back to the main road and turned south. A few hundred yards of nothingness before a metal Quonset hut loomed to his right. Patches of snow gathered in the galvanized steel grooves. He drove into a half-empty parking lot and swung in front of the structure—two hundred feet long and twenty-five feet high at its peak, like a cylinder sliced in half and slapped on a concrete slab. One door cut into the center with a pair of high-set windows on either side. A hand-painted sign hung above the door, white with pink lettering featuring a busty brunette in a bikini emerging from a clam. The Fuzzy Clam. Obviously a strip joint and, given the décor, probably a sticky-floored venereal disease factory.

Was Snell still tracking Keats's moves? The timing on the money train robbery and Snell's disappearance were dead on. Might be a coincidence.

He cruised back to the road, seeing nothing but snow-covered farmland to his right, and headed back toward town. In his rearview mirror, he spotted a black sedan roll from the exit ramp and slide in behind him, keeping a distance. Two guys inside, both wearing sunglasses. His lizard brain activated. The car sat at the exit ramp with plenty of time to turn north on 2nd Avenue long before Jake passed it. He'd been tailed enough times to know what it looked like.

He cruised past their hotel, more fast food restaurants, and a bevy of businesses and gas stations lining either side of the road. Past 17th Street, a bridge arced over a Coca Cola bottling plant. In the distance to the west, a giant white grain elevator shot to the sky with the letters ETC emblazoned on the side in red paint.

Would Keats actually hurt Jake and his family if he didn't come through on finding the money train robbers? He'd given Jake a lot more leeway over the years than he would anyone else, but could Jake continue to count on his good graces? What if Foster couldn't come up with an address on the tattoo guy?

He passed the Good Samaritan Hospital at 31st Street—hopefully his drama-free mission wouldn't require a visit, but based on his past, it was always good to know where medical care was. After a major intersection at 39th Street, he passed a partially abandoned mall and the small local businesses gave way to the big box stores of Target, Walmart, and Builder's Supply. A Menard's home improvement store marked the seeming end of civilization, the lone structure in sight was a gas station on the northwest side of a roundabout.

Gas station. Good Lord. A phonebook. Maybe he didn't need Foster.

Jake pulled into a slot in front of a rusty propane tank at the gas station called Glenwood Corners. He climbed out and headed toward the entrance, holding the door open for a couple of farmers clad in dirt-covered boots and Carhartt coveralls. The inside of the convenience store was tight, crammed with assorted snack foods and other essentials. A large cooler stocked with beer strung along the back wall.

An attractive girl with dirty blonde hair in her early twenties managed the register. High cheekbones, wide emerald eyes, and a button nose and a black eye she tried to hide with a thick layer of makeup. Her nametag read "Iola". He wandered around the store before grabbing a Coke Zero and bag of honey roasted peanuts. He set them on the counter in front of the girl.

"Anything else?" she asked.

"Hey, Iola. You have a local phone book?"

Her eyes narrowed. "How'd you know my name?"

Jake pointed to her nametag.

Iola glanced down and rolled her eyes, her thin shoulders dropping. "God, I'm such a ditz."

She dug around under the counter, producing a red book labeled the Frontier Pages with Kearney Regional. Jake took the book and stepped out of the way, thumbing the thin white pages until he arrived at the Ps. He drew his finger down the page and found three Parkers—two R Parkers and Marjory. He almost ripped the page from the book before he noticed the girl eyeballing him. Instead, he snapped a pic of the page with his phone.

"You can rip the page out. I don't care."

"And get you in trouble for destruction of company property? No way."

"You looking for someone in particular? Maybe I can help."

The corner of her mouth crooked up, eyebrows raised. A peek to the ring on his left hand. She was flirting with him. The two farmers dropped a couple dollars on the counter for their coffees and headed out, leaving Jake alone in the store with her.

"How'd you get the black eye?" Jake asked.

The smile disappeared and narrow shoulders pumped once. "Occupational hazard, I guess."

"Someone try to steal a Twinkie, or do you have another job as a prison guard?"

She giggled. "God, no."

"Wait. Nurse in a psych ward?"

"You're funny. New in town?"

"Nah, from Lake of the Ozarks. Couple hours southeast of Kansas City. You should leave him."

"Who?"

Jake tapped a finger on his eye. "The asshole who

gave you that shiner."

Iola looked down at the register.

Jake rolled his head to the side. "Women shouldn't get smacked around. Saw enough of that growing up. Never ends well."

"Maybe I ran into a door."

"Maybe. Door with a left hook?"

Her hands popped on her hips. "I don't even know you. You stick your nose in the wrong place around here and you're gonna get it busted off which would be a shame with that handsome face. 'Sides, if my boyfriend—"

The front door swung open and a gangly guy stomped in, stained denim jeans, mud-crusted boots, and a mop of brown hair spilling over the collar of a thick blue jacket. The girl's mouth clamped shut and she turned away from Jake. She said, "Mornin' Wendall."

Wendall grunted a reply, scratching his thick beard as he passed the two of them. He slowed, eyes sweeping Jake up and down, then headed toward the coffee in back. Whatever dirty laundry the girl had, she wasn't spilling it in front of this guy.

Jake handed her the phonebook and whispered. "Thanks. Watch out for those doors."

He headed back out to his car and found the black sedan he spotted from the other end of town parked next to his. Rapid footsteps clomped behind him, and Jake spun in time to spot two guys coming in hard and fast. One with raised brass knuckles and the other with a lead pipe. This couldn't be good.

CHAPTER THIRTEEN

The guy with the brass knuckles reached Jake first. He stood an inch taller than Jake with a barrel chest and beady eyes under cropped black hair. He swung wide and hard, going for the knockout blow on the first punch. Jake had used brass knuckles often in his early years working for Keats and figured out early why they're illegal in many jurisdictions.

Jake deflected the punch and used the guy's momentum to grab the side of his head and slam it into the hard steel of Bear's Expedition. Jake cracked him in the ribs with his knee for good measure. Air whuffed from the guy's lungs, and he staggered backward on the cracked asphalt and dropped on his ass.

The second guy was a head shorter than his partner, wiry with fire brewing in deep-set owl eyes. He jabbed the end of the pipe into Jake's solar plexus. Pain erupted and Jake's breath burst into the cold afternoon air. The guy chambered the pipe and took a head shot. Jake ducked, the metal combing his hair as it passed. He dropped low, then coiled and unleashed a hook to the pipe guy's ribcage, hard enough to loosen his shoe laces. The man spun and careened off the side of the Expedition, the pipe clanking across the parking lot.

Climbing back to his feet, Brass Knuckles advanced again, cautious this time, eyes a bit dazed but determined. Jake squared up, but the man's eyes grew wide, focusing over Jake's shoulder. He stopped, shoved his hands in his pockets, and walked toward the driver's side of the sedan.

Jake turned to see a Kearney cop car roll in front of the gas station building. A female cop with chestnut hair pulled back to a shoulder-length ponytail climbed out of the car and cast a slanted eyebrow in their direction. Jake had no desire to be on the local police radar.

"Everything okay?" she asked, hand still on her door.

"Sure," Jake said, walking a few steps and yanking the lead pipe guy to his feet. "My buddy slipped on an icy patch. Thanks for checking."

The cop appraised Jake for a moment. Her eyes narrowed, flicking back and forth between Jake and the other two. She wasn't buying his story. His mind was spinning up the story he'd have to tell when she let him off the hook.

"Be careful," she said.

Jake waved with his free hand. "Will do."

The cop disappeared inside the building with one last glance over her shoulder and Jake slammed the lead pipe guy against the sedan, cranking his wrist up between his shoulder blades. The guy howled.

"Who are you?" Jake hissed, keeping his voice low but fierce.

The guy grunted as Jake raised his wrist another inch. "Fuck you."

As Brass Knuckles moved around the front of the sedan, Jake said, "You come one step closer and I'll pop your buddy's shoulder out of his socket."

Brass Knuckles stopped, slipping his hand inside his jacket.

"Yeah," Jake continued. "That's a great idea. Shoot me with a cop thirty feet away. Now you better tell me who you are unless you want me to explore how flexible Skippy here is."

"Let him go and we'll talk," Brass Knuckles said, his voice low and deep. At least his hand dropped from where he undoubtedly stashed a piece.

"We coulda talked first and avoided all this," Jake said.

"That cop'll be out any minute now. I don't think any of us want to get caught up in answering a bunch of questions."

The guy was right. Though Jake hadn't done anything wrong, the cop would suck up time he didn't want to waste. Jake had his suspicion who these guys were, but since they weren't talking and time was short, he pressed Lead Pipe into the side of the sedan and yanked his wallet from his pocket. With the wallet free, he shoved the guy toward Brass Knuckles.

The two started toward Jake but stopped when the bell over the convenience store door jingled. The cop glanced to him, and Jake began laughing as if one of his opponents just told a hilarious joke, widening his eyes toward his two attackers.

"Oh damn, that's a good one," Jake said. They caught onto the ruse and joined him.

The cop climbed in her squad car, a puzzled look

on her face. The merriment stopped the second her door closed.

Jake opened the wallet and checked Lead Pipe's driver's license. Maxwell Marden. Missouri license, Kansas City address. It confirmed Jake's suspicions.

"You assholes work for Lunetti, don't you?"

Brass Knuckles opened and closed his fists, like a bull getting ready to charge the matador. "The second she leaves, you're getting your ass kicked, Caldwell."

"That's a yes," Jake said. "Look, it's not my fault your boss is a dumbass. You want to kick my ass, fine, good luck with that. At least wait until I get back to Kansas City. I have shit to do here."

The cop rolled forward and did a U-turn in the wide parking lot, heading back their way. Jake took advantage of the cover and slid to the door of the Expedition.

The cop dropped her window. "You sure you're good, gentlemen?"

Jake gave her an A-Okay sign. "Just fine, officer. Right, Max?"

Max offered a weak nod.

The cop narrowed her eyes, flicking them between the three men. She had to notice the signs of the fight from the disheveled clothes and the goose egg blooming on Brass Knuckles' forehead.

Jake opened the door and climbed in. The cop rolled forward, drove to the other side of the lot and parked with a clear shot of the three of them. She had good instincts. Jake buzzed the window down halfway and held the wallet out.

Max walked forward and snatched it. "This ain't over."

"That's what I figured, but I was serious when I

said not here."

"Franco doesn't give a shit about your time schedule."

Jake started the car and put it in reverse. "You two had the element of surprise and still got your asses kicked. If I lay eyes on you again, I won't be so nice."

"You won't see us coming next time."

Lunetti's guys climbed in their sedan and Jake backed away. He drove to the cop car and lowered his window. The cop reciprocated.

"I wanted to say thanks for checking on me."

She ticked her head toward Lunetti's guys. "Buddies, huh?"

"Not in the least. I thought they were going to rob me or something."

"Is that a fact?"

Jake bobbed his head. "In fact, the big guy had a gun in his jacket and a set of brass knuckles he tried to hit me with. Those legal in Nebraska?"

The cop considered the question. "To own, but illegal to carry concealed unless they have a license or permit."

"Those guys are from Missouri. Doubt they have either. Might be worth checking out."

She tracked the sedan as it headed south on 2nd Avenue. "It might be indeed."

"Any way I could find out for sure? I'm in town for a couple of days and would hate to be looking over my shoulder the whole time."

The cop handed a card to Jake. "You can give me a call later and I'll let you know. You drive safe, sir."

"Will do," Jake said, taking the card that read Amanda Hunter. "Thank you, officer."

Hunter drove forward, turned south on 2nd Avenue,

and turned on her lights and sirens, speeding after the sedan. Hopefully, it would keep them out of his hair for a while.

How did Lunetti even know where he was? Jake sat in the truck and racked his brain. Then it dawned on him. That woman from yesterday calling about the surveillance case on her husband when he and Bear drove up. Jake had given out too much information about the college visits, giving Lunetti's guys a trail to follow. He'd have to keep his head on a swivel. There could be more thugs waiting in the weeds.

CHAPTER FOURTEEN

Jake punched in the three Parker addresses on his phone. Marjory Parker lived in Gibbon, a few miles east of Kearney and wasn't who he was looking for. The other two were right here in town. As Jake entered the first R Parker address into Google Maps, Wendall emerged and climbed into the driver's side of an abused Ford F-150 with a large metal toolbox strapped across the sides. Manual laborer.

Wendall pulled back on the road and Jake's map kept him on the same path. He followed at a distance. They passed through the roundabout, heading east along Highway 10. After a couple of miles, Wendall turned north on Antelope Avenue in front of a decrepit barn that was more walls than roof. Even though the map told him to go straight to the Parker address, Jake followed him. His beady eyes and the way Iola clammed up when Wendall came in struck Jake as wrong. Maybe he was the abusing boyfriend.

A mile later, Wendall turned onto an inclined asphalt drive, bending its way toward a sprawling brick-faced house a few hundred yards away. Even at this distance, Jake could tell the house was massive. He stopped at the driveway entrance and zoomed on the map on his phone with a flick of his fingers. Husker Road. Traveling down Antelope a bit farther, Jake swung around in the empty lot of The Elks golf course and followed the map again to the Parker address.

R Parker number one lived east of Glenwood Corners down Highway 10. After a mile drive, Jake headed south on Imperial Avenue, slowing as he approached an old, dirty white farmhouse screaming abandoned. He stopped the car, wiping the fog on the driver's side window with his coat sleeve. A compact red barn that hadn't seen paint in a decade sat on the other side of a gravel drive. The north face of the house bore the wounds of a fire that had gutted and scarred but hadn't quite brought the structure to its knees. Snow blanketed the exposed, charred beams. Long forgotten farming implements and a rusted, red diesel fuel tank lay scattered about the yard. It was obvious nobody lived there. Given the look of things, he wasn't sure if anyone wanted to live there even before the fire.

Jake rolled forward, the smell of manure blowing through the vents. Up ahead on his right was a huge feedlot, hundreds of cattle tromping through the mud and snow. Ironically, the feed lot sat on Sweet Water Avenue. He plugged in the second R Parker's address and followed the directions back into town, past the Buffalo County Fairgrounds and into a subdivision of cookie cutter ranch homes squeezed onto narrow lots.

His cell rang. Foster. "What's up?"

"Snell's last signal bounced off a cell tower outside

of York, Nebraska off I-80 two weeks ago."

"Is that where her phone is now?"

"Can't tell. There's no signal. Battery's dead or she's turned it off. I'm worried it's the former."

Jake tapped the steering wheel, thinking. York was halfway between Omaha and Kearney. Snell, or at least her phone, was last headed this direction. There could be any number of reasons why her cell phone hadn't signaled the world in two weeks, but none of them were good.

"I'm going to keep digging," Foster said. "I'll keep you posted."

The home of R Parker number two sat on a corner lot on Avenue E. Tan, vinyl siding surrounding a large bay window. Cracked concrete steps led to a white front door with a ragged wreath, withered to the sticks like the owner hung it last year and never bothered to take it down. He turned the corner and spotted a heavy-duty black Ford truck parked in a forty-foot driveway in front of a closed garage door. Mud caked the wheels and sides of the truck, and a layer of ice obscured the windows. A set of balls positioned to look like testicles, hung from the trailer hitch. A definite redneck mobile.

Jake continued past the house and backed into a side street which gave him a clear view of the truck. He put the Expedition in park and waited, thinking about the girl in the convenience store. The way she clamped up when Wendall walked in. Afraid. The imposing ranch up on the hill on Husker Road Wendall had traveled to. Uninviting. Maybe he read into something that wasn't there.

Thirty minutes later, the garage door to the house opened and a man emerged. Weathered and wiry, he looked like the man from the photo Cat sent—Randall Parker. Jake couldn't make out the man's hands from this distance but would lay a sizable wager this was the guy he was looking for.

Parker started the truck and let it warm for a few minutes before backing from the drive and winding his way back toward the hotel district. Jake followed at a respectable distance.

A text from Bear vibrated. *I'm thirsty.*

Parker turned east off 2nd Avenue at 4th Street and angled his way to a massive brown-sided building, parking in the back of the crowded lot. The Big Apple Fun Center. Parker hopped from the truck and clipped across the parking lot. When he disappeared inside, Jake headed toward the hotel to grab Bear.

It was time for a beer and the Big Apple was now the perfect place to have one.

CHAPTER FIFTEEN

The Big Apple Fun Center was within walking distance of their hotel, but it was too freaking cold so they drove. The building was a combination pool hall, sports bar, bowling alley, putt putt, arcade, laser tag, go cart and children's play area. Jake wasn't sure what else they could cram in there. Nice place, clean, spacious. It was a week night and though the action in the pool room side was sparse, league players packed the bowling alley.

Bear wanted to shoot pool. Though the pool room was out of the bowling alley's line of sight, Jake spotted Parker in action on a far lane when they came in and figured he'd be there awhile. Jake served his time in a bowling league once and would rather have a root canal with no anesthesia than do it again. They had the pool room to themselves, except for a trio of farm boys in their early twenties who played an unending stream of crappy songs on the juke box.

The Warsaw boys were several beers deep and Bear was already thirty dollars in the hole to Jake. Jake peeked in on Parker during a couple of bathroom breaks while Bear racked the balls on the table. At ten bucks a game, Jake missed shots on purpose to keep Bear's diminishing wallet from emptying completely.

"Didn't you used to be good at pool?" Jake asked.

Bear missed a straight shot that a blind man could have made. "I've been a little busy arresting bad guys to work on my game."

Jake drained the ten ball in the corner pocket and chalked his cue. "Shooting pool is like riding a bike or having sex. The skill's supposed to come back to you eventually."

"Well, that explains it. I can't remember the last time I did either of those. There might be a statute of limitations on skill recovery."

"You want me to shoot left-handed to make it fair?" Jake missed the next shot on purpose.

"Don't tank the game on my account, you little asshole." Bear lined up a difficult bank shot, stroking the cue between his meaty fingers. "Any updates on Snell?"

"You know what I know."

Bear straightened. "Spill it, man. You being cryptic always makes me nervous."

"I'm not being cryptic. Foster said she was more or less on vacation after being shipped to Omaha for failing to leave Keats alone."

Bear's bushy eyebrows drew together. "How can you be more or less on vacation?"

"It sounds like it wasn't a voluntary two weeks off."

"What does Keats say?"

"Dude, Keats and I aren't fucking girlfriends exchanging gossip over mani-pedis. I haven't talked to him since the deal with the trafficked girls."

Bear rubbed chalk on the end of his cue, sniffing as

if he smelled Jake's lie. "What else did Foster say?"

"Just that nobody has heard from Snell in a few weeks, including her daughter. She's nervous and so am I. Foster thinks Keats had something to do with it."

"What do you think?"

Jake drained his beer. "Keats is too smart to risk taking out a Fed. Snell was a pain in his ass, but he wouldn't kill her. I told Foster I'd dig into it when we get back."

Bear checked his phone for the hundredth time before leaning back over the table.

"You expecting a call?" Jake asked.

"Landry hasn't texted me once. I don't even know where they are."

"Halle texted me. They're watching a movie in the dorm with the soccer girls. I think the girls are going to end up better than the shot you're about to take."

"Fuck you, Caldwell. This sum bitch is dropping in the corner pocket."

Jake waggled the money he'd won in the air. "Double or nothing you miss."

"Now you're really hustling me. No bet." Bear took the shot. The red three ball careened off the felted rail, missing the corner pocket by two inches, setting Jake up to close the match out. "Goddamn it."

"At least I know you aren't spending your work time shooting pool at the bars," Jake said. Three shots later, the game was over.

Bear dug in his wallet and pulled out another ten, slapping it in Jake's outstretched palm. "I forgot how good you were and how bad I suck. Buy me a beer."

"That I can do." Jake wanted eyes on Parker and motioned toward the alley. "Let's go watch the locals bowl. I can't take any more of this shitty music."

They paid for the pool, headed out of the bar area and down a wide carpeted hallway, dodging a group of screaming eight-year-olds heading toward the blinking lights of the arcade. The thump of heavy balls smacking the polished maple lanes and clashing plastic-covered wood pins greeted them. Jake steered them to the far end of the bar, closer to Parker and his bowling team. A minute later, they sat with frosty mugs of beer at a set of tables near the bar, twenty feet back from the bustling lanes.

Bear took a healthy swig and wiped foam from his dark beard. "We're getting old, Caldwell. We almost have girls in college."

"And I'll have one in daycare soon."

"You gonna find out if it's a boy or girl?"

Jake shook his head. "Maggie wants it to be a surprise. Life's last great mystery she calls it."

"I know the PI business has been a little slow for you. You figured out how you're going to pull off a new baby and a college girl?"

Thoughts of Keats's offer fluttered across his brain. He swatted them away with a wave of his hand. "We'll figure it out."

Bear drained the last of his mug. "Better go grab us another."

"I kicked your ass on the pool table, man. You're supposed to buy."

Bear smacked his last ten spot on the table. "There. You fly, I'll buy."

Jake snatched the bill and stood. "No wonder you're out of shape."

"I'm round. Round is a shape."

Jake sauntered to the bar. An older man who smelled like he was allergic to deodorant slid up in blue jeans over scuffed boots. A grizzly beard sat below an egg-shaped head. Parker. Jake moved a subtle step to the side to tamp down the odor and held the empty pitcher up to the bartender who offered an acknowledging dip of the chin.

The bartender set the two pitchers in front of Parker. "Here you go, Randall."

Parker grunted and tossed a twenty on the bar top. He grabbed the two pitchers, sinewy muscles flexed in his tanned forearms protruding from a red button-down shirt with the sleeves rolled to a two-inch cuff. Jake locked in on Parker's left hand.

Parker strode past a half-dozen lanes. He set the pitchers on a table where a trio of similarly dressed, but younger men swarmed the beer. Jake nabbed his pitcher, returned to Bear and poured fresh beers. Bear was talking about something from Warsaw, but Jake's attention was locked on Parker.

"Hey," Bear said, rapping the table with his walnut knuckles. "Did you hear a word I said?"

Jake yanked his attention from Parker. "Sorry."

Bear craned his head toward Parker's crew. "What the hell is so interesting about those guys?"

"Nothing. One of them looked familiar is all."

Bear cocked an eyebrow. "Bullshit. You've got that look in your eyes, like a coon dog who picked up a scent."

Jake waved him off. "Nah, it's nothing."

"Uh huh. Pull this leg and it plays jingle bells." Bear's cell phone dinged. "Girls are ready. Let's go."

Jake stood, threw one last glance toward Parker, and strode toward the exit. He didn't want to leave but couldn't dig into Parker without a lot of explaining. Plus, he had a place to track him from if necessary.

Bear's heavy footsteps plodded behind him.

All signs pointed to Parker as being the guy he was looking for. It wasn't just the way the man carried himself, a cocky swagger with his chest puffed out and neck elongated, like a rooster strutting in the barnyard. This man had the markings of a bad apple, like a shimmering black aura. What held Jake's attention was the tattoo on the man's left hand. It looked like the one from the grainy video—a stag with giant antlers from the first knuckle to the wrist. The one etched in the skin of the man who robbed Keats's money train.

CHAPTER SIXTEEN

The girls wouldn't stop chattering about their great time with the soccer team. The Kearney girls treated them like they were on the team. Landry would have signed an offer letter on the spot if the coach slid one under her nose. Halle liked everything fine, but she asked if they could swing by the store to buy a Husker sweatshirt. Jake made a mental note to Google the tuition cost again.

Once he and Halle were alone in their room, Jake tried to focus on her, but he kept thinking about Parker from the Big Apple. He was sure it was the right guy, but doubt crept in as he lay in the musty hotel room. Was the presence of the tattoo in and of itself enough? Was Snell dead? Was she headed this way voluntarily when she disappeared or was she abducted?

"Dad? Hello?"

Jake pulled focus on his daughter, sitting cross-legged on the bed across from his. Her long blonde hair thrown over her shoulder, her ice blue eyes narrowed. "I'm sorry, sweetheart. What were you saying?"

"Where's your head at?"

Maggie said the same thing to him all the time. Kids were sponges.

"Smartass," he said.

"Better than being a dumbass."

She didn't miss a beat. One of Jake's favorite sayings. "Just thinkin' about things."

"Money?"

"What?"

She played with her hair. "You know, being able to afford to send me to school. I'll understand if you guys can't swing it."

He plopped down and draped his muscular arm across her shoulders. "Honey, don't you worry that beautiful brain of yours. We've got it covered. Well, at least initially. Your heart set on Nebraska?"

A wry grin crossed her face. "I look really good in red."

He kissed her forehead. "Then a Husker you shall be."

"I have to get accepted first."

"They'd be crazy not to take you. Go get ready for bed. We're heading home early."

While she was in the bathroom, Jake slipped into shorts and a t-shirt and climbed in bed. As much as he tried to focus on the basketball game flickering on the room's television, his mind kept wandering to Parker at the Big Apple, the tattoo on his hand and Keats's "offer". A strong wind rattled the window frame as if telling him to knock it off.

He should call Keats and relay the information. If it panned out, Keats would reward him with Halle's undergrad tuition. If it didn't, Keats could let Jake off the hook because at least he tried. But what would

Keats's guys do to Parker? They'd kill the guy and quite painfully. Jake already had enough bad deeds weighing on his conscious if Parker turned out to be the wrong guy.

Jake could also ask Keats about Snell. Jake and Snell's heroics had cost Keats a pretty penny over the years. Snell's obsession with Keats grew over time, like a cancer. Jake would bet a decent amount of dough Keats had nothing to do with Snell's disappearance, but how much? While doubtful, Keats's hand in this wasn't implausible.

He cut his eyes to his phone charging on the nightstand. He could make the call to Keats, relay the info about the stag tattoo guy, go home and not worry.

Or he could stay and find out more information. The coincidence of Snell starting vacation at the exact time of the money train robbery wouldn't leave him alone. It was like a drip from a faucet in the wee small hours of the morning. He could try to ignore the annoying plink all he wanted, but it bored into his brain.

Halle emerged from the bathroom, clad in a Warsaw Track t-shirt, the normal summer tan on her long, muscular legs faded to oblivion. She kissed Jake on the cheek and slipped under the sheets in her bed. She typed a couple of text messages before turning off the lamp and rolling to her sleeping side.

Jake listened to her breathe, matching her cadence, his racing mind slowing, his body relaxing and slipping. His best ideas appeared in this state, before he faded to dreamland. His eyes drooped and his mouth fell open. The man's swagger. The tattoo on his hand. Parker. Just before he gave up the last of his consciousness, Jake knew what he would do. The problem was, nobody was going to like it much.

CHAPTER SEVENTEEN

At eleven in the evening, Darius Frost breached the dimness of the Dome Lounge, a sports bar off K Avenue, eyes sweeping the crowd. Though you could no longer smoke in the bar, decades of nicotine caked into every nook and cranny. You could replace the carpet, replace the ceiling tiles and paint the walls, but still get a nicotine buzz after a few minutes in the place.

The Dome was one of his usual watering holes. Low ceilings, neon beer signs plastered along the walls, and a chair at the end of the red topped bar with Darius's ass imprint pressed in the cushion. Nobody sat in the chair when Darius was in the bar. It wasn't like the bar reserved the seat for him exactly, but he'd more or less claimed it. The bartender informed unwitting patrons they might want to find somewhere else to sit when Darius entered. The urgency with which the bartender relayed the information was dependent on whether Darius walked or staggered in. Darius liked to kid himself the chair was reserved due to his prowess on the football field when he played for the Huskers but knew his father's reputation had more to do with it than anything. He planned to change that soon enough.

Phil and his wife Rita sweated behind the bar, popping tops off ice dripping beer bottles and mixing drinks. Phil spotted Darius first and nudged Rita who wandered to the end and whispered to an old farmer in a John Deere hat. The farmer slipped off the stool and moved to the other end of the bar.

"What's up, D?" Phil asked.

"You seen Ronnie?"

Phil threw a thumb over his shoulder. "Playing foosball with Stumpy. You want a beer?"

"And a shot."

As Phil flipped the cap off a Budweiser bottle and poured a shot of Crown Royal, Darius slid Conover's picture across the bar top. "You seen this guy?"

Phil squinted at the pic. "Doesn't look familiar? Should I know him?"

Darius threw the Crown to the back of his throat and snatched the picture from the sticky bar top. "No. If you do see him, give me a call."

"He do somethin' wrong?"

Darius set his jaw. "Just call me. That too fuckin' hard for you, Phil?"

Phil threw up his hands in surrender and found something to do at the other end of the bar. Darius grabbed the beer bottle and clomped toward the back, wearing his bad mood like a black cloak. He offered a curt wave to a few of the patrons, but most in the bar avoided eye contact with him.

Ronnie Sykes and his twin brother Lonnie leaned their chunky, six-foot frames over the foosball table, spinning the handles on opposite sides. Lonnie was nicknamed Stumpy because he lopped off his middle, ring, and pinky fingers at the second knuckle running a bandsaw at the chicken processing plant in Lexington. The disability made him an awful foosball player since he couldn't grip the rods well, but it didn't stop him from trying.

Darius stood at the end of the table and gripped the edges, watching the white ball bounce between the plastic figures. Ronnie lined up a shot, spun the stick, and the ball smacked in the back of the goal.

Ronnie's lips slid over chicklet teeth. "Game over, bitch. Pay up."

Stumpy flipped him the bird with his good hand. "What's up, D?"

Darius dropped the picture of the old man on the foosball table. "You two seen this guy?"

Stumpy bent over for a closer look. "Who is he?"

"Some guy named Conover. A private investigator asking about Juan Hidalgo."

"Oh shit."

Darius nodded. "Oh shit is right. Showed up at Elevator B today poking his old ass nose around. Neither of you seen him?"

"No, but we've been here since five."

"Can either of you drive right now?"

Stumpy exchanged looks with his brother. "Like I said, we've been here since five. We technically could drive, but it don't mean we should."

Darius drained half the beer in his bottle and scanned the crowd again. "Tomorrow, you two comb the town and get eyes on this guy. When you find him, call me and nobody else. Don't do a damn thing until you call me."

"Your dad know about this guy?"

Darius curled his upper lip. "Unfortunately. But that's all he knows, and I plan to keep it that way. If Xavier asks you, Juan didn't show up for work after pay day three weeks ago. That's it."

"But if he finds out—"

Darius jabbed a meaty finger into Stumpy's chest. "You worry about you. That should keep you busy. Just find this Conover asshole."

"You got it, boss."

Darius drained the rest of his beer and thumped the empty bottle on the table. "One more thing. The cartel is sending a crew our way. Don't know when they're gonna be here and don't know what they want, but if you run into any of them, remember if one of us cracks we'll be buried together in a cold hole with Juan."

***

Marc Conover parked his rental car in the darkness provided by a broken street light outside the Dome. He watched the giant of a man stomp inside the bar after tailing him from the ETC Elevator to the swanky country farmhouse and now to the bar. Tailing people inconspicuously in the middle of nowhere was a hell of a lot harder than Los Angeles.

Conover was tasked with finding Juan Hidalgo, and this buzz-cut behemoth was his best lead. Any trace of Juan vanished right here in the middle of Nebraska and Conover trusted his gut. The kid was still here somewhere. Probably dead, but he was paid to know for sure.

Over the last two days, everything he found seemed to lead back to Juan's place of employment:

the grain elevator. The fact the Giant skidded into the elevator parking lot an hour after Conover left and stormed back out with Conover's picture in his meaty paw was significant. He needed to find out who this guy was.

He put his binoculars to his owlish eyes and jotted the plate number of the Giant's truck on a notepad, hand shaking with what he feared was the beginning stages of Parkinson's. At fifty-eight, the disease seemed to be striking him early. But, his uncle had it and Conover knew that increased his chances. He'd eat his gun before he let it get as bad as his uncle.

Conover scrolled through the contacts on his cell and found the number for Lena in L.A. The woman could track down the Lost Ark of the Covenant. She answered on the third ring.

"Hey, Lena. It's Marc Conover."

Lena's smoky voice dripped with annoyance, her default tone. "I can read my caller ID. What do you want?"

"A favor. Can you run a plate for me and do a simple background on the owner?"

"Don't you have a guy for that?"

Conover ran a hand through his cropped silver hair. "Dino retired to Mexico last month. If I give you the plate, can you do it? I'll pay you."

Lena sighed. "I'd have to run it by Ray. He's got me busy tracking down a Hollywood starlet who's gone off the radar."

"Who?"

"Holly Lauren."

"Did you check her new condo in Malibu? I bet I know the guy who set up the security system last month. Run this plate for me and I'll give you the address."

Lena thought it over for a beat. "Fine. It'll save me time. I have a date tonight."

Conover hung up and made a quick call back to LA. There were a handful of guys who would do security work for the stars. He was lucky on the first try. He dialed Lena back, read her the plate, and gave her Holly Lauren's new address. Lena would have found it in a matter of minutes anyway. The girl had game.

"You have a date?" Conover asked. "What happened to the girl with the tattoo on the back of her neck?"

"Don't ask." Lena disconnected without another word. A habit she learned from her boss. Ray Donovan was a man of few words and hung up on Conover more times than he could count.

Conover reclined back in the leather seat and waited for the Giant to exit the bar. If there was one skill he mastered as a private investigator, it was waiting.

CHAPTER EIGHTEEN

Bear dropped his fork on his plate. "What are you talking about? If you're staying, I'm staying."

The girls exchanged questioning glances over the top of their avocado toast. They were elbow deep in breakfast fare at a Perkins on 2nd Avenue. Bear, as usual, had twice the amount of food of Jake, Halle, and Landry combined. And he was eating the bacon off Landry's plate.

Jake pushed his eggs around on his plate. "I need you to get the girls back home. Besides, you have a warrant sweep to do tomorrow."

"Dockery can handle that."

"Ken couldn't find his ass with both hands and a flashlight. Look, I'll rent a car to get me around town and I'll call you if I need you."

Halle stopped chewing and cut her eyes to Jake. "Why would you need him, Dad? What do you need to stay for?"

Jake curled his toes in his boots, pissed he didn't have this conversation with Bear before breakfast and away from the girls. "I got a call about a job here in town. Simple surveillance gig. But, it's going to take a couple of days."

"Surveillance of who?" Halle asked.

"Yeah, surveillance of some stranger from a bowling alley?" Bear asked.

Jake kicked his partner under the table. "Can I talk to you outside?"

"Hell no. It's ten degrees."

Jake stood and stomped toward the lobby area. An old couple waited for a table, but there was nowhere else to have this conversation without freezing. Bear followed, chewing on a piece of bacon.

Jake turned his back to the geriatric couple, keeping his voice low. "Snell may have been heading in this direction. I talked to Foster and she said the last signal they had from her pinged outside of York."

"So? York's gotta be like a hundred miles away. What's that have to do with you staying here?"

"I have to find out what happened to her. I know you don't like her, but she saved my life. I owe her."

Bear frowned. "Look, I don't hold any warm and fuzzies for the woman, but I wouldn't want anything bad to happen to her. I still don't get what finding her has to do with you staying here and conducting surveillance."

This was getting complicated. "I need to find the guy from the bowling alley."

Bear bit off another piece, gnawing on the pork and Jake's statement. "He just looked familiar, my ass. You didn't seem to care last night."

"I changed my mind."

"Bullshit. Something's up and I ain't leavin' here until you tell me."

Bear could read him like a book. He had to know

with certainty if this was the guy who ripped off Keats's money train. He didn't want to lie to his best friend, but if he mentioned the name Keats, Bear would throw a hissy fit in the middle of the restaurant and tell Maggie, and Jake would be in a world of hurt. So, he decided to tell Bear the truth, kind of.

"You remember the investment banker?"

"The money laundering job."

Jake checked on the old couple who dropped to a bench a few feet away. "They couldn't identify faces from the surveillance video but did pick up one distinguishing feature. One of the guys had a stag tattoo on his left hand."

"So?"

"The guy from the Big Apple had a tattoo of a stag on his left hand, same size and positioning as the video."

Bear's eyes narrowed. "That's some pretty long odds it's the same guy, Caldwell. I mean, you just randomly bump into him at a bowling—"

"Not randomly. I found the tattoo in a database, found his address, ran his plates and tailed him to the Big Apple."

"When did you do all this?"

"While you were napping," Jake said. "Look, I know it's a long shot, but it's worth checking out."

"And if you find out it's the right guy, what exactly are you gonna do?"

Jake threw up his palms, surrendering. "Nothing. I'll report it to the banker and head home. He sends his guys up. If they make a recovery of the stolen funds, I get a hefty finder's fee."

"Define hefty."

"Impressively large."

Bear's eyebrow shot up in a questioning slant. "So, we're going with vague this morning. What's all this got to do with finding Snell?"

"According to Foster, Snell may have been working on a case involving the stolen funds. If those funds lead here, maybe she came, too."

"And you won't take any sort of action yourself other than making a phone call?"

"Nope. Snell's a long shot. I'll poke around and see what information I can find on this guy. No drama. Can you please take the girls back to Warsaw? If I get a bead on Snell, I'll call you."

Bear chewed on his upper lip, eyes probing Jake's face. "No drama?"

Jake raised two fingers in the air. "Scout's honor."

"Scout's honor is three fingers, dipshit." Bear thought for a beat and growled. "All right, goddamn it. Let's get the girls together so we can hit the road."

Jake cringed, knowing he was pushing the limits. "Hey, can I get my gun out of your truck first?"

Bear's shoulders dropped. "No drama? You are such a fucking liar."

"A Scout is always prepared."

Bear held up three fingers, then turned them toward Jake and let two of them drop, giving Jake the bird.

***

Twenty minutes later, Bear dropped him off at the Enterprise Rent-A-Car lot. After asking Halle not to say anything to her mother before he had a chance to talk to her, Jake waved goodbye, his Sig Sauer on his hip and overnight bag in his hand. He headed inside where a pimple-laden twenty-something kid handed him the keys to a newer, charcoal gray Ford Fusion after Jake signed and initialed his life away. He didn't anticipate drama, but the way his luck ran, he played the odds and paid for the extra insurance.

He started the car and let the engine warm, his breath a cloud in the freezing exterior. Slipping his cell phone from his pocket, he called Keats. His old boss answered on the fourth ring.

"Caldwell? What time is it?"

"Morning. Sorry to wake you. I might have something on the situation we discussed earlier."

Keats yawned. "You find my money?"

"I may have stumbled upon a stag."

"Jesus, you do have something. Where are you?"

"Nebraska. I need to do some poking around but will let you know if I find out anything interesting. Thought I'd tell you so you don't send your goons with bags of doorknobs to beat me with."

"Very considerate of you."

"One other thing," Jake said. "Did you know your favorite FBI agent is missing?"

"Which one? I love so many of them."

"Snell."

Keats grunted. "If that bitch is missing, I didn't have a fucking thing to do with it."

"She hasn't contacted you recently?"

"I spotted her outside the warehouse a couple of months ago watching the place. Nothing since."

"I'll call you on the other deal if I find anything. I wanted to let you know I'm working on it. Oh, and one more thing."

"I thought Snell was one more thing."

"Well, I have another. Lunetti sent a couple of goons to try and rough me up."

Keats laughed. "Just two? How bad did you hurt 'em?"

"They were able to walk away, well limp away. I'd appreciate it if you could tell him to back off."

"I'll see what I can do."

Jake clicked off and called home, praying Maggie wouldn't kill him. With the pregnancy, her hormones raged, and it was a coin flip on how she'd take the news he wasn't coming back with Bear. He considered just telling her about Snell and leaving out the piece about the money train, but if she found out he lied to her, no amount of praying would save him.

She was less than thrilled, but after Jake made a dozen no drama promises, she relented. Maggie owed Snell, too.

"You think Victoria's there?"

"I don't know. It's a long shot but I'm going to do some poking around."

"And what if this is the guy you're looking for with the stolen money?"

"I make a simple phone call and leave the dirty work to someone else. I have to find out if it's the right guy. How's the baby?"

"Nice change of subject. Baby is jabbing its foot into my ribs. Think we might have a field goal kicker on the way. So, when do you think you'll be back?"

Heat seeped from the vents, a musty smell but a welcoming warmth. He spotted the button turning on the seat heaters and pressed it. "A couple of days at most. I'll keep you posted. Love you."

"Love you too, babe. Be careful."

He scanned the traffic on 2nd Avenue, pondering his move. He had little information on the man he was after and would have to be careful how he went about it. If he was on his home Kansas City turf, he'd know what doors to kick down and which lowlifes to shake, but he was in unfamiliar territory.

He cruised to Parker's house. No truck, and the garage door was closed.

Pulling out Officer Amanda Hunter's card, he dialed the cop's number. After a transfer and brief hold, she answered.

"Officer Hunter, this is your almost assault victim from the gas station yesterday."

"I got the feeling you weren't going to end up much of a victim."

"Probably not. I just wanted to check the disposition of our two knuckleheads."

"Knuckleheads is putting it kindly," she said. "Both had guns with the serial numbers filed off, a pair of brass knuckles and, surprise, a pound of meth in the trunk. It was a nice bust for me. Thanks for the tip."

"Glad I could help. I assume they won't be any trouble for me while I'm in town."

"I think you're safe. Be careful out there."

Lunetti's goons locked up was one less thing he'd have to worry about. He cased Parker's place for an hour with no results. Even if the man was home, there would be no casual way to approach him. He could break in and snoop around the house. But the lots were small enough to spit out one kitchen window into another, and he'd get spotted.

Jake called Cat and asked for a background check on Randall Parker. Per their usual arrangement, Cat bitched and moaned but agreed to do it. Setting the phone back on the console, Jake backed up and headed for the Big Apple. It was the only other lead he had.

CHAPTER NINETEEN

The Big Apple parking lot now held a half dozen cars and two oversized pickups. Jake backed into a spot and jogged inside, racing against the frigid wind trying to bite his face off. How did people live in this? The Ozarks turned cold as hell in the winter, but this was a whole other level, like comparing the prowess of a minor league baseball team versus the majors. Maybe he was getting old.

A ragged, raging band of five-year olds savaged the play area to his right as he passed the entertainment zone. Mothers huddled around a sea of floating mylar balloons, wearing haggard expressions of exhaustion as they sipped beers and tracked their kids. Jake passed the arcade, heading for the bar on the bowling alley side. Unlike last night, all but three of the thirty lanes were empty, unsurprising for noon on a weekday.

A disgracefully fat man with a dour face underneath a mop of auburn hair waddled along the bar. Thirtyish, he moved with the speed of a sloth who had popped a mouthful of valium. When he glimpsed Jake at the end of the bar, Jake could all but hear the gears in his head spinning, calculating the number of calories he'd have to burn to make the trek to the other end of the bar. Jake went to him instead.

"What can I get ya?" the bartender asked. His nametag read "Tank".

"That your real name?"

"It's what they called me in high school. Lineman."

Jake didn't figure the guy for a running back. "Gimme a beer, Tank."

"What kind?"

Jake spread his hands wide. "Surprise me."

Tank grabbed a pilsner glass and poured something from a tap labeled Snow Beast Winter Ale. "Here you go. Made in Broken Bow."

"Where's that?"

"About an hour northwest of here. Given this weather, it seems appropriate."

Jake sipped the Snow Beast. Cinnamon and malt with a vanilla finish. It wasn't his normal kind of beer but was pretty tasty. "A lot deader in here than last night."

Tank pulled beer bottles from a box and set them in the well. "Last night was league. It's also noon on a Tuesday."

"I was here. Made a guy a bet he couldn't pick up a split. He didn't make it and he disappeared. Thought maybe he'd be here."

Tank wiped sweat from his reddening face with the bar towel draped over his shoulder. "Who was it?"

"Guy named Parker. Randall Parker, I think."

Tank stopped, beady eyes narrowing. "You think?"

"I had quite a bit to drink."

"You're not from here, are you?"

Jake took another drink. This was an interesting reaction. "In town for work. Why?"

"Because if you were from here, you'd know if the man you made a bet with was Randall Parker. My advice would be to let it go."

"Why's that?"

Tank pressed his lips together and finished setting bottles in the well. "Trust me. Messin' with Randall and the crew he runs with isn't worth pursuin'. Enjoy your beer."

Tank waddled to the other end of the bar and washed glasses. Jake alternated his attention from the television showing highlights from Monday Night Football to Tank at the end of the bar. The man didn't seem nervous about Jake's question, but it was obvious it wasn't going to be a free flow of information. After a few minutes, Jake set the empty glass on the bar top and stood.

Tank waddled back over. "You want another?"

Jake pulled a twenty from his wallet and held it between his first two fingers. "Nah. But if I did want to find Randall Parker, where would I find him?"

Tank's eyes blinked like he tried to send a Morse code message. "I'm telling you, you should let it go."

Jake waggled the twenty in the air. "Just for shits and giggles."

Tank scanned the area for onlookers and snagged the twenty. "Try the Dome Lounge."

"Where's that?"

"K Avenue. North of Railroad Street. Best time would be after seven o'clock. You didn't hear it from me."

"Thanks, Tank."

Tank wiped his hands on his bar towel and turned away. "It was nice knowing you."

CHAPTER TWENTY

With no other immediate leads, Jake killed some time on a foot tour of the charming red brick-paved downtown filled with boutique shops and bars. What was it with this town and red brick? Someone made a fortune somewhere in the long history of Kearney.

Around one in the afternoon, he stopped in a sports bar called the Chicken Coop for a beer and a burger. He dropped to a black leather stool at the bar, a bank of round tables behind him half full of locals. He clicked on Snell's cell number. Straight to voicemail. Hearing her voice and carrying the uncertainty if she was dead or alive made his palms sweat.

After ordering, he called up a Google search on his phone and found a news article out of Omaha covering the discovery of Vinny V's bullet ridden body at a rest stop off I-29. No mention of the victim's name which wasn't surprising. Keats had made Vinny burn off his fingerprints when he started running Keats's dirty money to make it harder to trace Vinny back to him. The Feds would figure it out if the case ever hit their desk. Any information on Snell came up snake eyes. Not surprising.

The beer was cold and the burger better than average. He even managed to win a hundred bucks playing Keno using Halle's birthday as his number. His cell rang as he stuffed the bills into his wallet. Cat.

Jake plopped back in his chair at the bar, eyes locked on Sports Center on a flat screen above the bank of liquor bottles. "That was quick."

"You asked for simple license plate and background check. Frankly, you should be able to do this yourself by now. I already showed you how."

"Did you find anything or not?"

"I just emailed you the file. My bill, too."

Cat disconnected and Jake opened the email. There wasn't much. Truck was registered to a Randall Patrick Parker. Local Kearney address where he spotted the truck. Born June 24, 1972 in Gilman City, Missouri. Multiple addresses over the years, gaps when he spent time in various prisons for larceny, assault and a longer stretch for armed robbery in Jefferson City. Released from prison in 2012 and moved to Nebraska in 2014 after his parole ended. A flimsy record of a misdemeanor assault in Buffalo County last year but seems like he managed to keep his nose clean since. Other than robbing the Kansas City mob boss's money train, of course.

He wandered back to the street after paying his tab, the burger mixing with nervous energy to form an uncomfortable ball in his stomach. He found himself standing outside the World Theater, an old school movie theater housed in a tan bricked building on a corner of Central Avenue on the north end of downtown. Jake recalled seeing some news story about the place last year on YouTube. The guy who wrote the television series *The Blacklist* was from Kearney and renovated it.

With a couple hours left to kill before seven o'clock, Jake returned to the Days Inn and crashed on the bed. He threw his arm over his eyes to block out the light streaming through the window, the lack of sleep from the previous night and the afternoon beer weighing down his limbs, too tired to get up and close the blinds. Sleep came fast and hard.

Jake sat at the dining room table. Stony was in the kitchen at the Warsaw house, cooking eggs on a cast iron skillet and singing an old Don Williams song called "I Believe in You." Jake hadn't heard the song in twenty years, but he bet he could still sing every word. A young version of his sister Janey sat on the couch, eyes locked on the television with the foil-covered rabbit ears, twirling her curly red locks around her index finger. His brother Nicky sprawled in Mom's old easy chair, dead eyes staring at the stained ceiling, the heroin needle that spewed the fatal dose into his ravaged veins poking from his arm, right in the middle of the forehead of a stag tattoo he never had.

"Here you go, Jake," Stony said, another stag tattoo he didn't have either etched on his forearm. The stag's antlers reached out and shoveled eggs from the pan onto Jake's plate. The eggs were black with streaks of red. Jake poked them with his fork. The red oozed blood. The copper scent bit at his nose.

Jake looked up. Stony's skin sagged down his skull, forming lined bunches of flesh on his neck. "When did you get the stag tattoo?"

Stony raised the pan as if he were going to crack Jake over the head with it. Instead, he dropped it on the table, blood from the eggs splattering Jake like he sat next to a gunshot victim. Stony leaned in, the odor of death and decay and cancer wafting from him. "Eat it, you little shit. We can't go wastin' good food."

Jake stared at the eggs. Maggots wriggled through the blackness.

On his right, Snell sat with her hands in her lap glaring at him, clothed in the blue dress they buried their mother in. She spread open a Bible, finger tracing the pages as she brought up a cell phone with her other hand and ate it like it was a cookie. The plastic crunched and sliced open her mouth, blood droplets splattering on the Bible pages. She used a finger to trace a picture of a stag with her own blood.

Stony dropped to the chair across from Jake. "And tell your worthless brother to get off his lazy ass and come eat."

"Nicky's dead."

The skin dropped from Stony's skull completely, falling across his chest like a bloody apron. He peered over Jake's shoulder to the living room, nothing but bulging eyes set deep in a crimson streaked skull of a stag, antlers growing toward the ceiling. "Oh, yeah. Guess he is. Shoulda been you, Jake. Shoulda been you."

Jake cried out and jerked upright in bed, covered in sweat and eyes probing the dimness of the room, chest heaving.

Outside, the night had all but conquered the light. The clock on the dresser read six o'clock. He slapped his cheeks until the nightmare faded. Son of a bitch. What the hell was that about?

After a moment, he rolled from the bed and climbed into the shower, letting the hot water beat away the dream, but it wouldn't fade entirely. The image of the maggots wriggling from the eggs and the stag's naked jaw bone flapping up and down played in an unwelcome loop with the soundtrack of *Shoulda been you, Jake.*

He didn't need a psychologist to interpret that dream to tell him it was time to go to the Dome bar and find Randall Parker and the stag tattoo.

CHAPTER TWENTY-ONE

The Dome was dim and half full as Jake strode through the door. A U-shaped bar with a dozen stools in front and a dozen round tables behind it along with a pool table in the corner. Neon bar signs and Nebraska Cornhusker football memorabilia lined the walls. A young guy with a bushy, untrimmed beard ran the Keno game from the corner. This state loved Keno. Other than the hotel, every place he'd been ran the game.

He sidled to the bar and ordered a beer from a leather-faced man with white hair dropping from the back of a red Husker's hat to the top of his stooped shoulders.

"Any particular kind?" the bartender asked.

"Don't care. As long as it's cold and in a clean mug."

"Cold we got. Clean mug? That's another story."

Jake dropped one of the tens he won off Bear on the mahogany and settled into a stool at the end of the bar with his back against a wood-paneled wall, where he could get a good view of the entire bar and nobody could sneak up behind him. The bartender set Jake's change in front of him along with a bowl of peanuts before walking back to his perch at the other end of the bar.

Luke Combs played on the jukebox near the Keno guy at a perfect volume. Loud enough to hear, but you could still have a conversation without screaming. A few sad souls searched alone for life's answers in their drinks. A trio of local farmers howled and swapped stories denigrating each other. They'd obviously been there a while. Another half dozen patrons sat in twos and threes at the round bar tables, a mix of young and old. Two harder characters shot pool in the corner with the competency of two drunk chimpanzees with sticks. Jake liked the vibe of the place.

As Jake finished his second beer, the door to the bar flung open and a hulk swaggered through. Mid-twenties, thick beard, maybe six foot five, two-hundred fifty pounds and as solid as a brick shithouse. He surveyed the bar as he wiped a hand over his slicked back nutmeg hair, his mouth set cruelly. Jake smelled the arrogance seeping from his pores. The hulk held up four fingers to the bartender who popped the tops from four beer bottles and set them on the end of the bar. It might have been Jake's imagination, but the volume level of conversation in the bar seemed to drop once the hulk entered, like when the black hat in a Western breaks through the swinging doors of the saloon.

Randall Parker trailed in with two ridden hard and put away wet dudes in ripped jeans and scuffed boots lagging behind him. One was Wendall, the guy Jake followed to the mansion on Husker Road.

Parker's narrow eyes scanned the crowd, settled

on Jake for a moment before following the hulk back toward the pool table, grabbing the beer bottles from the bar on his way and leaving a twenty to the bartender. Even though the two rough guys were in the middle of a pool game, the hulk shoved the balls toward the end and told the other two to rack 'em up. Wendall and the other guy perched on barstools to watch.

The pecking order of the group of six was clear. The hulk was the alpha, Parker the beta, Wendall and the other guy who came in with Parker were grunts and the two rough guys playing pool were comic relief. Who was the hulk?

The bartender shoved the twenty into the register and spotted Jake's empty beer mug and sauntered over. "I'm Phil by the way. Want another?"

"Sure. Who's the big guy at the pool table?"

Phil's beady eyes narrowed as the beer filled Jake's mug. "Why you askin'?"

"Just wondering. He looks familiar."

"You must not be a Husker fan."

"He played?"

Phil set the mug on the bar top, white foam spilling down the side. "And you ain't from here. Otherwise, you'd know who Darius Frost is."

Jake stuck his index finger into the beer foam to knock it down. "He related to the coach?"

Jake was more of a Big 12 conference follower, but knew the Huskers hired Scott Frost as their head coach and fans were batshit happy. *That* Frost was a football legend in the State of Nebraska who quarterbacked the Huskers 1997 national championship team.

"Darius ain't related to Scott, and don't even think about asking him if you like having all your teeth."

"Sore subject?"

"All his life. But, he did play for the Huskers. For a while, anyway."

"What happened?"

Phil opened his mouth to respond, and then, as if he thought better of it, closed it and wandered back to his stool. Interesting response. Jake sipped his beer and watched Parker from his peripheral vision. The man was a pretty good pool player, beating Darius Frost soundly. As Frost racked the balls for a new game, Parker clipped across the bar and past Jake to the bathroom.

Jake spotted the older man a few stools down tracking Parker as he walked to the bar before turning his attention back to the pocket-sized notepad in front of him, scratching a few notes and sliding it into the pocket of his pressed khaki's. He was in his late fifties, thin with white hair cropped close to his skull. His face was distinguished, like he was a high-born person in another life. Definitely out of place in the bar, from the notebook to his white button-down shirt.

A minute later, Parker returned and stepped to the bar beside Jake, signaling to the bartender for a beer and a chaser. He placed his wiry arms on the bar and cranked his head toward Jake. "How you doin'?"

Jake spun a quarter turn in Parker's direction. "Better than I deserve. You?"

"Can't complain. You were at the Big Apple last night."

"Shot some pool and had a couple of drinks."

Parker's eyes probed Jake's face. "First there, now here. Kinda weird."

"Coincidence. This town isn't that big."

"No, it ain't. I'm also wondering why you keep

staring at me from across the bar. Either me or the pool table, and I seriously hope it ain't me. You wanna play? Twenty bucks a game."

Jake was pretty sure he could take Parker on the green felt but didn't want to wallow in the middle of his crew. "Nah, you'd clean me out. I didn't mean to stare. You look familiar, like someone I should know but can't quite place. Where you from?"

Parker threw the shot to the back of his throat and smacked his thin lips, his eyes locked on Jake. "Live right here in Kearney."

"But you're from somewhere else."

"Why you say that?"

"The twang in your voice. It's faint, but it's there. Not the Deep South, but south of here. Missouri or north Arkansas maybe."

Parker drew back for a second and turned his body to face Jake, left elbow resting on the bar top, tattoo close enough for Jake to touch. "That's a pretty good read. And who are you?"

Jake supposed asking the question *Why did you rob the money train of a vicious Kansas City mobster and shoot his bagman to death?* seemed a little obvious. "I'm nobody."

"You look like a cop."

"No way. Just passing through town. Buy you another shot?"

Parker sipped his beer. "Why?"

"Seems like a friendly thing to do."

"Since you were starin' at me and all, I wanna make sure you're not gonna roofie me."

"I don't swing from that side of the plate."

"Phil. Two shots of Jack." After Phil delivered the glassware, Parker offered his shot glass. "Here's to swimmin' with bowlegged women."

Jake clinked his glass against Parker's and downed the shot, the whiskey burning its way down his chest. "Nice tattoo. You a hunter or it mean something else?"

Parker sucked his tongue against his teeth, smacked the shot glass on the bar top and leaned in. "Thanks for the shot, friend. As for the tattoo, it roughly translates to mind your own fuckin' business. You have a good night."

Parker held the stare down for a beat and swept back to the pool table, putting Jake no closer to finding out for sure if Parker was involved with the money train and potentially Snell.

CHAPTER TWENTY-TWO

Darius Frost and his crew carried themselves with a swagger and volume growing exponentially with each beer and shot they downed. They drank like prohibition would go into effect at midnight.

Jake sipped his beer and scoured the internet on his phone for stories about Darius Frost. Verizon's service was spotty in the bar and it was slow going. Best he could tell, the team dismissed Frost for violation of team rules which could mean anything. Old comments on chat boards surmised he'd gotten in one fight too many on and off the field for the Huskers. Out of the corner of his eye, he spotted the khaki pants man idling his way.

"Mind if I sit?" the man asked, motioning to the empty barstool.

"Be my guest."

"Name's Conover. Marc Conover."

Jake shook the outstretched hand, thin bones, but firm shake. "I'm Jake."

Conover adjusted his coaster so it lined up parallel with the bar and ensured his mug sat in the dead center of the cardboard square. "So, which of these guys are you keeping your eye on?"

"Seems like the same ones you are," Jake said. "Figured we'd talk sooner or later. You a Fed?"

"I'm not that important."

"Who said Feds are important? Most of 'em I know are a pain in the ass. You're definitely law enforcement, though. Too old to be a beat cop. Maybe a detective? And you're too tan to be from around here. Maybe Florida or California."

"Los Angeles. Retired. Homicide. Not bad, Jake."

"Blind squirrel, broken clock." Jake liked the man. He had a handsome, but weathered face, deep lines around his eyes born of hard work on the streets. "I'm guessing you aren't in Nebraska in the middle of winter on vacation."

The man reached into his pocket and extracted a simple white card. Thin stock with black lettering. Marc Conover, Private Investigator with a phone number and an address in Vernon, California. "I'm looking for a guy."

Jake thumbed the card. "One of the guys over there?"

"You know any of them? Saw you talking to one."

"Just met him tonight."

"I think they might know something about the kid I'm looking for. Came out here for work from L.A. Last seen with some of those guys, but nobody's seen him for weeks. Family is worried. Hoping these guys can lead me to him."

"So, go talk to them."

Conover nursed his beer. "Not here. Bad shit can happen in a bar when you start asking strangers questions. What's your interest?"

"I thought bad shit can happen when you ask strangers questions."

"But there's six of them and one of you."

"Who said I'm interested?"

"Me and my thirty plus years of experience," Conover said. "You've been eyeballing them for the last hour. Subtly, but enough for me to notice."

Across the bar, Frost drilled the eight ball in the corner pocket and howled triumphantly. The howl died in his throat when he noticed Jake and Conover. His grin turned to a scowl as he unfolded a sheet of paper he pulled from his back pocket, alternating glances between it and Jake and Conover sitting side by side across the room. With pool cue in hand, he stomped toward them.

Jake's gut tightened. "Oh shit."

Conover nodded. "I see it. Coming for me or you?"

Jake slid to the edge of his seat. "Not sure it matters."

As Frost rounded the bar, pool cue swinging by his side, the nearby patrons found some compelling reason to check out another section of the bar or to head out the front door. The two comic relief guys stayed behind at the pool table, happy to gain back their access to the felt. Wendall and the other lackey positioned themselves on either side of Frost as he stopped in front of Conover's barstool. Parker took a seat at the end of the bar near the door, leaning back in the chair and sipping his beer.

This trio swaggered like an ass kicking posse in the making, and Jake's immediate instinct was to wade in, puff his chest, and dare them to make a move. Maggie's no-fists reminder rolled through his brain so he remained seated. He thought, in this case, she'd be dead wrong, but he'd give her the benefit of the doubt and wait it out.

His lizard brain analyzed the situation. One exit to his left past the bathroom, and he'd have to get past one guy. Another on the other side of the bar he could get to by hopping past Phil. The last exit was out the way he came in, but he'd have to wade through Frost and his crew. Maybe Parker as well. Frost gripped a pool cue. One of his buddies had a knife shoved in his right rear jean's pocket—Jake noticed when they first came in. Wendall flicked his eyes between Conover and Frost, like an attack dog waiting for permission from his master to move. Scars crisscrossed Frost's knuckles. He was no stranger to a dust up and, given his size, he hadn't lost many of them.

Frost jabbed Conover with the skinny end of the pool cue, leaving a streak of blue cue chalk on his white shirt. "Hey, old man."

Irritation flickered in Conover's denim-colored eyes at the chalk mark. "What can I do for you?"

"I'm wonderin' why you're poking your nose around my family business."

"And what business is that? I went to a lot of them today."

Frost's scarred knuckles blanched white, gripping the cue. "The grain elevator."

Jake already knew where this was going. Conover's demeanor screamed calm, his years of police experience helping him do so. But, Frost would make this encounter bloody. He was a bully and a drunk one at that. Inebriated assholes loved getting into bar fights. Conover could probably handle himself if he was forced to deal with one of them, but he gave up a lot of size and age to Frost. And there were the

HUSKER ROAD | 127

two other guys on either side of him to worry about.

Conover placed his hands palm down on his khaki's. "It was Juan Hidalgo's place of employment and I'm looking for him. His people are worried."

"Did they tell you nobody's seen him since he collected his last paycheck?" Frost asked.

"That's what they said in the office at the elevator."

Frost slipped a half step closer. Jake tensed. It wouldn't be long now.

"Then what are you still doing here?"

Conover jerked his chin toward Jake. "Just having a beer. Besides, I'm still looking for Juan. Maybe you and I could talk tomorrow?"

Frost took the business card Conover offered, crumpled the paper in his meaty paw, and dropped the ball to the floor. "Maybe you should get the hell out of here and stop poking your nose around where it don't belong before something bad happens."

Jake slid forward, still on the edge of the stool, but his boots now touching the floor.

Conover's eyes darted between the trio of men standing before him. "You boys have something to hide? You're awfully defensive over a few simple questions from an old man."

Frost jerked the cue up, and Jake leapt from the stool and blocked Frost's downward speeding forearm with his own. Bone met bone and sent a shockwave of pain through Jake's upper arm. Jake grunted in pain, then jabbed a palm hand strike under Frost's chin and sent the behemoth stumbling back and the pool cue clacking to the floor. Shithead One threw a lazy haymaker. Jake ducked but the follow through hit Conover in the face. Jake unleased a side kick to the knee of Shithead One, then spun and cracked

Wendall with an elbow to the chin. Both men dropped to the floor as Frost collected himself.

Blood dripped down Frost's chin, and fire blazed in his eyes. A snarl curled his lip as he charged toward Jake. If he was smart, Frost's prefrontal cortex would have registered the scene in front of him. He was bleeding, one of his guys writhing on the ground in pain clutching his knee and the other out cold on the bar room floor with their assailant standing combat ready. But Jake wasn't surprised Frost charged. He expected nothing less from a drunk bully transformed into a bull charging red in the ring.

Frost came in too hard and too fast, telegraphing a round house punch. Jake ducked the punch with little effort and let Frost's momentum carry him past. He created maximum torque with a twist of his muscular torso and unleashed a vicious back fist to Frost's passing skull. Bone met bone once again, the force of the blow buckled Frost's knees and he tumbled down, his head cracking the wood paneling by Jake's bar stool. Frost tried to get his knees under him but chose to roll to his side instead.

He glared at Jake with fiery eyes, chest heaving and blood from a split lip trickling down his chin. "You're dead, motherfucker."

Jake smirked. "Like I haven't heard that one before. Remember, you started it."

"And I'm gonna finish it."

"It's your funeral."

Jake spun to movement in his peripheral vision. Parker walking toward him from the end of the bar, hands raised in surrender.

"I'd get out of here if I were the two of you," Parker said, baring his chicklet teeth. "I don't just mean out of the bar. Get out of the county as fast as you can."

Jake wiped the blood from his knuckles on a bar napkin and dug a twenty from his pocket. He tossed it on the bar toward Phil. "Sorry about the mess."

The bartender eyed the bill like it was covered in Ebola. "Screw the county. I'd get the hell out of the entire State of Nebraska if I was you two."

Conover led the way and Jake backed toward the door, his eyes glued to Parker. When the frigid night air struck his face, he turned to Conover. "We should talk."

Conover squinted against the wind, gingerly probing the side of his head. "Probably."

"Meet me at the Days Inn on 2nd Avenue. Room 206. I'll supply the beer."

CHAPTER TWENTY-THREE

Twenty minutes later, Jake opened the door to his hotel room and let Conover pass inside. While buying the beer, Jake had Googled Conover to ensure he was who he said. Jake bumped the thermostat up a couple of degrees. The heating unit, along with the wall, rattled on, then smoothed out by the time Jake set the twelve pack of beer on the desk against the wall. Conover dropped to one of the two queen beds and took the beer Jake offered.

Conover twisted the cap from the bottle and stuck it in his pocket. "Well, that was fun."

Jake dropped to the desk chair. "For us, not them."

"No, for you. I got hit. You didn't get a scratch on you."

"Not true," Jake said, flexing his fist. "I skinned my knuckles on the back of Frost's head. Damn thing was like hitting a bag of cement."

Conover drained a third of the beer. "You jumped into a three-on-one situation without thinking."

"Three on two. And I thought about it plenty as they made their approach."

"I wasn't much help, I'm afraid."

Jake waved him away. "You distracted the big guy and allowed me to surprise him. As dumb as he looks, I doubt he'll make the same mistake again."

Conover's eyes swept over Jake. "Where'd you learn to fight like that?"

"I had some martial arts training years ago. Most of it evolved over time, learning what works and what doesn't through trial and error."

"You don't look like you lose much."

"Losing's how you learn what not to do," Jake said. "But, fighting multiple guys at once isn't hard, because the idiots almost always take turns."

"What happens when they don't take turns?"

"You get your ass kicked. You were a cop. Didn't you ever have to take on more than one at a time?"

Conover's eyes dipped to the floor. "Once. Two eighteen-year-old kids wanted for murder. But I had a gun."

"What happened?"

"One went away in cuffs and the other in a body bag."

"Jesus. Sorry about that."

Conover shrugged, a slow, sad rise and fall of his shoulders, and drained the rest of the bottle. "It was me or him. Doesn't mean I don't think of them every day. What I could've done different which would've led to a different outcome."

"Come up with anything?"

"No. Can we talk about something else?"

"Sure. You want to tell me why we're both looking at the same group of guys?"

"Give me another beer first." Jake handed him the bottle, and Conover pocketed the cap again. "I'm here to find a kid named Juan Hidalgo, as you heard."

Jake grabbed another beer. "Right."

"He worked for the giant in the bar. His mother and father are Mexican immigrants from El Aguaje. The town is like many others in Mexico, controlled by the cartels. They wanted a better life for Juan and his sister. Armando, the father, started a hardware business and managed to make a pretty good middle-class life for his family. Juan was supposed to take over the business but had other ambitions."

"Like what? Working at a grain elevator in Nebraska?"

Conover removed his jacket, folding it with care and precision before placing it like a newborn on the bed. "More like not scrimping and scraping. He ended up working his way northeast from California, taking jobs along the way for a few weeks at a time before ending up here in Kearney. He'd send money back to his family, though they didn't need it. His father thought Juan was trying to make a point."

Jake took a drink. "What happened once he got to Kearney?"

"He started working for the grain elevator. Instead of working a few weeks and moving on, he stayed. Found himself a girlfriend and moved in with her."

"Maybe the love of a good woman kept him here."

Conover's eyebrows shot up. "Definitely love based on an interview with one of his neighbors. But Juan loved the money as well. The father told me the money Juan sent back kept getting larger. The last FedEx envelope was thirty-five hundred dollars. No way Juan made that much as a grunt at a grain elevator. He did something on the side. Maybe something with the crew we ran into tonight."

"You talk to the girlfriend?"

"Not yet. Keep missing her. She lives in a mobile home park off Grand Avenue."

"Any chance the lovebirds ran off together?"

"Possible, but my gut's telling me something different. Your turn."

Jake's brain spun up a story. How much did he want to tell this stranger? Certainly not the whole story. But maybe he could spit out the lie he told Bear. It was close enough to the truth. Did the source of Juan's new-found wealth have anything to do with Keats's money train?

"I took over a PI business from a guy in Kansas City when he retired to the Florida Keys. I'm not licensed or anything, but people still come to me because I get things done."

"Why aren't you licensed?"

"Because I wouldn't pass the background check. Long story we don't have enough beer for. Anyway, this investment banker hires me to track down some money taken from him for a cut of the recovery."

"Like embezzlement?"

"Not exactly. Let's say he needed a good dry cleaner."

"Gotcha. And you traced the money here?"

"Not exactly," Jake said. "See, the money was headed to the cleaner, and a group of guys took down the shipment. They shot and killed the courier. The only distinguishing feature of the gunmen was the stag tattoo on one of the gunmen's hands."

"Like the member of Frost's crew who stayed out of the fray then warned us to run? The one who stopped and talked to you before I came over."

"You noticed that, eh?"

"I was a detective for thirty years. So, you think these guys might be involved in ripping off your investment banker. How'd you trace them to Kearney?"

"Associate of mine tracked him through a federal database."

"Smart."

"His name's Randall Parker. Has a half-decent rap sheet. Seems like he'd be the type who—"

Three loud, rapid knocks sounded from Jake's door. He and Conover jumped up and exchanged wary looks. Jake grabbed the Sig Sauer from his overnight bag and approached the door, hugging the wall with his back. The knocks turned to thumps and someone from the other side raised their voice and spoke Jake's name. Jake stuck his eye to the peephole, his face crunching with confusion at who was on the other side.

"Just a sec," he shouted, darting back to the bed and shoving his Sig under the mattress. "Cops."

Conover's face fell. "The fight at the bar. Somebody must've tailed us."

Jake opened the door and two Kearney cops stared him down. The one in front wore a nametag reading "Raasch". He was around Jake's age, shorter and heavier with a shaved head and banjo eyes. The other guy, a kid who was probably carded when he went to the liquor store stood to the side with his hand resting on the butt of a nine-millimeter, still in the holster with the strap undone.

Raasch studied Jake and looked over Jake's shoulder to Conover. "Evening, sir. Were you at the Dome tonight?"

"Why?"

"Because I'm asking. Were you?"

"I'm guessing you already know the answer or you wouldn't be here."

Raasch plucked handcuffs from his belt. "Please place your hands on the wall, sir, and spread your legs."

The other cop's hand tightened on the butt of his gun, so Jake complied as Raasch patted him down. He firmly moved Jake's arms behind his back and cuffed him. "You're under arrest for the assault that took place at the Dome."

"How'd you find me?"

"Someone called it in and told us where you were."

Jake craned his head over his shoulder. "Nobody at the bar knew who I was."

"Man, I'm just doing what I'm told."

Conover stepped to the door. "It was self-defense, officers. He was protecting me."

Raasch scanned Conover from head to toe. "You can meet us at the station and make a statement."

Raasch jerked Jake down the hall.

Conover shut the door and trailed behind. "Jake, anyone you want me to call?"

Jake craned over his shoulder. "Call James Parley with the Benton County Sheriff's Office in Warsaw, Missouri. Tell him what happened."

Raasch stopped and turned Jake to face him, his eyes wide with surprise. "You know Bear?"

"He's my best friend. How do you know him?"

"Small world," Raasch said. "He's my old boss. I used to work in Benton County."

"No shit? Is that a good thing or a bad thing for me?"

Raasch tugged him back down the hall. "It's not anything for you. I like Bear, but it isn't going to help you. You pissed off the wrong hombres tonight."

CHAPTER TWENTY-FOUR

Darius Frost strangled the steering wheel of his truck, licking the blood seeping from his split lip. His head ached like it was being crushed in a vice, and the Kearney street lights wore halos. Another goddamn concussion. He'd suffered more of them than he cared to count playing football, and the guy in the bar added one to the tally sheet.

Parker smoked in the passenger seat. Ronnie, Stumpy and Wendall slumped in the backseat of the truck, all smart enough to keep their mouths shut after watching their boss get his ass kicked.

"Xavier say what he wanted?" Parker asked, blowing a stream of smoke through his hooked nose.

"Just said for us to get there."

"Jesus, think my jaw's busted," Wendall moaned from the backseat.

"Shut up," Darius snarled. "Or I'll make sure it is."

A red haze covered Frost's field of vision, pulsating and blotched, like blood splatters. He was furious, but mostly embarrassed. His swollen, split lip and goose egg on his forehead were a shameful billboard he would have to display to his father. Frost and his crew did pretty much whatever they wanted, and anyone who challenged them wound up in the hospital or worse. Tonight, the entire bar watched one guy kick the hell out of half his crew in three seconds without breaking a sweat. Probably the reason for the summons from Xavier.

Darius swung east on the highway, heading toward Husker Road. The fight replayed on a loop in his head, the anger mounting with each successive run. He glared at Parker. "Where were you when that dude was wadin' through the three of us?"

Parker met his eyes. "Watching from the end of the bar."

"Goddamn coward. Then you disappear."

"Wasn't a thing I was gonna do to him. Besides, one of us needed to be coherent enough to trail him when he left."

Frost pulled back. "Where is he?"

"Days Inn on 2nd. Don't get your panties in a bunch getting over there. I called our contact. Cops picked him up a few minutes ago."

"For what?"

"Assault."

Frost ran his thick fingers through his hair, lip curled. "Goddamn it. I want this asshole, not the cops."

Parker pulled a cigarette from the pack in his pocket and lit it off the butt of his existing smoke. "Relax, D. You're not gonna file charges, so they're gonna hold him for a while, question him, and let him go. Gives us time to regroup, figure out who he is and come up with a plan."

Frost fumed and turned north on Antelope, his father's ranch lit up in the distance. "He was sitting with Conover."

"Yup, which is why we should figure out who he is. Might be he was some random good Samaritan who stepped in when you lost your shit. Might be he's with Conover and somebody we should keep an eye on."

"He might be someone we need to bury in a deep fuckin' hole next to Juan."

Parker blew a plume of smoke out the window as they turned up Husker Road and rolled up the hill toward the house. "Might be. Time will tell."

Darius's brow wrinkled. A pair of black Chevy Tahoes he didn't recognize sat in the front circle drive. "Who the hell is that?"

Darius and his crew climbed from the truck and headed up a stone walkway bordered by ornamental accent lights. He paused at the double doors, wiped his clammy palms on his coat, and went inside, careful to wipe his feet. Track dirt in Xavier's house at your peril.

A figure stepped from the shadows, as thick as Darius with dark skin, black hair, and soulless eyes in a midnight blue suit bulging at the seams. The man's arms crossed in front of him, held together by the silver-plated Smith & Wesson in his hands.

Darius stepped back. "Who are—"

"Darius." His father waved him forward, worry lining his face. An unusual expression for Xavier. "Come inside. We need to talk. Now."

Darius stepped toward his father as if he navigated a minefield, afraid one wrong move would blow him up. His crew followed, giving the gunman a wide berth. Darius glanced one last time to the gunman before Xavier pulled him around the corner into the living room. The gunman's smile sent a shiver down

Darius's spine.

"Who are these guys?"

Xavier pulled Darius close as they stepped toward the study, voice dropping low. "Our friends from south of the border and they are pissed off. Keep it together."

The tremble in his father's hand resonated on Darius's shoulder. Fear wasn't an emotion he'd ever seen from his dad. As they turned into the study, Darius knew why. Five Hispanic men scattered around the room, dressed in slacks and jackets with stern faces which said they could cut off a man's digits with a rusty, dull knife without raising their blood pressure a single point. A sixth man rose from the chair his father normally sat in. A striking figure in a silver suit, black shirt, thick peppered hair combed back.

He crossed the room and extended his hand. His accent was present, but not overwhelming. "Ahhh, the prodigal son returns. You must be Darius. I'm Armando Diaz. Please, have your men warm themselves by the fire. It's such a cold night."

Xavier taught Darius to shake a man's hand with enough pressure to make him wince a bit as his bones ground together. Establish dominance. However, the man in front of him looked like the type who wouldn't appreciate such a display, so Darius kept his grip on the weaker side of firm. "Nice to meet you, Mr. Diaz."

Diaz tracked Frost's crew as they were herded around the roaring fire. "What happened to your face?"

Darius glanced at his father. Xavier's lips drew in and his nostrils flared, the worry morphing to anger as he got a good look at his son in the light of the study.

"Just a misunderstanding in a bar," Darius said. "You should see the other guy."

A stoic wave dropped like a veil across Diaz's dark complexion and he released Darius's hand. "I'll get right to the point, Darius. As I was telling your father, my employer has some concerns about your operation out here in this arctic wasteland."

"What kinda concerns?"

"Two million dollars' worth. Two million dollars which was supposed to be transferred to our accounts last week and wasn't."

Darius's knees buckled a little. The La Familia men glowered at Darius and his crew like they'd slept with their sisters.

Diaz stepped closer. Though six inches shorter, the man exuded power with death on his breath. "What do you know about our two million dollars, Darius?"

"It's all there. We just haven't transferred it."

Diaz closed in, face hovering below Darius's. Darius willed his feet to anchor to the floor as they wanted nothing more than to turn and run from this man, not an option with the La Familia men surrounding Darius and his crew.

Diaz's voice dropped low, a whiff of scotch and cigar exuding from his mouth. "Don't lie to me, Darius. Ever. We have nothing without trust. Where is my employer's two million dollars?"

"I...I can get it."

Xavier cursed and turned toward the door. One of Diaz's men cut him off and directed him back in the room with the barrel of his gun.

Diaz whispered. "I'm confused. You just said it was all there. Why is it gone in the first place?"

"There was a problem with our money launderer, but I'm working on it. You'll have your money by next week. I swear."

Diaz stepped back and nodded toward his men. La Familia sprang into action and forced Darius and all four members of his crew to their knees. They left Xavier standing. Though his father's face remained neutral, his wide eyes screamed panic.

Diaz slid a gun from his jacket, a black M&P Smith and Wesson, .45 auto. "I swear I just told you not to lie to me, Darius. It's like you don't trust me."

Darius hated the panic creeping into his voice. "I'll have it to you by next week."

"Not good enough." Diaz turned, aiming the barrel two inches from Wendall's forehead. He craned his head back to Darius and Xavier and shot Wendall between the eyes, sending a spray of blood and bone against the hearth, the sound splitting the room. Wendall's body teetered and crumpled to the ground. "You will have it transferred by this time tomorrow night. Do we understand each other?"

Darius trembled on his knees, the anger from the car and the beating he took at the bar replaced by naked fear at the site of the blood puddling on Xavier's hardwood floor from Wendall's corpse. The man at the bar knocked Darius's cloak of invincibility loose, and now Diaz ripped it away entirely.

Diaz smacked Darius on the head with the tip of the pistol. "I said, do we understand each other?"

Darius's head wobbled like a bobblehead doll with a busted spring, a million thoughts flying through his head. Wendall's brain sliding down the mantel. The stash of cash hidden under the floorboards in Twila's place. The blackness in Diaz's eyes. Where he could get a fake passport.

"Oh, and one other matter," Diaz said, turning back to Darius. "Where is Juan Hidalgo?"

Every muscle in Darius's body locked. *Why was he asking about Juan?*

"He left three weeks ago," Darius stammered. "He collected his last paycheck and I ain't seen him since."

"Three weeks ago." Diaz walked a slow circle around Darius's kneeling body. It was maddening. Each time Diaz left his line of site, Darius was sure his body would join Wendall's on the floor. "That's the last time we heard from him as well. You see, Juan is a dear member of our family who was sent here to discretely keep an eye on things. To see if there was a problem."

Darius closed his eyes. It wouldn't be long now. If Juan was a member of La Familia sent to spy on them, he knew what Darius had been up to. If he reported those activities up the chain...

"You bring Juan back to me along with the money. After all, he was like a son to me. Comprendes, Darius?"

Darius's mouth fished open and closed, lost in the chaos unfolding in front of him, his eyes sweeping the frightened faces of his crew. The two million would be a stretch. Producing Juan was an impossibility unless they dropped his rotting, dirt-encased corpse in the middle of the study.

Diaz turned and shot Ronnie in the head. Ronnie toppled sideways into his brother. Stumpy let a single cry loose and bit more of them back, eyes locked in horror at his dead brother.

Diaz squatted and pressed the hot barrel into Darius's cheek. "I said, do you understand me?"

Darius jerked his head up and down, piss dribbling down his leg.

Diaz stood and turned to Xavier, sliding his pistol

into a shoulder holster. He offered a tight-lipped smile. "Thank you for your hospitality, Xavier. You have a lovely home. We'll be in touch."

As the remaining Triad members gawked in shocked silence at the bodies on the floor and the crimson mess on the fireplace, Diaz and his men slipped out into the cold Nebraska night.

CHAPTER TWENTY-FIVE

Jake was no stranger to sitting in a police interrogation room. The last time was when he was knocked out cold by a mountain of a bouncer in a Kansas City strip club because of a suitcase full of a deadly bioweapon. He should start writing this stuff down. Maybe write a book someday.

He swept his eyes across the room. There must be a standard blueprint police stations followed. Beige walls. White linoleum floors with chips at the corners and black skid marks from years of chairs being dragged in and out. And the standard wood table with hard, unforgiving chairs on either side. Jake was in the middle of pondering a nap when the door opened, and Raasch entered with a folder in hand. He set it on the table and sat opposite of Jake.

Raasch drummed his fingers on the folder and watched Jake for a moment before speaking. "You want to tell me why you started a fight with three guys at the Dome?"

"You have a first name?"

"Bill. My friends call me Billy."

"I didn't start anything, Billy. I protected a fellow citizen from getting beat with a pool cue by a hulk."

"So, it was self-defense?"

"Pretty much. Can't say I didn't enjoy knocking the arrogance out of the guy."

Raasch rapped his knuckles on the table. "You'd have to beat Darius Frost with a bag of bricks for a few hours to even make a dent in that mound of arrogance."

"Sounds like you have some experience with him."

Raasch rolled his eyes. "Unfortunately. How come we never met in Warsaw?"

"Beats me. But, I left Warsaw when I was eighteen and didn't come back until a couple of years ago. Our ships must have crossed in the night."

"What brings you to Kearney?"

"My daughter was checking out the local college. Same with Bear's."

Raasch smiled. "Wow. Laurel, no wait, Landry is old enough to go to college? That makes me feel like a dinosaur."

"What brought you to Kearney?" Jake asked.

"Followed a woman. She hated Warsaw and had family up here. I grew up in Springfield and lived in Warsaw for a couple of years. She was more fun to look at than the lake, so I came with her."

Jake shifted in the chair. It was killing his ass. "You two still together?"

"Nah. She dumped me for a pharmaceutical sales guy in Omaha. I like the job and the town and stayed. What were you doing in the Dome?"

"Having a beer. Didn't know it was against the law."

"It isn't but beating the crap out of three guys is. Especially those three guys."

Jake leaned forward. "What's special about Frost?"

"All I'll say is he has connections."

"To who?"

Raasch pressed his lips together, the corners of his thin mouth arcing up. "I said connections was all I'll say."

"That's pretty vague. Am I getting charged with beating on all three of them?"

"Depends."

"On what?"

Raasch stretched and locked his hands behind his head. "On you."

Raasch fell silent, eyes locked on Jake, waiting. But waiting for what? Jake thought back to the bar. The way the conversation died when Frost walked into the bar. The way everyone cleared out when Frost approached Conover. Parker told them to get out of the county. Phil the Bartender told them to get out of the State of Nebraska.

Darius Frost was a big deal. Because he played football for the Huskers? Doubtful since he got kicked off the team. Hard to be a local legend when you get disgraced. Darius was too young to carry that kind of clout on his own. Somebody else had pull in town.

Wendall was in Frost's crew. Jake followed Wendall from the convenience store to the country. To the mansion on Husker Road. Daddy's house.

Jake raised his eyebrows to the stained popcorn ceiling. "Getting charged doesn't depend on me. It depends on whether or not Darius Frost's daddy wants me charged. And I'm going to go with a big fat no because Big Daddy is already embarrassed by his disgraced son and doesn't want the publicity that'll come from some stranger whipping his ass five ways from Sunday in a local watering hole. I get it right?"

"Bear said you were a smart son of a bitch," Raasch said.

"Smart or smart ass?"

"Both."

Jake settled back in the chair. "When did you talk to him?"

"Fifteen minutes ago. Your friend Conover called him, Bear called here and I picked up the phone. It was nice to catch up. He's on his way."

Jake tensed. If Bear headed back to Kearney, his wife would call Maggie in a heartbeat. "Bear's coming back here?"

Raasch raised his palms. "He told me to tell you, and I quote, tell Jake I won't tell Maggie shit."

Jake's stomach released. The last thing his pregnant wife needed was to hear the local police picked up her husband for a bar fight. Especially after he promised her there'd be no drama.

"So, who is Frost's daddy?"

"Xavier. Has his fingers in a lot of different businesses in town. Someone you don't want to get on the wrong side of."

"I keep hearing that. Tell me more."

Raasch spoke in a low voice. "Not here. Sit tight and cool your heels, or I can put you in a cell if you want to get some shuteye on a crappy mattress. Just don't blue light it. We'll release you when Bear gets here, assuming none of those Neanderthals change their minds and file charges. They won't."

"So why do I have to wait until then?"

Raasch picked up the folder and thumped it against his palm. "Because you'll need someone in your corner when you walk out of here besides the geriatric private eye. Looks like you're going to be our guest for a while. You can chill here, or we can stick you in a quiet cell, your call."

He weighed his options. Bear was at least six or seven hours away. The thought of sitting in this uncomfortable chair for that long lacked major appeal. "Would I have a roommate?"

Raasch's eyebrows shot up. "Do you want a roommate?"

"Think I'll pass on the offer, Billy."

"You're in luck. It's been a quiet night. Can't promise it'll remain that way, but for now you're safe."

Jake was pleased he wasn't going to be charged. He wasn't pleased with Raasch's ominous warning. *You'll need someone in your corner when you walk out of here.* He had a strong feeling he would butt heads with Darius Frost and his crew again soon.

CHAPTER TWENTY-SIX

Raasch released Jake to Bear's custody at seven the next morning. Jake trudged out of the police station rolling his neck and shoulders, trying to work out the stiffness from sleeping on a mattress the thickness of a legal pad and the comfort of a granite counter top.

Bear lounged against his Expedition parked on the street, the corners of his mouth pushing back his ears. "Morning, sunshine. Sleep well in Shangri La?"

Jake ignored the question. "You look chipper for having driven through the night."

Bear opened the passenger door for Jake. "That's because I have enough caffeine in me to raise the schlong of a dead man. Plus, I've been looking forward to the big ass breakfast you're gonna buy me including all the bacon I can eat."

"In that case, we'd better swing by the bank so I can take out a loan."

Ten minutes later, they parked in the same booth at the Perkins where they'd eaten with the girls twenty-four hours earlier.

Jake yawned and rubbed his eyes. "Thanks for

coming."

"I was gone for less than a day, and you get arrested for beating the shit out of three guys in a bar? You need a remedial class on the definition of no drama."

"They deserved it."

"Don't they all?"

"I was protecting a guy."

Bear dumped sugar in his coffee and stirred. "The PI from California? He and I had a nice chat when he called. We're all supposed to hook up this morning after breakfast. And before you say anything, yes, I'm staying this time."

"What about your warrant sweeps? Won't your constituents miss you?"

"Not the asshats we'd be tracking down. Besides, the action around here sounds like it's getting mighty interesting."

They ordered and Jake filled Bear in on what he and Conover discussed at the bar and Raasch's warning to be on the lookout for the Frost clan. While they talked, Jake's cell dinged with a text message from Special Agent Foster.

Case wrapped up early. Just got to Snell's apartment. Meet me?

Jake texted back he'd call her in a bit. He wanted to figure out what was going on in Kearney in case Snell and the missing money train were linked. "What do you know about Raasch? He seemed like an okay guy, but you know him better than I do."

"Billy's a good dude. Handy."

"Handy? What the hell does that mean?"

Bear pointed the spoon. "It means if you give the man a ball of steel wool, he'd knit you a bicycle. Handy.

But if you're too sleep deprived to understand such simple vocabulary as handy and drama, try smart and capable. A good shot and a scrapper in a fight. Was sorry to lose him, but his girlfriend was a royal pain in the ass who hated Warsaw."

"Can we trust him?"

"For sure. Unless something's changed in the few years since I saw him. In fact, he's meeting us along with Conover."

Their waiter brought the food. Oatmeal and toast for Jake and the eighteen-hundred calorie Hearty Man's Combo for Bear with two extra sides of bacon.

Jake appraised the mountain of food in front of his best friend. "That's a lot of pork. You trying to have a coronary before nine in the morning?"

Bear shoved a greasy slice of meat candy in his mouth. "I like pig butts and I cannot lie."

***

Thirty minutes later, they were out the door and headed back to the Days Inn. Jake wanted to shower away the scent of the jail cell before they met with Conover and Raasch.

Bear turned south down 2nd Avenue, alternating his gaze between the road in front of him and the rearview mirror. "We have a tail. Silver F150 with two dudes. Two cars back. Saw them when we left the police station."

Jake avoided the urge to turn around. "Switch lanes. I wanna check them out in the side mirror."

Bear complied and Jake leaned against the window. Through the windshield of the silver truck, Jake recognized one of the guys. He'd been playing pool at the Dome when Frost interrupted their game. Jake suspected he was a low man on the Xavier Frost totem pole. He didn't recognize the driver of the truck from the Dome or anywhere else.

Bear asked, "They ring any bells?"

"One of them was at the bar last night. Think they're part of Frost's crew."

"Want me to try and lose them?"

"Nah, let's go to the hotel. Park in front and we'll go in. Once I shower, we'll head out the back and take my rental. Hopefully, Tweedledee and Tweedledumb won't see us leave."

Thirty minutes later after Jake showered, shaved and tucked his Sig Sauer in his hip holster, they snuck out the back of the hotel. In Jake's rental, they left the rear lot and cruised up the access road, sneaking a peek to the front of the hotel as they passed. Tweedledee and Tweedledumb sat in their truck watching the hotel entrance, oblivious to the fact their target just slinked away.

"Not very bright, are they?" Bear asked.

"Open mouth breathers make life easier."

Bear grinned. "Hey, that rhymes."

"I'm a poet and don't even know it."

Conover and Raasch waited for them in Conover's room at the Ramada, each with a Styrofoam cup of coffee. After introductions, each claimed a chair or the edge of the bed to sit.

Raasch started the conversation. "Conover filled me in on Juan Hidalgo and this money train you're tracking, Jake. Looks like they may be related?"

"Maybe. We're going to have to do a little digging."

Raasch set his coffee on the table. He rubbed his hands as he leaned forward, taking his time composing his thoughts. "This is an unofficial consultation. I'm going to warn you to be very, very careful about how deep you dig and where around Kearney."

Jake asked, "Because of Frost's daddy?"

Raasch's head bobbed. "If there's one thing I learned early on in this lovely little town is that Xavier Frost is one dude you do not want to get on the wrong side of."

"Who is he?" Bear asked.

"You didn't hear any of this from me. If my boss heard I told you any of this stuff, she'd have my ass in a sling. Xavier Frost runs a group called the Triad."

"Is that a company?"

"It's not any kind of legal entity. Just what people call it. It's three guys who own grain elevators and trucking and warehouse companies. All seem legit and profitable. There's Xavier Frost who owns grain elevators across Nebraska including the one Conover visited. Walter Roth owns Roth Trucking, and John Browers owns Monster Logistics. Roth and Browers are kind of silent partners who help with logistics. Xavier is the brains and the brawn of the operation."

Jake rested against the backboard of the bed. "So, how does this trio of guys have this much power in town?"

"Kearney has some viable industries. There's Baldwin Filters, the Eaton Corporation, and Marshall Engines. Good Samaritan Hospital is also a major employer. But, agriculture is Kearney's bread and butter. Hell, over ninety percent of Nebraska is made up of farms and ranches. Buffalo County ranks in the top ten counties in the production of alfalfa, hay, corn and beef. Factor that with our location right off I-80 and there's some serious money to be made in shipping those commodities."

"And Frost and this Triad control it all."

Raasch bobbed his bald head. "Most of it. But, there's rumors they're shipping out more than corn and soybeans."

"Like what?"

"Guns and drugs. Some feds poked around a couple of years ago, but nothing came of it. The Triad knows nobody's going to come at them hard, especially the local police."

Bear stroked his beard. "They pay them off?"

"I've heard rumors but don't have any hard evidence. The Sheriff seems solid as are most of the cops in town. But, others will look the other way, help make sticky situations go away or flap their gums for a little cash in their pocket. The Triad also supports a lot of local businesses and charities which gives them a lot of leeway. Any serious competitors to their business don't seem to last long. When those competitors leave town, they are limping away—financially and sometimes physically if they raise a stink."

Jake asked, "So how does Darius and his crew fit into the business model?"

"Darius was a local high school football legend. He was one mean bastard, both on the field and off. People around here live, breathe, and shit Husker football and once he signed with the football team, he was given more latitude than he already had, given who his father is. When the coach booted him off the Huskers, he dropped out of school and came back here with a major chip on his shoulder."

"What fun for you guys."

"You have no idea. His natural aggression, humiliation from getting kicked off the team, and his father's umbrella of protection makes for a tense situation for everyone. He's always hanging with the same five or six guys who have a mix of some petty charges. Any serious charges seem to get dropped."

Jake grabbed a four-dollar bottle of water from the counter and took a long swig. Jake wondered who else Frost hung out with besides his regular crew. "Any girlfriends?"

"Darius gets more ass than a toilet seat. But he does have a pretty regular girl. Stripper named Twila Meadows who works at The Clam. The dumpy strip club south of town."

"I drove by it. What about Randall Parker?" Jake asked.

"Parker's a reasonable character until he drinks too much. Then he gets belligerent. He's been in town for a couple of years and kept his nose pretty clean until last year when he beat the hell outta some guy, but the charges were dropped. I'll tell you this. That man is smarter than he looks."

Jake thought back to the bar fight. Frost and his two henchmen had waded into the brawl, while Parker sat at the end of the bar watching the action and drinking beer.

Conover chimed in. "What's this mean for Juan Hidalgo?"

Raasch's bald dome teetered from side to side. "There's a thin file on him. His parents called a few weeks ago and filed a missing person's report when they didn't hear from him. A couple officers did a cursory check at ETC Elevator where he worked and were told he took his last paycheck and skipped town."

"Same bullshit story I got," Conover said. "Anything

in the file on his girlfriend?"

"Nothing. I think she works in housekeeping at one of the hotels, but I don't remember which one. Listen, I gotta go home and get some sleep before I pass out. I wanted to give you the lay of the land before you start poking around much further. Jake, I'd grow eyes in the back of my head. Darius Frost isn't the type to let things go."

"I know. A couple of his guys tailed us from the police station. We lost them before we came here."

Raasch spread his hands wide. "Exactly what I mean. If I were you, I'd either forget about this money train trail or get out of town for a while and let the dust settle. Either way, remember you didn't hear a word from me about Frost or the Triad. And be careful."

They thanked Raasch and waited until the hotel room door clicked shut behind him. They stared at each other, soaking in what they'd learned.

Jake broke the silence. "Where does this leave you, Conover?"

The older man ran his hand over his silver hair. "Still looking for Juan Hidalgo."

"What's your cop gut telling you?"

"He's dead. I don't have anything to base it on, but it feels that way. But I'm not getting paid to lay low. I'm still trying to track down Hidalgo's girlfriend and do some sniffing around the elevator where he worked. I can't leave Kearney until I know for sure what happened to him. What about you two?"

Jake thought back to Foster's text. "I'm going to take Raasch's advice and lay low. Bear and I are going to Omaha."

Bear flinched. "Omaha?"

"Lead on Snell. Foster's there. With two guys trying

to tail us, we should let things here simmer down a notch."

Conover's eyes darted between them. "Who's Snell and Foster?"

"Long story. We'll tell you over a beer when we get back. You've got my number. Use it if you get in a jam. We'll check in with you later."

They shook hands, and Bear and Jake headed down the hotel hallway.

Bear grumbled. "I hate Omaha."

"Why?"

"Last time I was there I lost a shitload of money at the casino and got food poisoning."

"Sounds like you lost a shitload twice," Jake said. "No offense, partner, but I don't want to be within five miles of you if you unleash today's breakfast."

They popped out the back exit of the Ramada. Jake placed his hand on the door to the rental car. "You know, your bad behavior isn't the city of Omaha's fault."

"I think it was the bacon at the buffet. I don't trust any town that fucks up bacon."

Jake pointed at him. "You have a point."

They headed south to I-80, passing by their hotel. With no sign of the two guys tailing them, they swapped back to Bear's Expedition for comfort and headed west toward Omaha. If Snell was onto Keats and Randall Parker was involved in robbing Keats's money train, they would be back in Kearney in short order.

CHAPTER TWENTY-SEVEN

Two and a half hours later, Jake and Bear hit the outskirts of Omaha. Nebraska's largest city housed just north of four hundred and sixty thousand residents, almost a million if you include the entire metropolitan area. Jake hadn't spent a ton of time there but enjoyed his brief stay. Years ago, he'd tracked down an administrator at the famous Omaha Zoo who owed Keats twenty grand. For letting Jake hold a baby chimpanzee, Jake allowed the guy to keep three of the five fingers on his dominant hand in working order.

Bear plugged the address Foster provided to Snell's apartment in the Expedition's touch screen. They turned off I-480 and headed north on Abbott Drive past the TD Ameritrade Park where the College World Series is played. A few twists and turns later, they pulled into the parking lot of an apartment complex. Three story buildings covered in cream siding topped with forest green tiled roofs held up patches of snow that resisted the melting rays of the morning sun.

Jake slowed, checking the numbers on the sides

of the buildings. In front of the farthest apartment, nestled near a grove of pine trees, Jake found an empty space and pulled in. He texted Foster they were there, and the duo climbed out into the cold.

Bear grunted as they climbed the stairs toward the third floor. "Why couldn't Snell get an apartment on the first floor?"

"You could use the exercise after eating six pounds of bacon this morning."

Bear wheezed. "The grease is keeping me going. You seen Foster lately?"

"Not since she put a half dozen holes in the Wolf's chest last year."

A year ago, Jake was caught between two Russian spies at war with each other on U.S. soil. Foster turned one of the spies, called the Wolf, into Swiss cheese. Justice was served, but the shooting might be deemed questionable in the eyes of the law. She was a good lady and Jake and Bear had no problem covering for her with the FBI to make sure she came out of the ordeal clean.

They hit the third floor and strode down the concrete floor to Apartment 3D. Foster opened the door before Jake could knock.

"Hey, strangers." Her once shoulder length dusky hair was now in an attractive pixie cut. She slid her athletic build to the side to let them in. "Thanks for coming. Wish it was under better circumstances."

Jake moved inside Snell's apartment, sweeping his eyes across the living room and kitchen. It was like a sterile, show model, devoid of any personality except for a picture on the counter of Snell and her daughter Beth. Cardboard boxes were stacked along one wall beside a credenza holding a modest flat screen television. The place smelled musty, unused. The only signs of life were in the dining room where manila folders scattered on a dining room table that could seat six. A large corkboard leaned against the wall, a mishmash of pictures and notecards pinned to it with red strings connecting them

Jake stepped to the table. "Jesus, how long have you been here?"

"Most of this is Snell's handiwork, but I've been here long enough to figure out what she was into." Foster shoved her hands in her pockets, shifting her weight from foot to foot. "Listen, I never got a chance to thank you two for what you did covering for me with—"

Bear waved a hand. "Not necessary. The asshole deserved every bullet you gave him."

"Still, I could've lost my job. I won't forget it."

Jake thumbed the folders on the table. He hated getting thanked for doing things any decent person would do. "Tell us what you've learned so far."

She pointed to the chairs. "Have a seat. This could take a minute."

They dropped to the hard, wooden chairs surrounding the table, Jake's eyes drawn to the familiar face pinned at the center of the corkboard. Keats. Why did it always come back to Keats? He sat back and let Foster tell her tale.

She ran her fingers through her short hair. "I don't know if you're aware of why Snell was shipped to Omaha in the first place."

"Keats," Jake said, pointing to the corkboard. After working for the mob boss, Jake knew most of Keats's operations. Over the years, Snell tried to pump Jake for information which could help her nail Keats, but

Jake would never rat Keats out. It would be too dangerous for his family, and Jake was a huge fan of breathing.

Foster's shoulders slumped. "It's always been Keats, going back to her old taskforce days with Bear. I'll admit sometimes her evidence was flimsy, but I really think she was onto something this time."

Jake wouldn't bet a nickel on her speculation. Keats was like Teflon. Nothing stuck to him.

Foster laid pictures on the table from one of the folders. Pics of Vinny leaving Keats's warehouse with duffel bags. Vinny loading the bags into his van. A time stamp dated those photos over a year ago. More recent pics of Vinny entering the Horseshoe Casino and coming out empty handed. Pages with Snell's pinched handwriting logging dates and times. She snagged the pics from Keats's warehouse before she was shipped to Omaha.

Foster continued, "But, her obsession with Keats began to affect her other cases. She was letting things fall through the cracks. Paperwork wasn't filed when it should have been, and a surveillance case on a drug trafficker was botched. The bosses know what a valuable agent she is but couldn't let her continue down this road. So, they shipped her to Omaha, a few hours from Keats and near her daughter Beth who is attending Creighton."

Bear waved his hand over the information scattered before them. "But it didn't stop her from digging, obviously."

"No. In fact, it gave her something tangible to go after Keats." Foster stood and pulled the corkboard to the table.

Snell pinned Keats's picture to the middle. An

unflattering shot of him at Garozzo's Italian Restaurant in Kansas City before he dropped twenty-five pounds. To his left, connected with a red string, was a picture of Vinny V. Above Vinny V was a surveillance picture taken from a distance of Vinny with...*holy shit*...Darius Frost. Connected to Frost were pictures of a grain elevator and a warehouse Jake recognized as the one from Kearney near the barbecue joint. Monster Logistics which, according to Raasch, was owned by one of the Triad members. The most interesting thing was a blue string connecting Darius Frost back to Jason Keats.

Foster pointed at each picture while she talked. "Based on what I can figure from her notes, this is Vincent Verano. He must have been some kind of courier for Keats."

"Vinny V," Jake offered. "He was a bagman. Picked up money from Keats's operations."

"Who was found outside an I-29 rest stop full of bullet holes," Foster said. "Snell had pics of Vinny V meeting with this guy outside the Horseshoe Casino in Council Bluffs, a few miles from here." She jabbed a finger to a picture showing Vinny and Frost exchanging duffel bags. "She didn't have a name of the other guy in her file. They tracked the plates of the truck, and it was registered to a company called ETC Elevator in Kearney."

"That's Darius Frost," Jake said. "The guy whose ass I kicked in the bar last night in Kearney."

Bear leaned in for a closer look. "That's him? He looks like a big dude. Who else helped you?"

Jake ignored the jab. "ETC Elevator is also where Juan Hidalgo worked."

Foster asked, "Who's Juan Hidalgo?"

"Missing kid who went to work at ETC," Jake said. "There's a PI from California searching for him. He got mixed up with Frost's crew."

"Juan started sending home a lot more money in the past few weeks," Bear said. "He disappeared right around the time Vinny got ripped off."

"Bear and I talked to one of the local Kearney cops, and he said Frost's daddy is a bigwig in town." Jake pointed to the corresponding pictures as he continued. "Tied to grain elevators, trucking companies, and Monster Logistics through an organization called The Triad. Rumor has it they're shipping guns and drugs."

"Makes sense," Foster said. "Snell pulled a case file from a couple of years ago on the Triad. There was some surveillance done on the elevator by a couple of field agents and some suspicion of drug activity, but they couldn't nail anything down. The bosses pulled agents to work on something else, but her notes say Frost made regular monthly trips down here to the casino."

Jake traced the links between Roth Trucking and ETC Elevator. "If these two were involved in shipping guns and drugs, it could be they're using the casino to help launder the profits. I know that was one of Vinny's methods of cleaning Keats's cash. Might be Frost's as well."

"But how does it explain Vinny and Frost exchanging bags?"

"It doesn't." Jake's first thought was drugs, but Keats had an exclusive arrangement with the Mexican cartel La Familia for his supply. Maybe Vinny ran something on the side? He batted the thought away. Vinny was too smart and loyal to Keats to run a side job like that. Or maybe Keats wasn't as exclusive as

Jake thought he was.

Foster searched the table for a manila folder. She found the right one and pulled out a piece of paper with Snell's pinched handwriting. "This was the latest thing I could find in Snell's files. Vinny V was heading to Omaha with a substantial haul and she was heading out to tail him."

"How'd she know he was coming?"

Foster pinched her lips together. "She put a tracker on the van he drove."

Bear asked, "She have a warrant?"

Jake elbowed him. "Like lack of a warrant ever stopped you. How'd she get a tracker on the van if she's in Omaha."

Foster blushed. "I put it there. Against my better judgement."

"Anyone else know?"

"Just me and Snell."

Jake was surprised Keats hadn't found it yet. He used to be pretty diligent about sweeping his vehicles and offices. "Who in the FBI was Snell working with?"

"Nobody I know. Her notes say she reached out to an Agent Lance Brakeville who was involved with the initial inquiry to the Triad but I couldn't find him."

"He doesn't work with the Feds anymore?"

"He's still on the payroll but on assignment somewhere. But she couldn't dig too deep. If anyone found out she worked on anything related to Keats, they'd throw her ass to the curb. Looks like she tried to build an ironclad case before she ran it up the chain. This note on tracking Vinny in her file is the last thing I could find."

"When was it dated?"

"Three weeks ago. The same night they found

Vincent Verano shot to death at the rest stop. Jesus, I'm really starting to get worried."

Jake worried about Snell as well. She disappears the same night Keats shipped one point five million dollars with Vinny. The same night video showed four armed men robbing Vinny, one of whom had a giant tattoo on his hand. Had Snell been there?

"What does the FBI say about Snell's disappearance?"

Foster's jaw trembled. "Not a thing. She took vacation and is a couple of days overdue. I brought up my concerns to her boss, but he's a prick who's probably started documenting her not showing up for work so he can fire her. There's some hot and heavy domestic terrorism threat coming out of Washington that's sucking up resources. But, he doesn't know what we know now."

"Maybe he should. This doesn't sound good."

"If I show him this, Victoria is done with the Bureau. Let's see what we can come up with before I dump this shit show on someone's desk."

Jake scratched the stubble on his chin. Now that he was aware Darius Frost and Vinny V were connected, it solidified the fact Frost and his crew robbed Keats's money train and killed Vinny. But, if Frost knew Vinny, he knew who Vinny worked for which made robbing Keats an act of incredible stupidity or desperation on Frost's part. Having met the guy, Jake could make a case for either one, but desperation smelled more on point. Still, there were questions.

Why was Frost desperate for money?

Was Juan Hidalgo in Frost's crew the night of the money train robbery?

What was in the bags they exchanged at the

Horseshoe Casino?

What happened to Snell that night?

Jake pressed to his feet. "Bear and I are going to head back to Kearney."

Foster blinked rapidly, mouth ajar. "But, you just got here. We have to find out what happened to Victoria."

"I got a feeling the answers lie with Darius Frost and his crew. And they're in Kearney."

Foster stood. "I'm coming with you."

"Nope," Jake said. "You should finish combing through this paperwork and her notes, maybe find leverage we can use against Frost. These guys are well-connected in Kearney and aren't gonna roll over and confess what happened. Frost robbed the money train for a reason. Juan is probably dead for the same reason, and Snell...well, let's cross that bridge when we get to it. Get your hands on the previous investigation with the Triad and see if there's anything we can use. Please."

Foster's eyes hardened and her jaw clenched, the enamel on her teeth grinding. "And what do I do when I find this leverage?"

"You call me. You gather this information together into a concise little package, and you deliver it to whoever at the FBI will listen."

"You think she's dead, don't you?"

Jake didn't want to answer the question, and Bear locked his attention on the carpet like he was counting the number of fibers per square foot. "It doesn't look good. But, she's crafty and resilient."

They walked back to the Expedition in silence. Jake offered to drive, started the car, and stilled. Mental pictures of Snell rolled—the coldness in her office when they first met, her soft face in her car when

Jake told her he wanted to marry Maggie, the joyful tears when they recovered her kidnapped daughter.

Bear turned to him. "You think she's dead."

Jake let the question sit for a beat, reluctant to answer for fear it might be true. "Feels like it. Otherwise somebody would've heard from her."

"Why would they leave Vinny's body and not hers if she was there?"

It was a good question. "Maybe they thought leaving the body of a dead Fed would bring too much heat?"

Ten minutes later, they were back on the highway headed to Kearney. Bear drummed his knuckles against the window. "You know, I was thinking about Vinny and his shipment Snell tracked."

"And?"

Bear cranked his head slowly. "I'm guessing the shipment was in the ballpark of one point five million dollars."

Jake's mouth went dry. "You think?"

A razor-sharp edge crept into Bear's voice. "And I don't think Jason Fucking Keats got his investment banking license recently either. So, Jake Caldwell, I'm thinking you are a lying sack of shit, and I'm going to whip your ass when we're not going eighty miles an hour with you behind the wheel."

Jake's testicles crept toward his body for safety.

CHAPTER TWENTY-EIGHT

Marc Conover hit the Kearney hotels again in search of Juan's girlfriend, Maria Almodavar, after checking she still wasn't at her trailer. His deadline clock ticked hard and loud. Going back to California empty-handed wasn't an option. He hadn't given up on a case in thirty years and he wasn't starting now.

Lena scored him Maria's picture from the Nebraska Department of Motor Vehicles and Conover spent the morning showing it to hotel managers. Cooperation was spotty among the staff who were convinced he was with Immigration and Customs Enforcement. Abandoned housekeeping carts littered more than one hallway he traveled down.

He struck pay dirt at a Holiday Inn Express south of I-80 behind some barbecue restaurant. The petite manager's face fell with concern when Conover flashed Maria's picture. Though a relatively new employee, Maria was sweet and hardworking but hadn't shown up for work for a couple of days. She'd heard Maria talk about Juan, but never met him. She rounded up the housekeeping crew, and Conover explained why he was looking for Maria and received a sea of blank, disbelieving stares. Except for one.

A slender Hispanic woman in her mid-twenties with long, midnight hair tied in a braid stood in the back, unwilling to meet Conover's eyes. She shifted on her feet and chewed her fingernails. The second the manager dismissed everyone, she darted out the back door. Conover asked the manager about her, but she declined to give out any information. Conover walked the halls of the hotel again and lurked in his car for an hour but saw no sign of her.

He slumped in a booth at Freddy's Burgers around noon, rubbing the white band of skin where his wedding ring used to rest while waiting on his burger and fries. His cell rang. Mabel from the trailer park. Conover jerked upright. Neither Maria nor Juan was at their trailer, but a woman just entered.

Conover darted out the front door, abandoning his food order. "Let me guess. Hispanic woman, long hair, mid-twenties?"

Mabel exclaimed. "How on earth did you know that?"

"Lucky guess. What's she driving?"

"Something white. I told you I'm not good with cars."

"I'll be there in ten minutes. Will you please call me if she leaves?"

"Certainly, Mr. Conover. Shall I put out the Sara Lee cake?"

***

At the trailer park, Stumpy Pitt rested his chin on the padded steering wheel of his battered pickup, thoughts of his brother weighing him down. Thank God his mother passed two years earlier. If the cancer hadn't killed her, Ronnie's death would have. Memories of his brother filled the hours, each one like an ice pick to the stomach. He even missed Ronnie's drunken, incoherent rants and stupid conspiracy theories. Stumpy wiped his misting eyes.

Speaking of incoherent, ever since Frost's beat down at the Dome and the subsequent run in with the La Familia psychos, his boss was insane. The guy kicking Frost's ass in the bar and Diaz executing Wendall and Ronnie knocked his last remaining screw loose.

As the low men in Frost's hierarchy, Stumpy and Ronnie were given the worst jobs like watching empty trailers and bagging up dead bodies. He couldn't purge the image of Juan's head exploding in the circle of lights from pickups in the field. Juan's one intact bulging eye accusing Stumpy as he bagged and buried him in a shallow grave in a cornfield outside of town. Ronnie's eyes had regarded him in the same accusatory way. Stumpy had seen too many dead eyes in the last month.

There was no way he could cross Frost now. If he tried to leave, he was a dead man. If they didn't find the money and figure out how to solve the Juan Hidalgo problem, they were dead men. If the cops caught him, Stumpy would end up in prison. The only way out of this disaster was to find the money.

He thumbed through pictures of him and Ronnie on his cell phone when a white Jeep Liberty with rust-kissed wheel wells pulled in front of Juan's trailer. Stumpy perked up and watched a pretty young woman jam a key in the door and dart inside.

Stumpy punched the speed dial icon on his phone for Frost. "Somebody's at the trailer."

"Who?"

"I don't know. Some Mexican chick with long hair."

"I'm on my way. Don't let her leave."

The coldness in Frost's voice sent a chill down Stumpy's spine.

CHAPTER TWENTY-NINE

Jake white-knuckled the steering wheel. Bear's verbal assault was starting to take its toll. "Can we focus on finding Snell and what happened with this Hidalgo kid, for the love of Christ?"

Bear spent the last two and a half hours chewing Jake's ass up one side and down the other over Keats. The fact Jake didn't accept Keats's offer didn't matter. The fact that, even if he did accept it, Jake's only obligation would be to point Keats in the right direction for a hundred and fifty thousand dollars didn't matter. Bear felt betrayed because Jake lied to him and, deep down, Jake's stomach housed a pit the weight of a bowling ball, because he knew Bear was right. That said, the tirade started to feel a bit sanctimonious.

Jake took advantage of Bear drawing a breath and called Conover to let him know they were on the outskirts of Kearney. He punched the speaker button so Bear would have to shut the hell up.

"My trailer park spy let me know a maid Maria Almodavar works with went into her trailer," Conover said. "I just pulled into the trailer park. Valley View

Mobile Home Park."

"We'll meet you there. What do you think she'll—"

"Ah shit. How far away are you?"

Jake's foot dropped on the accelerator. The Expedition lurched forward. "Maybe five minutes. What's up?"

"One of Frost's goons just went in the trailer. I recognize him from the bar."

"That can't be good."

Conover growled. "It's not. I'm going in."

"Dude, wait for us. Five minutes tops."

A car door clicked open through the phone. "I'm not taking a chance on what this guy might do to her. I'll be fine. If you can take out three of them by yourself, I can handle one. Get here as quick as you can. Main entrance road. Look for a silver Explorer and a white Jeep Liberty parked outside."

"Conover?" The line was dead. "Son of a bitch."

Bear punched up the mobile home park on the navigation touch screen. "Why would this Frost guy be interested in Juan's girlfriend?"

"Loose end?" Jake offered.

It was a good question. The people at the grain elevator told Conover that Juan took his last paycheck and bailed town. At the bar, before Jake embarrassed Darius, Frost threatened Conover for poking his nose where it didn't belong. If Conover only asked the last time anyone saw Juan, why the hypersensitivity concerning his whereabouts?

A line of cars at a stoplight halted their progress. Jake whipped right, past a Daylight Donuts, up a side street and turned right on Highway 30. "Something isn't adding up. If Frost is interested in Juan's girlfriend, it means he cares Juan is in the wind. Which blows

Conover's gut theory Juan is dead."

"Or he cares about what she knows." Bear craned his neck and peered out the back window.

Jake flicked his eyes to the rearview mirror. "We have a tail?"

"There was another Taco John's back there calling my name."

"Jesus, can we focus here?"

"Sorry. Chewing your ass out worked up my appetite. Conover could be right. Juan's dead and Frost is covering his tracks and is worried what the girlfriend knows." Bear thought for a moment. "Maybe we should call Raasch."

"Probably a good idea. Do it."

Raasch was on the other side of town on a call but promised to get there as soon as he could. "Or should I drop everything and blaze in with lights and sirens?"

"There'll be three of us and one of them," Bear said.

"You realize if you take on one of that crew, you take on all of them?"

Jake followed the red line on the navigation screen and swerved left, gunning it up Grand Avenue. "I guess I'm already in a world of shit then."

Raasch was quiet for a beat. "I'm on my way. You guys are gonna get me fired."

"You can come back to Warsaw," Bear said. "I'll hire you."

A minute later, they whipped through the entrance to Valley View Mobile Home Park marked by a squat, standalone building. The paint was faded yellow and mailboxes were embedded in the wall. A neighborhood directory hung on a pole. The place was nicer than any of the mobile home parks in Warsaw. Jake slowed, eyes scanning ahead until he spotted the silver Explorer. He jerked to a halt, jumped out and jogged toward the trailer, Bear hot on his heels. Thumps emanated from inside and the trailer rocked followed by a woman's muffled scream.

Jake leapt up the steps and yanked the trailer door open. A narrow hallway and kitchen stood to his left, cabinet doors ajar and dishes everywhere. A claustrophobic dining area and living room to his right, crap scattered everywhere as if an F5 tornado had blown through. Either Juan and his girlfriend were incredible slobs or someone tossed the place.

Conover wrestled on the ground with a thick guy in blue jeans and a tan Carhartt jacket—one of the pool shooters from the Dome. Conover lay underneath the man, but had his arms locked in a choke hold around the man's neck. The man gagged and pulled at Conover's arm, but Jake managed to wrestle him to his stomach and jammed a knee in his back. A Hispanic woman with an emerald green uniform huddled in the back corner of the trailer, clutching her torn blouse, dark hair disheveled and eyes wide at the struggle at her feet.

Bear crowded into the living room. "You okay, Conover?"

Conover winked, blood trickling from his thin nose. "What took you so long? I'm getting too old for this shit."

***

By the time Darius Frost and Randall Parker pulled to the entrance of Valley View, the flashing lights of one of Kearney's finest bounced from the sides of the nearby trailers. He stopped the truck, watching

Raasch climb out and slide a baton into his belt.

"Fuckin' Boy Scout Raasch," Parker sneered. "What's he doing here?"

"Better question is where's Stumpy?"

"My guess would be in the trailer with the girl which is why the cops got called."

Frost thumped the steering wheel. "Goddamn it. I told him to wait until we got there."

"You said make sure she didn't leave. Looks like he may have gone in there to make sure she didn't."

"That ain't what I meant."

Parker lit a cigarette and blew smoke through a cracked window. "You gotta be specific when you're giving instructions to morons."

Frost slipped a plastic baggie from his shirt and scooped a bump of cocaine with a long pinky nail. After snorting it, he let the drug jolt his brain and held the baggie to Parker.

Parker waved him away. "Not a good time to be doin' that shit, boss."

"Gotta stay sharp," Frost said, dropping the package back in his pocket.

"You been staying sharp a lot lately."

Frost's lip curled and he lit a smoke of his own. "You sound like my old man."

They sat in the truck, eyes locked on the trailer until Raasch came out with Stumpy in handcuffs. The man who almost broke his skull at the Dome and the private eye Conover followed out the trailer door.

Frost sniffed. "What was the asshole's name again?"

"Which one?"

"The big one who took the cheap shot on me."

"Jake Caldwell."

A fourth man with a beard and a beer gut brought up the rear. He ducked out the trailer door with the girl in tow, clutching her torn blouse. Parker sat upright in the truck and squinted.

"That ain't Maria," Frost said.

"No, it isn't."

When Raasch loaded Stumpy into the squad car, Frost released the brake and rolled down Grand Avenue.

"What the hell was she doing in the trailer? You seen her before?" Frost asked.

"Didn't look familiar. What now?" Parker asked.

"Call that lawyer Bernstein and get his ass to the police station before Stumpy says something stupid."

"Stumpy won't roll on us."

Frost shot daggers at Parker. "After that wetback blew his brother's head off in front of him, I'd say all bets are off on knowin' what any of us would do."

"What are we gonna do about Juan? Even if we find the money—"

"I don't know. Ah, man. We are so screwed. I gotta figure out a way to spin this to buy us some time."

Parker flicked his cigarette butt out the window. "We're down to hours. You'd have to be Steven fuckin' Spielberg to come up with a way to spin this story."

A ball of nerves ate at Frost's gut. It was possible Diaz would accept the money with no Juan Hidalgo, even though they didn't even have the full two million. There's no way the man knew for sure Juan didn't hightail it out of town. He didn't tell Diaz that, in addition to looking for the money, they were trying to track down the girlfriend, Maria. Darius couldn't spin the story of Juan bailing if the girl was still around.

Xavier had been no help whatsoever after Diaz

went psycho. He'd told his son to clear out the bodies and clean up the mess before he walked out of the room. Darius formulated and repeated the simple plan in his head as they mopped up the blood. Find the money. Find the girl. Don't admit shit about Juan to La Familia and pray for the best. He wasn't religious by any stretch of the imagination, but it was all he had at this point. If he couldn't find the money, Juan Hidalgo's body wouldn't be alone in the cornfield.

CHAPTER THIRTY

The girl from the trailer was named Lucinda Ramirez. She said she lived in nearby Gibbon with her husband and a one-year-old daughter. She worked with Maria at the hotel and the two became fast friends. Raasch put her in his office for the time being.

Lonnie "Stumpy" Pitt was a high school teammate of Darius Frost. Moved to Kearney from Minnesota as a freshman with his twin brother and latched onto Frost's high school crew early. After depositing Stumpy in an interrogation room, Raasch crammed Jake, Bear, and Conover into a twenty by twenty conference room with sky blue walls waiting for the Buffalo County Sheriff to show up. The room stank like burnt coffee and body odor.

Jake took advantage of the quiet time to step to the hall and call Maggie. He gave her a generic status update and said he hoped to be home in a couple of days. She was helping Halle fill out the application for the University of Nebraska.

"She needs some reference letters. You know anyone?"

"What makes you think I know any respectable people?"

"Talk to Bear, smart ass," she said. "I'll work on the rest. Stay safe."

Jake hit the bathroom and grabbed a Snickers before returning to the conference room.

Raasch scratched at a coffee stain on his shirt. "Stumpy is like a loyal dog. Doubt you'd ever break him. He'd go to jail before he rolled on Frost."

Jake sat on the edge of the conference table, wincing at the candy bar. It tasted like it was a decade old. "Why's he called Stumpy?"

Raasch waggled his fingers. "Lost a battle with a bandsaw at a chicken plant."

"Hoped he had a little dick or something. That'd be more fun to throw at him."

"Hell, try it. I have no idea what he's packin'. Might work."

"We have any leverage we could use on him? Girlfriend? Sick mother?"

"Just the dim bulb upstairs," Raasch said. "Street smart, but enough academic brain power to lightly toast a piece of bread. Stumpy had some D1 looks from some low-level football teams coming out of high school but didn't have the grades to get in. Rumor is he scored like a twelve on his ACT."

"Thought they gave you at least twelve points for spelling your name right."

"They do. He spent a few weeks at a community college in Arkansas but quit the team a week after classes began. Guess he saw the writing on the wall, assuming he can read. Worked some low-level jobs around town, drank too much and was on a bad trajectory. Stumpy was ecstatic when Frost returned to Kearney. It put him back on the map."

Bear said, "So we can't roll him, but we could trip him up."

"Wouldn't be hard," Raasch said. "Something's up with him, though. It's like he's not all there, more than normal."

"So, how do we go at him?"

A gravelly voice sounded from the doorway. "You aren't going at anything."

Jake and Bear swiveled to find a stout African American woman, late fifties with silver hair pulled back into a bun. Her lantern jaw was set and hazelnut eyes flicked over the strangers in the room.

Raasch waved a hand toward her. "Sheriff Wilma Airy, this is Jake Caldwell, Sheriff Bear Parley from Warsaw, Missouri, and Marc Conover, a private investigator from Los Angeles.

Sheriff Airy crossed the threshold and offered her gnarled hand which they shook in turn. She dropped her hat at the head of the table and sat, motioning to Raasch to close the door. "You the Sheriff Parley he used to work for?"

"Don't believe everything he told you," Bear said.

Her eyes narrowed, a hint of a southern drawl seeping out as she spoke. "You better hope I do. Raasch speaks highly of you. Which is why I'm surprised a man of your experience didn't bother to give me a courtesy notice you were following a case in my county."

Bear motioned to Jake. "I wasn't following any kind of case. Just came to help a friend out."

Airy turned to Jake. "A friend who gets in a bar fight with the son of the most powerful man in Buffalo County. While I can appreciate you kicking the crap out of Darius Frost, something I've wanted to do since he showed back up in Kearney, I do not appreciate the hornet's nest you kicked over."

"My apologies, Sheriff." Jake jerked a thumb to Conover. "I was stopping Frost from burying a pool cue into the head of my new friend. I had no intentions of starting any trouble."

"The road to hell is paved with good intentions, son." The corner of Airy's mouth curled. "I heard Frost squealed like a girl when you put his head into the wall at the Dome. Wish I could've seen it."

"Well, he had it coming."

Airy's grin slipped away. "Well, let's not make a habit of it. So, is somebody going to tell me what's going on? I have three strangers in my town stirring the shit pot, and I want to know why."

Jake didn't know Airy from a hole in the wall. Could they trust her? Raasch already said Xavier Frost owned the town and law would turn a blind eye toward them. Standing behind Airy, Raasch gave him a thumbs up to go ahead. Jake spent ten minutes explaining how they arrived at this point, leaving out any mention of Snell and Foster's potential tie to the money train.

Airy probed Jake's face before turning to Conover. "You have anything to add, Mr. Hollywood?"

Conover considered the question for a beat. "No, ma'am. I only want to find out what happened to Juan Hidalgo."

Airy steepled her arthritic fingers under her chin. She said nothing for a minute. Jake started to say something, but Raasch shot daggers in his direction, so Jake closed his mouth and waited.

She pushed forward to the table. "Here's what

we're going to do, and it's not up for negotiation, so don't even try. Raasch and I will get a statement from Ms. Ramirez about what happened at the trailer. Assuming it goes as I think it will, she will be free to go. You three will accompany Raasch on your way out of town to ensure she gets back home safely to Gibbon. After that, I suggest Mr. Conover heads back to California, and you two keep going southeast to Missouri."

Jake's nails bit into his palms. "What about Stumpy?"

"Raasch and I will question Stumpy and book him for assault and any other charges I can think of. But, it won't be your concern since you won't be in town any longer. How's that sound to you? Actually, scratch that. I don't care how it sounds to you. That's what's going to happen."

Conover raised his hand. "And what about Juan Hidalgo?"

Airy batted his question away. "I personally talked to Mr. and Mrs. Hidalgo when they filed their missing person's report. I've got people on the lookout and have notified the sheriffs in the surrounding counties to keep an eye out for their son."

"You and I both know the Triad is searching for Juan," Conover said. They all noted the irritation crossing Airy's face as she frosted a glance over her shoulder to Raasch when Conover mentioned the Triad. "They tried to bust me up after I poked around, and Juan and Maria's trailer was tossed. They're not just looking for Juan. They're looking for something Juan had."

"You have a theory, I suppose?"

"Juan was involved in the money train robbery

along with Frost and Randall Parker. Maybe Stumpy too for all we know. Given how Frost is reacting to us poking around and the way he ransacked the trailer, they're on the hunt for something."

"Something like what?"

"I don't know. Maybe some kind of evidence documenting what they did?"

Airy clucked her tongue, unconvinced. "Or maybe it's Juan."

"Maybe both. Look, Sheriff, I can appreciate your position, and if you came to LA on the hunt like I am, I'd tell you the same thing you're telling me. But, I was hired to do a job and find out what happened to Juan, and that's what I intend to do."

Airy pressed her thick lips together. "I was afraid you would say something like that. When I suggested you get out of town, it wasn't me playing the big bad sheriff card, but for your own protection from the Triad. I can't force you to leave, but you should know there isn't a whole hell of a lot I can do to protect you. If the Triad comes at you, they won't leave any evidence for me to come back at them."

Conover pumped his shoulders. "I'm not exactly a helpless kitten, but that's why I have these two guys in my corner."

"No, you don't because they're leaving town."

"That's not fair, Mom," Jake said. "Why do we have to leave and he gets to stay?"

Airy curled her lip. "Don't be a smartass, Caldwell."

A knock sounded at the door, and Raasch popped outside for a moment. When he came back in, disappointment hung on his face like a wet blanket.

"Stumpy's lawyer showed up. So much for tripping him up."

"That was fast," Jake said. "He didn't call anyone, and nobody knew he was here."

"Plenty of people knew," Airy said, using the table to push herself up. "Let's get this Lucinda's statement and then you three go with Raasch to get her back home. I'll have a go at Stumpy after letting him stew for a while and follow-up with Raasch. I have a feeling Stumpy will be sprung before morning. Xavier Frost plays poker and golf with the local judge."

***

An hour later after too much sludge playing the part of coffee and going in circles about what to do next to figure out the mystery of Juan Hidalgo, Raasch brought Lucinda Ramirez into the conference room. Her dark eyes locked on the floor. There was a half-moon bruise under her right eye and a safety pin held her torn blouse closed. They'd agreed at least one of them would stay at Lucinda's house to protect her and her family until Raasch could get someone he trusted to relieve them.

Raasch said, "Jake, you want to ride with me and Lucinda? Bear and Conover can follow us to Gibbon."

Lucinda's eyes grew wide and she pleaded, her English heavily accented but precise. "Please, no. You do not need to come to my home."

Raasch touched her shoulder gently. "Lucinda, we discussed this. We have to make sure you're safe. You said your husband won't be home for another couple of hours."

She wrung her hands. "My husband will protect us once he gets home. I will be fine until he gets there. Please."

Jake's brow wrinkled. Lucinda's instant panic at them going to her home was curious. She was just assaulted. One would think she'd welcome the protection. Especially since she'd given a statement against one of them. She appeared more concerned about their going to her house than the safety of herself and her family. A light bulb flicked on. He knew why.

"Tell you what, Lucinda," Jake said. "Let us get you home safely. We can sit outside in the car until your husband gets home. How about that?"

Raasch shot him a quizzical look, but Jake held out a palm. Lucinda agreed and followed Raasch out the door.

Bear grabbed Jake by the arm. "I've seen that look before in your eyes. What's up?"

Jake patted him on the back. "I know where Juan's girlfriend is. Maybe she can help us figure out what's going on."

CHAPTER THIRTY-ONE

Gibbon was a sleepy town of less than two thousand residents located twelve miles northeast of Kearney. Jake rode in the back of Raasch's patrol car, Lucinda in the front. The woman spent the fifteen-minute journey in silence with her head resting against the cold window, eyes tracking the snow-covered landscape as it whizzed past. Bear and Conover trailed in Bear's Expedition.

Once they hit the outskirts of town, Lucinda directed Raasch through a series of turns into a residential neighborhood of tiny houses near a United Methodist Church. Raasch pulled into a cracked concrete driveway in front of a modest but well-maintained ranch with white vinyl siding. Bear and Conover pulled in behind them.

Lucinda turned to Raasch. "Thank you for the ride. You do not have to stay. As you see, there is nothing but an empty house."

Raasch propped his elbow on the steering wheel. "Can we come in and walk through the house to make sure there's no bad guys?"

Lucinda flicked her dark eyes between Raasch and Jake. "There is no need. I will be fine."

"Lucinda," Jake said. "I'm sure Deputy Raasch explained who the man was at your trailer who attacked you."

Her accent was heavy, each word enunciated. "But he is in jail and cannot get to me."

"But the men he works for could. I don't even know if they know who you are. The man wasn't at the trailer looking for you, he was looking for Maria. You were in the wrong place at the wrong time."

"Then I am safe."

"Maybe, maybe not. I'd rather not take the chance. Let us walk through the house with you to make sure everything's good. If it is, we'll hang out in front until your husband comes home."

She wrung her hands in her lap, chewing on her bottom lip, eyes locked on the house as she contemplated Jake's offer. "You stand at the door? I will go through the house. There are four rooms. It will not take long."

"Fine," Jake said. "Lead the way."

They climbed from the squad car. Jake pushed a hand to Bear and Conover indicating they should stay in the car. A pungent aroma wafted across the afternoon wind as Raasch and Jake followed Lucinda to the front door.

Jake wrinkled his nose. "What's that smell?"

Raasch jabbed a finger to the north. "Slaughter plant a couple miles away."

"It's almost enough to make a guy turn vegan."

"Don't let Bear hear you say that. This is stupid by the way."

"What?"

He jerked a thumb toward Lucinda. "Letting her go first."

"It'll be fine. Trust me."

Lucinda unlocked the door and motioned for them to stay as she went inside, leaving them in front of the open door. The remnant odor of spices floated to them from the adjacent kitchen, faint but enough to kick start Jake's salivary glands.

"It doesn't feel fine," Raasch said. "What are you up to, Caldwell?"

Jake tracked Lucinda as she crossed the living room to the kitchen and down a hallway out of earshot. She shot sideways peeks to the two men at her door, obviously going through the motions and putting on a show.

"Maria Almodavar is here."

"You sure?"

"Pretty sure," Jake said.

"And you know this how?"

"Lucinda worked—"

An ear-piercing scream erupted from the interior of the house. Raasch beat Jake through the door, sliding a Glock from his holster. Jake trailed close behind, down the hall, and to a back bedroom where Lucinda stood, shaking like a leaf. Her bony hands covered her mouth, noisy gasps like she struggled to breathe. It was easy to see why.

Maria Almodavar lay face-up on a queen mattress in the cramped bedroom, arms spread to the side, mouth ajar and dead eyes locked on the ceiling. Crimson stained the front of her white sweatshirt, spreading from the point where three black holes pierced the fabric—and Maria.

"Jesus Christ," Raasch muttered, holstering his

weapon. "You going to stick with 'it'll be fine', Jake?"

Raasch checked for a non-existent pulse before yanking out his radio.

Lucinda wobbled and Jake guided her to the living room. He sat her on the couch and swept the rest of the house. No other occupants, but the back door had been forced open. He went to the kitchen to get Lucinda a glass of water. She accepted the glass and managed a couple of swallows. Raasch's muffled voice sounded from the bedroom. Jake dropped beside Lucinda on the couch.

"How long was Maria here?"

Lucinda didn't answer, her wide eyes locked on the coffee table in front of them. Jake repeated the question.

"A few days," she said, her cadence slow and shocked. "I hide her. My husband did not even know she was here. There were men looking for Juan. She said she get worried because they came more often and more angry each time. They search her trailer, threaten her but she did not know where Juan is."

"That's what she said? She didn't know?"

"It is the truth. She was worried. Had a hard time working. Wondering where Juan could be. She was such a nice person."

Lucinda cried, her thin body trembling, and Jake patted her on the back.

Raasch emerged from the bedroom. "Local PD's on the way. I also called Airy and let her know."

Jake waited for the sobs to pass. "Lucinda, I know this is hard, and I'm sorry for your friend. But did Maria ever tell you why people were after Juan? Why they were at his home when you showed up?"

"He took something he should not have. I ask her

what, but she would not say. Maybe that is why their place a mess when I walk in."

"What did the man say before he attacked you?"

The tears flowed again and her voice climbed in pitch. "Where is Juan? Where is Juan? Tell me now, stupid puta. I do not know and I tell him this. That is when he hit me and tore my work shirt. If the older man does not come in..."

Raasch crouched, his eyes soft. "Why didn't you tell me this at the station? About Maria?"

"She beg me not to. Said police would not help. Said I couldn't say anything to my husband. The men after Juan, after her too. They tear her place to pieces looking for something. Maybe what Juan take from them."

"And you have no idea what it might be?"

She shook her head, but Jake had a pretty good idea now what it was. "Lucinda, you worked with Maria every day?"

"Almost. Same floor. We eat lunch together. She was my best friend. She and Juan were the only two people at my wedding."

"And did she talk about Juan a lot?"

A bout of fresh tears dropped across her cheeks. "She love Juan very much. He ask her to marry him. Had beautiful ring. They were happy together."

"And when was this? When did he ask her and give her the ring?"

Her chocolate eyes swept the ceiling. "A few weeks ago. He go to Omaha, to the casino. She said he got lucky at cards."

Jake offered her a smile. "You're doing great. This is helpful. Did she say if he went with anyone? To the casino?"

"Just men he works with."

"At the grain elevator?"

She nodded. "He must be good at cards. Once he start going, he always come back and spend money on her."

"Did you see Juan after he bought Maria the ring?"

She sniffed and took a tissue offered by Raasch, dabbing her eyes. "No. Maria worried because after the ring, Juan talk about leaving town with her, moving away. But he did not come home."

"One last question. What did Maria ask you to get at the trailer?"

Lucinda bit her upper lip, eyes darting away. "Just clothes. She had nothing to wear."

A lie. Biting her lip to keep from talking, eyes shooting away. "Lucinda, look at me." When she didn't comply, Jake turned her chin toward him. "This is important. We're here to help you. To find out who did this to Maria, what happened to Juan, and to make sure whoever did this can't get to you or your family. What did she ask you to get at the trailer?"

Tires squealed outside the house, a distant sound like a car taking a turn too fast. The hairs on Jake's arms prickled, sending goose bumps across his forearms. When a second screech sounded from the front of the house, he moved. He'd heard that sound before.

"Get down," he yelled to Raasch as he yanked Lucinda from the couch to the floor.

A second later, the front window exploded with bullets. Glass flew everywhere and hot lead whizzed overhead, slamming into the drywall behind the couch. Whether the gunfire lasted seconds or a minute, Jake wasn't sure. Fear clinched his gut. Bear and Conover were out there and in the middle of the shit.

CHAPTER THIRTY-TWO

The gunfire stopped, tires burned pavement, and a roaring engine faded in the distance.

Jake pulled himself to his knees, checking Lucinda. "You okay?"

She mumbled something resembling "Yes", her eyes wide with shock.

Jake turned and saw Raasch hugging the floor.

"Raasch? You hit?"

Raasch pushed himself to his feet. "I'm good. What the hell was that?"

Jake darted across the living room and burst through the front door. Bullet holes riddled Bear's Expedition, and the driver's side back tire was blown out along with the windows on Bear's side. Bear staggered from the driver's door, his beard glistening with shards of glass, gun hanging from his side. Crimson stained his left leg at the thigh.

"You shot?"

Bear spread the split fabric of his jeans with his fingers. "Grazed. Raasch, get on the horn. Late model black Taurus, at least three occupants armed with

AR-15s. Heading north down whatever the fuck the name of this street is."

Raasch bolted to his squad car. He jerked the handset and talked as he backed over the grass around Bear's SUV and tore up the street in the direction of the Taurus, lights and sirens at full attention.

Jake ran to the Expedition. Conover extricated himself from the floorboards in the front. A nasty gash covered his forehead, blood dripping down his nose.

"Conover, there's some napkins in the glove compartment for your head." Bear limped back a few steps and took in the damage. "Awww, Jesus. Look at my truck."

Conover grabbed a stack of Sonic napkins and pressed them to his forehead. "That was some serious firepower." He pushed open the passenger door and came around the front.

"You guys see who it was?" Jake asked.

Bear picked glass from his beard. "Nah. Heard the screech of tires, turned in time to spot those muzzles pop out the windows. The guys wore ski masks. They hit the house and before I could even pull my piece out they hit us. The girl okay?"

"One of them is."

"There were two. Lucinda and Juan's Maria."

"Which one isn't okay?"

"Maria. She's dead. Shot before we got here."

Sirens whooped in the distance as Jake headed into the house. Anger built, beating back the shock of the drive-by shooting. Ski masks or not, he knew who was behind this. Frost would pay.

***

Fifteen minutes later as they huddled in the living room, Raasch waded through the entourage of cops outside the house. The whole Gibbon police force must have been in attendance. Two paramedics attended to Lucinda. Bear and Conover were already treated and worked on Bear's bullet-ridden Expedition. Conover applying duct tape to garbage bags plastered over the blown-out windows, and Bear putting the spare tire on the driver's side rear wheel.

"Anything?" Jake asked Raasch.

Disappointment sagged Raasch's features. "Found the Taurus in a parking lot on the outside of town. Must've switched cars for the getaway."

"Had to be Frost and his goons. I'd get your folks stacked on the highway going back into Kearney."

"I'm not an idiot, Caldwell. We're already on it."

A knock sounded behind them. Two Gibbon officers filled the door, one lanky, the other shaped like a pear. Raasch crossed the room to meet them.

Jake moved to the couch where the girl sat, shaking under a reflective blanket. "Lucinda, we have to talk, and we're running out of time."

She trembled. "What if my husband was here? My daughter?"

Jake forgot about the daughter. "You check on her?"

"She is fine. At my mother's house."

"Say a prayer of thanks for that. But, there are other lives at stake here. Someone took a hell of a risk to try and kill you. What was in the trailer?"

Lucinda jammed her elbows on her knees, fingers massaging her temples. "She make me promise to tell no one."

"Please. We're running out of time. We can keep

you and your family safe, but to get the guys who did this and keep them from trying again, we need your help."

Stress lines furrowed her forehead. "A key."

"To what?"

"I do not know. She just ask me to get it."

"She say where it was?"

"In their bedroom," Lucinda said. "Loose board on Juan's side behind night table. The man got into the trailer before I get it."

Jake patted Lucinda on the back and stood. He maneuvered around the cops congregating on the front stoop and met Bear and Conover at the truck. Bear tightened the last of the lug nuts on the spare tire and chucked the wrench through the missing window into the backseat.

"This thing drivable?"

"She started right up. Will be colder than a penguin's pecker, but she'll run. What the hell is going on?" Bear asked.

Jake laid out what Lucinda told him.

Conover flipped up the collar to his jacket as the wind kicked up. He taped up plastic to the missing window as he talked. "Juan ripped off Frost, didn't he? Frost robs your guy's money train and Juan robbed Frost."

"That's what I'm thinking. But why shoot up the house?"

"Has to be the girl. They're afraid of what she knows. We were icing on the cake."

"I don't know. That's what I thought at first, too. But, that's a hell of a risk for Frost to take. Killing us and gunning down a cop as well?"

"What now?" Bear asked.

Jake scanned the horizon, the winter sun descending over the tree tops. "Let's go get the key. We find the key, maybe we find the money. We find the money, we have leverage to get the goods on Frost and his band of shitheads."

"Unless Frost already has the key."

"He doesn't, or he wouldn't have torn the trailer apart. And he definitely wouldn't have killed Maria."

Bear raised a finger. "Or he found the key and doesn't want to leave any witnesses behind, including us."

"True. Either way, we need to be sure by checking the trailer. Let me fill in Raasch, and we can head over there."

Conover tugged at Jake's arm. "Wait. You sure we can trust Raasch?"

Bear piped in. "I worked with him for a couple of years, and he never gave me a reason to doubt what side of the line he played on."

"That was a long time ago. People change."

Bear locked his eyes on the wrecked house. "I don't think so in this case. I trust the guy."

"But what about everyone else in the department? Think about it. The Triad is doing this illegal shit and keeps getting away with it? How did Stumpy get a lawyer so fast? How did they know we were here? You don't do that without someone on the inside. What do you think, Jake?"

Jake scratched his head as he ran through the last couple of days. "Conover has a good point. How did they know we were here?"

Bear said, "They could've followed us from the police station. Maybe they were still here from when they killed Maria, who knows? All I know is I trust

Raasch."

Jake was on the fence, but they didn't have a lot of choice. "He could come in handy, and I don't know if we should dive much deeper without keeping him in the loop. We have to make sure we're all rowing the boat in the same direction."

Conover bristled. "We also gotta make sure nobody in the boat is drilling fucking holes in it when we're not looking."

"Fair point, but if Bear trusts him then so do I. I'll talk to him and see if he can keep it under wraps until we find out more."

As Jake trudged back up the lawn to let Raasch know what they planned, he wished the bad feeling in his gut would go away.

CHAPTER THIRTY-THREE

Jake wanted to get the key Lucinda mentioned and had zero desire to be stuck with Raasch in Gibbon for hours wrapping up the homicide and drive-by scene. He jumped in Bear's bullet marred Expedition along with Conover, and they left a protesting Raasch behind.

Bear gunned the Expedition west on Highway 30. The trash bags secured with duct tape over the blown-out windows flapped, but slowed the frigid air from whipping through the vehicle. "Man, what I'm going to do to these pricks who shot up my goddamn truck."

"Didn't you pay it off last month?" Jake asked, his voice loud over the thwapping of the plastic.

Bear's neck craned slow enough to hear the tendons stretch. "You know I did. Now you're being an asshole."

"You seem more worried about the truck than getting shot."

"I didn't get shot. I was grazed. Big difference."

"What are the odds we find the key?" Conover

asked.

Jake searched the landscape for answers. "If Juan stole the money from Frost, he obviously didn't keep the cash at his trailer or Frost and his crew would've found it by now. Not like there's a ton of places to hide a million and a half in a trailer."

"What about the house in Gibbon?"

"Nah. Maria wouldn't have sent Lucinda for a key. My guess is a storage locker somewhere. Maybe a bus station or something?"

Conover piped in from the back. "No bus terminal in town. I checked when I got here to see if Juan caught one out of town. There's a drop off, but no station."

Bear swung the Expedition around a John Deere tractor rumbling half on the road and half on the shoulder of the highway. "Sounds like a storage locker is the best place to start. How many of them in Kearney?"

"Assuming it's in Kearney. He could've hauled it to Omaha to the casino."

"Juan would want to keep it close in case he needed to jet out of town, which he was already thinking about according to Lucinda." Jake slid his cell from his pocket and punched up a Google search on storage places in Kearney.

"Shit." Jake sighed. "There's a dozen storage places in town."

Conover's phone rang in the back. He answered, listened for a minute, asked a question, said thanks and clicked off. "My trailer spy Mabel said two guys just left Juan's trailer. A big guy and a skinnier older guy."

"Sounds like Frost and Parker."

Bear growled. "Let's chop off their hands and see if they smell like gunpowder."

Jake envisioned groping around an empty cut out in the wall of Juan's trailer. "If the key's not there, we know we have a leak to deal with in the Kearney PD."

"Nobody's said no to my hands idea," Bear said. "I think I have an axe in the back."

Jake shot his eyes sideways. "You're kidding, of course."

Bear's lip curled. "Look at my truck. Ain't a jury in the world would convict me."

Fifteen minutes later, they pulled into the Valley View Mobile Home park and bee-lined to Juan's trailer. The door to the trailer hung ajar, but there were no cars parked in front. They climbed out and Conover offered a salute across the drive to a well-kept trailer with an old woman waving through the blinds.

"That's Mabel?" Jake asked.

"Better than a surveillance camera. Play our cards right and we might even get coffee and cake after this."

Bear perked up. "What kind of cake?"

"A Sara Lee."

Bear's face beamed. "Works for me. Then again, any cake works for me."

Jake sidled to the front door, hand on the butt of his Sig Sauer at his waist. He peeked through the cracked door to a wreckage of furniture. He stopped, listened to the emptiness, and climbed inside.

The trailer appeared to be a victim of an F5 tornado last time they were there and now it looked like a Category 5 hurricane rolled through on top of it. Slashed cushions littered the floor, their stuffing scattered like a layer of snow. Furniture smashed or overturned; knickknacks from a bookshelf swept to the ground. The thirty-two-inch flat screen television lay on its side with a spiderweb of cracks cascading across the screen.

Jake kept a hand on the butt of his gun and led the way down the hall toward the bedroom, stepping over wreckage and debris.

Bear grunted as he stepped over a fallen dresser. "Left no stone unturned, didn't they? Looks like my daughter's bedroom."

Jake kicked over an ironing board blocking the hallway. "Landry's room is this nice? You should see Halle's."

They reached the bedroom. Pretty much in the same shambles as the rest of the trailer. As Jake went for the nightstand in the corner, Bear and Conover crammed into the room. The nightstand was cheap particle board thrown onto its face, it's base resting against the wall. Jake stood it up, noting the drawer had been thrown to the other side of the room after its contents were dumped on the bed. Nothing but phone charging cords, a Bible, and a pack of condoms. No key.

He slid the nightstand away from the wall and examined the white, chipped baseboard. Vertical seams a foot apart. Had Lucinda not said anything, he would've assumed bad carpentry, but now he had something else in mind. Holding his hand up, Jake asked for Bear's pocket knife.

Bear handed it to him. "Don't break it this time. It was a gift from my wife."

Jake flipped the blade out and squatted. "Not my fault she doesn't love you enough to buy you a decent one."

He stuck the blade into one of the seams and pried it out. The baseboard popped loose. Jake set it to the side revealing a cut out with a loaded .38 Special and a cigar box. He grabbed both and stood, dropping the gun on the mattress and flipping open the box lid. Inside was a grand in cash and a small brass key on a Nebraska Cornhusker red and white lanyard.

Bear whistled. "Bingo. That's a padlock key."

"Now if we could figure out where it goes. Look around for any paperwork to a storage place."

Jake took the bedroom, Bear the wrecked living room, and Conover all areas in between. After ten minutes they had nothing.

Bear sighed. "That would've been too easy."

Jake headed toward the front door, slipping the lanyard over his head and shoving the key down his shirt for safe keeping. "Let's find the storage unit."

As they stepped outside, two trucks rumbled to a stop in front of the trailer. Darius Frost and Randall Parker climbed out of the larger one. Three other guys Jake recognized from the Dome climbed out of the other. Two of the guys produced bats from the truck. Darius let a thick steel chain dangle from his paw, the metal links clinking together.

"Damn," Bear said. "These guys think that's going to stand between me and a Sara Lee cake?"

CHAPTER THIRTY-FOUR

Frost took a couple of steps forward, swinging the chain in a short, circular motion. "Find anything good in there?"

Jake stopped fifteen feet away. "Just the mess you made."

"What were you lookin' for?"

"Same thing you are, I'm guessing."

Frost set his jaw. "Thought you were told to get your asses outta town. You boys don't listen so good."

Jake shrugged. "And you don't speak so well. Guess we'll call it even."

In his peripheral vision, Jake observed Conover and Bear sliding away from him on either side. Smart move. It was five on three. Maybe five on two and a half—he wasn't sure how much he could count on Conover's fighting skills. Better to split the opposing forces if they decided to make a move.

"What do you want, Frost?" Jake asked.

"You know who I am?"

"Seems like everyone in town knows who you are. Juan Hidalgo knew it and I'm pretty sure Juan's girlfriend Maria knew it."

Frost grinned and spewed a lie. "Don't know anything about Maria."

"Sure you do. Either you or one of the shitheads in your merry band of misfits took her out right before you did a drive-by."

Frost's head cocked back and his brow furrowed. "What drive-by?"

"In Gibbon, dumb ass. When you turned a poor woman's house into a shooting range."

Parker stepped forward, face pinched. "What the hell are you talking about?"

"Too bad you guys couldn't hit water if you fell out of a boat. All you did now was piss everybody off. But you're kinda used to failing, aren't you, Frost?"

Frost twirled the chain in a slow loop, the weight of the rust-crusted steel links clinking together. "You got a big mouth for a man who's gonna get the livin' shit kicked out of him." Frost slid his jacket to the side revealing the butt of a pistol. "Or worse."

"You're not gonna shoot me in broad daylight in front of Lord knows how many witnesses," Jake said. "That's why you brought the chain and the bats. Don't think even your daddy could get you out of a murder rap. You don't scare me."

Frost's lip curled. "I should."

The men in the crew flicked their eyes between Jake and Frost, their nervous energy wafting off them in waves. They would attack if ordered, but they really didn't want to.

Jake slid forward as the veins in Frost's neck bulged in fury. "Your dumb ass stole over a million bucks from a *mob* boss. I should be the least of your worries."

Jake's hands tingled, each moment opening up the adrenaline valve a little wider.

He was still outside the range of the chain if Frost chose to swing it, but not by much. He needed to get the chain out of the equation or get close enough to Frost that he couldn't use it.

A phone rang behind Frost. Parker answered and edged back to the truck, out of the wind.

"What happened to the money, Frost?" Jake asked. "Did Juan steal it? Is that why you killed him? Is that why you killed Maria, too?

Parker walked up behind Frost and whispered into his ear. Frost's lips disappeared. He asked Jake the same question when they first pulled up, but this time his tone was different. It swam in arrogance because he already knew the answer.

"What were you lookin' for in the trailer?" Frost asked.

Jake flicked his eyes to Parker, who leaned back on the truck with a shit-eating grin pasted on his lined face. A phone call. A whisper. Frost knew about the key. Fucking Raasch.

"You want it," Jake said, spreading his hands wide. "Come get it."

CHAPTER THIRTY-FIVE

"You don't wanna fight me," Frost said, holding up the chain. "And your grandpa and fat friend don't wanna take on my crew. Things are about to get ugly."

Bear bristled. "I'm not fat. I just swell up because I'm allergic to assholes like you."

Frost and Parker both flaunted guns, and Jake assumed the other three packed weapons as well. He'd bet money Conover and Bear were better shots than Frost's crew, but Jake didn't like the odds presented by the sheer number of bullets that would fly in their direction. Besides, who knew how many innocent bystanders could get caught in the crossfire. A handful of onlookers had already emerged from their trailers.

"Tell me what you want, Frost, and maybe I'll give you a chance to get it."

"You know what I want. The key."

That confirmed Jake's suspicion that it was Raasch who called Parker. Over Frost's brawny shoulder, Jake spotted fingers spreading the blinds from the trailer across the road. Conover's friend Mabel. Frost and his crew came back so quickly because the old woman dropped a dime on them. There was no way anyone was leaving this scene without some measure of violence, just hopefully not gunshots. Jake wanted to drag things out until the police showed. Someone nearby would make the call. Maybe. But, if the cops were dirty, they might take their sweet time arriving.

Jake reached into his shirt and pulled out the lanyard. He dangled the key, taunting Frost. "You mean this key? I'll make you a deal. You and me, one on one. You beat me, you get the key and we leave town. Nobody else jumps in, no guns get drawn. Trust me, my two guys could shoot the asshole out of a housefly and your guys would be deader than fried chicken before they took a step. But gunshots are noisy and none of us want the Kearney PD showing up."

Conover and Bear flashed their guns now, too.

Jake imagined the gears in Frost's head turning, contemplating the proposal. Jake dropped the key back in his shirt and pulled the Sig from his hip, handing it back to Conover without taking his eyes off Frost. Now unarmed, his hands tingled with unease, especially considering his opponent had a gun.

Frost twirled the chain and Jake's neck prickled with worry. A smart man would keep the chain or use the gun, but Jake was counting on Frost's Mount Everest ego to trump his common sense.

"Unless you're a pussy who needs a gun and a chain against an unarmed older man," Jake said, throwing an arrogant sneer on his face.

Frost took the bait, dropping the chain to the ground and handing Parker the Glock in his waistband.

The two circled each other, boots scuffing the

asphalt beneath their feet, brushing across the winter burned weeds springing between the cracks. The onlookers drew in closer, and Jake had his doubts Frost's guys would stay out of the fray. But he realized he'd better keep his focus on the behemoth in front of him. He was confident he could take Frost if he could stay out of his range. If Frost landed those giant hands on him, Jake would be in deep trouble.

Jake raised his hands, tucked his chin, and dropped his height a few inches, weight balanced and pressed forward on the balls of his feet. He picked up the speed of the circling, wanting to study how Frost moved. The dude was a D1 college lineman, so Jake guessed his footwork would be excellent. He wasn't wrong. Frost moved nimbly, the fists at the end of his arms the size of hams, content at the moment to dance with Jake. Not surprising considering how poor his blind charge worked out for him at the bar. But the dancing wouldn't last long.

Normally, Jake would throw the first punch when he was outsized. Most of the time it ended the fight before his opponent could react. But such a tactic wasn't going to work with Frost. He was too big and, unlike the fight at the Dome, he was ready this time. Jake wanted Frost to initiate the fight, because it would give him a self-defense claim when the Kearney PD showed up which would be soon if his suspicions about Mabel were correct.

Frost took a half step in, and Jake dropped back, continuing to circle, bouncing on the balls of his feet. Frost stepped in two more times, fists cocked. The tension built in Frost's body, his limbs tightening. The first punch was coming. Considering Frost swung the chain in his left hand, that's where the first punch would come from. Jake squeezed his fists lightly, ready to counterpunch, elbows sucking into his sides to protect his ribs.

Frost threw a jab which Jake slipped, continuing to circle.

Two more jabs and a compact roundhouse that missed. Jake bobbed and weaved with ease.

The first seed of doubt crept on the giant's face. Four punches thrown with no pay dirt. Jake let a cocky smirk creep to his face. He didn't feel cocky, but he wanted Frost frustrated. If he got pissed off, he'd overextend and open himself up.

Jab. Miss.

"I hope you played football better than you fight," Jake said.

Roundhouse punch Jake slipped under.

"Quit dickin' around and hit him, Frost," Parker yelled.

Then it came. Frost stepped too close and swung too hard. Jake parried the punch and unleashed a hard slap to Frost's ear. A smack to the ear worked as good as a hook to throw off an opponent's equilibrium. Frost staggered forward and spun, face tomato red, spittle coating the corners of his mouth. He plodded toward Jake, a raging hulk with murder burning in his eyes.

As he drew close, Jake unleashed a hard kick to Frost's knee, but struck too low. It was like kicking a tree trunk and his balanced wobbled. Frost took advantage and unleashed a jab, striking Jake in the temple and sending him tumbling back into Bear who caught him before he fell. Stars danced in Jake's vision.

Bear whispered. "We could just shoot the fucker."

"No, I got him."

"I see that. Right where you want him." Bear made sure Jake had his balance and shoved him back into the makeshift ring. The next minute was a blur of punches and kicks. Jake delivered most of the damage, ducking in and out of Frost's range. But he took his own share of hits including one to his ribs which knocked his breath to Iowa. Did he hear sirens wailing in the distance or were his ears ringing from one of Frost's blows?

If this had been a boxing match, Jake would be dominating in points. But there were no judges issuing scores and, in terms of pure damage, Frost's size would win out in the long run. Time to quit screwing around and get dirty.

When Frost missed with a haymaker, Jake coiled his body and swung from the cheap seats, hitting Frost in the liver. Jake knew from experience what a hard liver shot did to the body. Frost would feel like his legs were paralyzed and on the verge of passing out.

Jake took advantage of Frost staggering back, bent over, hands dropped to the spot of the blow. He jumped forward and drove his knee under Frost's lowered chin. The crunch sent shockwaves up Jake's leg, and he stumbled back as Frost wobbled, his eyes glassy and distant. His body hit the ground as a couple of Kearney squad cars tore up the street and screeched to a halt.

Jake hobbled to Bear and Conover who stepped away from Frost's moaning figure. Across the lot, Frost's crew had ditched their weapons and rested against their trucks like they were just hanging out at a tailgate party. Two Kearney officers and Sheriff Airy climbed out of their cars, Airy's eyes narrowed and jaw set as she surveyed the scene.

"What in the holy hell is going on here?" she demanded as she stomped toward Jake.

CHAPTER THIRTY-SIX

"Nothing, Sheriff," Jake said, probing his sore jaw and drawing back bloodied fingers from a split lip. He wasn't telling Airy a thing. Somebody in the Kearney PD tipped off Frost about the key. Jake didn't know if the leak was Raasch or if Raasch reported things up the chain. Either way, there was zero advantage to being forthcoming.

Airy took in Frost who curled in the fetal position. "Doesn't look like nothing."

"Darius and I were talking and he slipped. Right, Darius?"

Frost groaned.

Airy tugged Jake back toward the trailer out of Frost's earshot, irritated lines furrowing her brown face. "Don't screw around with me, Caldwell. I told you to get out of town and let me handle this case. Did you not understand that simple order?"

Jake choked back the urge to confront her about the key and Frost knowing about it. If she and Raasch were in league with the Triad, there was no sense provoking her.

"Bear and I had to bring Conover back and get our stuff from the hotel," Jake said. "Conover wanted to have a last look at the trailer to see if he could find anything that would lead him to Juan."

"So this little trip had nothing to do with finding a key?"

"Doesn't matter because we don't have it."

"Maybe I'll search you to find out for sure."

Jake threw his arms up. "Have at it. You won't find anything. Place was picked clean, not that there was much there to begin with."

Airy cocked an eyebrow in a questioning slant. "Sounds like first grade bullshit to me, mister."

"It's the truth. Hold off Frost and his crew long enough for us to get out of town and you won't see me again."

"You promise?" she asked.

"Probably."

Her nostrils flared wide. "Probably? If I see you again, I'll throw your ass in a jail cell faster than green grass passes through a goose. You get me?"

"Sure thing, Sheriff." Jake motioned for Bear and Conover to follow him. They headed toward Bear's Expedition, walking past Parker who stood as the point of the triangle of Darius's crew.

Parker locked eyes with Jake. "We didn't shoot up that house, man."

Jake continued without a word, though it was an interesting unsolicited aside. As he clipped toward Bear's truck, he reflected on Parker's comment and their reactions about the drive-by—genuine surprise. They lied about killing Maria, but perhaps not about the drive-by. And if it wasn't Frost's crew, who did it?

***

Bear and Jake drove to the Taco Johns to silence his and Bear's grumbling stomachs. Conover grabbed his car from the trailer park and met them inside. As Bear wolfed down tacos, Jake jotted addresses of storage units on two napkins. His hands hurt, knuckles red and swollen from the fight. He ordered two extra large sodas, filled them halfway with ice and shoved his fists into them.

"Bear and I will hit the units around here," he said, nodding to one of the napkins to Conover. "You hit these and don't dawdle. It's getting late and they could be closing soon. I seriously doubt Juan used his real name. All we can do is show his picture around and hope for a hit. You get one, you call me. You have a picture of Juan?"

"I'll text it to you," Conover said.

Bear asked, "You sure we should split up? Things are spicy out there."

"Divide and conquer. A dozen sites shouldn't take long between two groups. I don't wanna waste time going back to get my rental. Everyone keep your head on a swivel. If Frost and his crew catch any of us in the wrong spot or Airy sees we're hanging around town, we're done. You see them, get somewhere crowded. I've whipped his ass twice now, so it'll be bullets flying next time."

Bear wiped his mouth with a napkin and tossed it on the sea of empty wrappers. "We have another issue. How did Frost find out about the key?"

"Either Raasch or Airy," Jake said. "They're the only ones who knew."

Conover said, "If Raasch called it in, there's no telling how many people heard it."

Bear swirled his drink, the ice sloshing in the

Styrofoam. "I know this guy, Jake. Can't believe it'd be him."

"You thought the same thing about Sad Dog Daniels."

Bear winced at the mention of one of his trusted deputies turning to the dark side a couple of years ago.

"The point is, we can't trust anybody outside the three of us. Stay alert, Conover, and keep in touch."

Conover grabbed his address napkin and headed out the door.

Jake turned to Bear. "You ready to hunt?"

"Let me grab another couple tacos and some extra hot sauce to go. Those damn things are like crack."

CHAPTER THIRTY-SEVEN

Jake and Bear covered the first three storage locations on their list in twenty minutes. They came up with the story of finding the key in the personal effects of their dead cousin. Two of the storage places seemed genuine they hadn't seen Juan and took the time to check if he came up on the computer. The third guy was a scrawny little twerp with a chip on his shoulder who barely took the time to glance away from his Clash of Clans game on his phone to look at Juan's picture. He mewled like a hungry kitten when Bear snatched the phone out of his hand.

"I wonder how you're going to be able to play your game with two broken thumbs," Jake said, drawing close and mustering a death glare. "Have you seen this guy or not?"

The kid looked at Juan's picture for a couple of seconds, bumbled around on the computer, and came up with nothing. Bear threw the kid his phone, turned and crop dusted the lobby with Taco Johns fumes before following Jake out the door.

"Glad I was in front of you," Jake said.

"I was going to save the blast for the truck, but the little douche deserved it more. I hope he chokes on that cloud of foul."

They hopped in the Expedition and took off to their next stop.

"Did you see the look on Frost and Parkers' faces when I brought up the drive-by?" Jake asked.

"They seemed surprised," Bear said.

"I mean, I wouldn't put it past them to have their lackeys do the deed, but I got the impression they didn't know what the hell we were talking about."

"They definitely killed Maria, though," Bear said.

"Oh yeah. But, why would they kill her and then circle back to the scene of the crime and try taking us out?"

"If it wasn't them on the drive-by, then who? The Triad?"

Jake rapped his knuckles against the bullet spared passenger window. "Maybe. Maybe Big Daddy Frost is trying to take care of what Junior can't seem to do."

Jake's brain worked through the scenario, though one other possibility floated across his brain: Lunetti.

They hit pay dirt at their fourth stop – Tyson Storage on 16th Street.

The manager was a slim man in his thirties, gnawing on a toothpick and reading a book called *The High Crown Chronicles*. He studied the picture on Jake's phone. "I recognize him. Was in here a few weeks ago and rented a unit."

Jake displayed the key. "He's our cousin. Died last week in a car wreck. We're putting his affairs in order and wanted to clean out his storage unit and see if there's anything in there that could help his widow."

The manager put down the book and swiveled to

the computer. "Name of the deceased?"

Jake and Bear exchanged glances. "Um...try Juan Hidalgo."

The manager's eyebrows shot up. "You don't seem sure of your cousin's name."

"I know his name. We're just not sure if that's the name he used. He was going through a messy divorce."

"I can tell you right now that's not the name he used."

"What was it?"

"Sorry. We value our client's confidentiality."

Bear put his paws on the counter. "He's dead. He doesn't need confidentiality. But Juan definitely rented a unit here?"

"Ayuh. I even remember which one."

"Which one was it?"

"Can't tell you that either." The manager waved toward a door to their right. A numeric keypad blinked near the door handle. "Seeing how you have the key, you're welcome to try the locks until you get the right one."

Bear growled. "Jesus Christ. We're on a tight schedule. How many units you have back there?"

"Seventy-two."

Jake stepped toward the access door. "Fine. Buzz us through."

The manager held a hand up. "Ooh, sorry. Can't do that either. If you don't have the passcode, you'll have to provide a copy of your credentials to the individual managing this guy's estate designating you as someone who's allowed access."

"The guy is fucking dead."

"So you say, but how do I know that? I'm not trying

to be a jerk."

"You're doing a damn good imitation of one," Bear said.

"How do I know you didn't take the key from the guy and he's still alive? Even if the guy is dead, he still has rights and the contents of the unit belong to his estate. Court has to decide who gets the property. Sorry."

Bear threw up his hands. "This is such bullshit."

The manager waved his hands apologetically. "I know, I know. Had someone come in last week in a similar situation to yours. Even had a picture of the dead guy in the casket. But, no key, no gate code means no entrance without court papers. I'd let it slide, but my owner is kind of a hothead."

Jake wondered if it was Xavier Frost. "Who's your owner?"

"Company called Enterprise Transition Management. Believe me, you don't want to meet the guy who runs it."

A light flicked on in Jake's head. Enterprise. Same company name Franco Lunetti tried to bribe him with. "I think I've already met him. Give me a second." Jake tugged Bear into the corner of the lobby. "You have contacts at the Jackson County Jail?"

"A couple. Why?"

"Enterprise Transition Management is the company Lunetti owns. Call your people and get him on the phone."

Bear scowled over his shoulder at the manager. "Or we bash this guy's forehead into the keypad until the door opens."

"And get Sheriff Airy dropping down on our heads? No thanks. Make the call."

Bear pulled out his phone, grumbling. "Would be faster if we leaned on this guy."

"Probably and we'll do it if this doesn't work."

As Bear made the call to the jail, Jake called Conover to let him know they found the unit. The call went to voicemail. Jake tried again with the same result. That didn't give him the warm fuzzies. He left a message as Bear handed him the phone.

"They're grabbing Lunetti from his cell. Listen to the hold music. I can't handle Hall & Oates right now."

It took ten minutes for Lunetti to get on the line and another five minutes of Jake listening to Lunetti explain how few shits he gave about what Jake wanted.

"You got two of my guys locked up in bumfuck Nebraska."

"That's on you for only sending two guys."

"Get me out of here, and I'll get you in the unit," Lunetti said.

"Man, I don't have anywhere near that kind of juice, especially not with the charges you're facing."

"Then I can't help you, not that I want to in the first place."

Jake thought about the shooting in Gibbon. "Do it and I'll forget your crew tried to kill me with a drive-by."

Lunetti paused. "I don't know nothin' about a drive-by."

"Bullshit. The good news for you is it didn't work. I'm still sucking oxygen, but I need your help. Do it and I won't blacklist your name with the wrong people."

"With who? You already said you don't know nobody."

"With Jason Keats. He already told you to back off me. He doesn't like being disobeyed."

Lunetti broke the silence following Jake's threat.

"You wouldn't."

"In a heartbeat. I'm doing a very important favor for Keats at the moment, and I need in the goddamn storage unit. You help me get in there, I won't tell him you tried to wipe me out after he ordered you not to. I'll actually tell him you helped me, which I'm sure will translate to something favorable on your end. You keep dickin' me around and I'll tell Keats you should be ass raped in the jail shower with a splintered broomstick."

Silence flowed from the other end of the phone. Lunetti cleared his throat. "I ain't sayin' I ordered the drive-by."

"Whatever helps you sleep at night."

"Put the manager on."

Two minutes later, Jake and Bear were through the door and standing in front of unit twenty-eight. A gold padlock held shut a forest green corrugated aluminum door. Jake slipped in the key and snapped the lock open. Bear rattled the door up, revealing a five-foot by five-foot unit. The only thing in it was a large, black canvas duffel bag resting on the concrete floor. Jake squatted and unzipped the bag. Stacks of banded hundred-dollar bills pushed out the sides of the bag.

"Sweet Mary Mother Joseph," Bear whispered. "That's what one point five million dollars looks like?"

"That's it. The question now is what—"

Jake's cell rang and Conover's name popped up on the screen.

"Hey, Conover, we—"

"Hello, Jake Caldwell," Darius Frost said, his voice oozing through the speaker.

Jake covered the speaker. "Frost has Conover."

He put the phone on speaker.

"Where's Conover?"

"Right here with me. Unhurt for now. Unless I don't get the key. Then I'm gonna hurt him real bad. Slow."

Jake stood and ran a hand through his hair. "Where are you?"

"The Clam. Come in alone with the key. I even smell those buddies of yours and I'll gut your boy here like a fish."

The call ended and Jake's mind raced, settling on a plan in a matter of seconds.

"What now?" Bear asked.

Jake zipped up the bag and hoisted it over his shoulder. "We're gonna give him the key and get Conover back."

Bear stroked his beard as he worked through the idea. "I like it. He'll come here and not find a damn thing. Then what?"

"I don't know. I'm makin' this up as I go along."

CHAPTER THIRTY-EIGHT

The gravel lot of The Fuzzy Clam held a dozen vehicles, mostly over-sized pickup trucks parked in haphazard fashion along the side of the steel-sided Quonset hut. Jake and Bear rolled toward the front entrance and backed into a spot.

"Now what?" Bear asked. "This another strip joint I don't get to go into?"

"Look at the place, man. I'm worried I'll get chlamydia just walking through the front door. Keep the engine running and stay here with the money. I shouldn't be more than a few minutes."

"I don't think you should go in alone."

Jake shook his head. "You heard him. No you, no Raasch. Besides, I think he picked a public place to avoid escalation since it hasn't worked out well for him the last two times. Place may be a shithole, but I doubt Frost is going to light it up."

Bear stroked his beard. "We should have a signal or something. You give it and I come runnin'."

"People running out the door screaming?"

"Smart ass. I'm gonna guess it'd be too late by

then. Call my cell, leave the line open and let me listen in. You say the word…I don't know…pineapple, and I'll rush in."

Jake scowled. "How the fuck am I going to work pineapple into a casual conversation?"

"Be creative."

Jake hit the speed dial for Bear's phone, they checked the connection, and Jake slid his phone into his pocket. This was stupid because there would be no way for Bear to hear a word through his jacket and the eighties rock music which would undoubtedly be playing inside the Clam. But, if it eased Bear's mind, he'd do it. Tucking his Sig in his waist holster, Jake strode past a couple of guys having a smoke outside the front entrance and into the club.

The inside of the Clam was nicer than the outside, but still had the vibe of a lower tier strip joint. Neon beer signs pierced the haze of smoky darkness. Poison's "Talk Dirty to Me" blared from overhead speakers. Ahead, a raised, thirty-foot wooden runway ran like a bowling lane splitting groupings of close-set circular tabletops. A handful of patrons ogled a dancing redhead with a tattooed pot-belly and sturdy legs she could crush a walnut between. To his right was the bar, bathrooms, and DJ booth. A stocky, but slack faced man in his mid-twenties in a black t-shirt with "Security" screen printed in yellow, perched on a stool scrolling through a phone, oblivious to the activity around him.

Jake's cell vibrated. Keats. "This isn't a good time."

"Where's my money?"

Jake pressed a palm to his opposite ear to block the noise. "I'm working on it."

"Shitty eighties music blaring? You in a strip club

or something?"

"As a matter of fact, I am. Following up on a lead. Let me call you later."

"Just remember, you don't find my money and—"

"You'll shoot me in the head and dump my body in the Missouri River. Got it. I'm making progress. Have a little faith, Jason."

"Fine. Don't make me regret it."

Keats ended the call without another word.

A blonde dancer in a sparkled blue G-string sidled up to Jake as he scanned the place for Frost. "Want a table dance, handsome?" She took in Jake's face and squinted. "Hey, I know you. Phone book man."

It was girl from the convenience store a couple of days ago. "Iola, right?"

She stroked his arm. "Good memory. I'm Jasmine here, though. How 'bout a dance? We got two for ones goin' for the next four songs."

"Maybe later. You seen Darius Frost?"

She stepped back. "Why would you want him instead of dancin' with me?"

"He and I have some unfinished business. Where is he?"

"In the VIP section with a few other guys. Be careful, he's super amped up for some reason." She jerked a thumb over her shoulder to a curtain drawn half-open on the right side of the stage.

The shiner she wore when he met her had faded, barely noticeable through the darkness of the club and a heavy application of makeup and glitter. "Thanks. How's it going with avoiding those doors?"

She shot her plucked eyebrows to the ceiling. "The door hasn't been home for two days, so pretty good. Come find me when you're done with Darius."

Jake wove his way around the tables toward the curtained area. He cracked his neck and stepped through the opening into a thirty by thirty room with a fifteen-foot bar top in one corner. The lighting was dim, offset by sparkles from a slow spinning disco ball in the center of the room. A handful of couches were scattered in the center of a ring of bar tables. Parker stood when Jake entered and rested his hand on the butt of the pistol tucked in the front of his jeans. A couple other goons Jake hadn't seen before spread out to either side of Jake, but maintained their distance. Frost stood at the end of one couch with Conover seated beside him. When Jake entered, Darius yanked Conover to his feet and held the blade of a hunting knife in front of Conover's throat.

Darius jerked his head toward one of the wall goons. "Search him, Wally."

Wally motioned for Jake to raise his arms.

Jake threw on a death glare. "You put your hands on me, and I'll put you in a coma."

"I gotta search you."

"You don't. I have a gun on my hip and that's where it's gonna stay. Back away."

Wally shifted his beady eyes between Darius and Jake and backed up slowly. His feet squelching against the sticky floor.

"You bring the key?" Darius asked.

Any previous trace of the bravado and arrogance from Darius was gone. His eyes were wide, wild, panicked. Either he was on something, terrified, or a clock ticked hard against him. Maybe all of the above. Jake pulled the key from under his shirt and let it hang from the lanyard against his chest. "Give me Conover and you can have the key."

Conover's eyes shot down and he licked his lips as Darius drew the blade closer to his neck. His lined face seemed to have aged another decade since they last saw him. The new abrasions on his face didn't help. "Key first. I don't have time to dick around, Caldwell. I got a deadline. Hand it over, and I let the old man go."

Jake slipped the lanyard over his head and balled the fabric in his fist, letting the key dangle for Frost to see. "I suppose you can understand if I have a little bit of a trust issue here with you. Nothing keeping you from taking the key and Conover with you."

"I got bigger shit to worry about than either of you," Darius said. "Now give me the goddamn key, or they'll kill all of us."

Parker pushed off the wall. "Darius, man—"

Jake cut him off. "Who?"

Frost pointed the knife at Jake, his voice rising. "They'll slaughter everyone in this room, the woman, my father, your family. I'm your way out and the way out is the key."

Jake stiffened. Woman? He wouldn't be referring to Maria. Maybe Lucinda, but it was Lunetti who did the drive-by. There was one other woman he knew who made any sort of sense. "What woman?"

Frost bit his upper lip, maybe to hold his mouth shut.

Jake dangled the key. "What woman?"

Parker drew a Glock from his coat and pointed it at Jake, stomping closer. "Shut the fuck up, Caldwell. You too, Darius."

Jake didn't like where this headed. Frost wore a mask of desperation, and desperate people did stupid things. The calm and cool Parker was now hot and bothered over the woman slipup from Frost. It had to be Snell. If Frost was worried about her getting killed, it meant she was still alive and kicking.

Jake held his hands up, cutting his eyes to Parker. "Take it easy, man. Don't get crazy. I'll hand over the key, you hand over Conover, and we can go our merry little way."

Frost asked, "You got him, Parker?"

Parker nodded. "Let the old man go. We can't drag his old ass along with us anyway."

Frost thought for a beat and released Conover from the knife. Conover took a few steps toward Jake, rubbing the bloody line on his throat.

"Now gimme the key, Caldwell."

Jake let the key dangle, giving Conover time to get a safe distance away. "You must want it pretty bad to go through all this trouble. Once you get it, what's keeping you from killing us both right here?"

"I could do that right now if I wanted to and take the key from your cold, dead hand."

"But you won't. Because even if you have the key, you don't know where it goes. I'm guessing you don't have time to screw around combing the town for the lock. Tell me about the woman, and I'll tell you where the lock is."

Frost sneered. "I don't know anything about a woman. Give me the key."

"You already mentioned her. You found her outside Omaha at a rest stop the same time you robbed the money train."

If Frost's jaw dropped any farther, it would fall off. Jake was fishing, but given the reaction, he was at the right watering hole.

Jake put his hands on his hips, closer to the butt

of his gun. "She alive?"

Frost swallowed his surprise. "She's alive and well. But one phone call ends that real quick. The key and I'll tell you where she is, *after* I get the money."

Jake weighed the offer. He had Conover. He had the money. He knew Snell was alive, though he didn't know where. Frost didn't know the location of the storage locker and while he hunted for it, Jake could find Snell.

Jake lobbed the key and Frost snatched it out of mid-air. "Happy hunting. Call me when you're ready to talk about the woman."

Frost ran the lanyard through his thick fingers, and with a dip of his square chin, his men edged toward them. Jake pushed Conover behind him toward the doorway leading back into the club.

Frost held up the lanyard like a prize. "No hunting needed. Only one place gives out Husker lanyards like this. Tyson Storage on 16th."

Jake gritted his teeth. Frost knew the location of the storage unit. Any leverage or time advantage they had flew across the room with the key. "Pineapple."

Frost's face crunched. "What?"

"Pineapple," Jake repeated, hoping his voice was audible through the phone over the blare of Motley Crüe jamming on the speakers in the club behind him.

Frost pointed the tip of the knife at Jake. "Kill these motherfuckers."

As the bad guys drew their guns, Jake drew his, yelling "Pineapple" and wishing Bear picked a better signal word.

CHAPTER THIRTY-NINE

Jake was a good fifteen feet from the door back into the club and didn't like his chances of getting through it without catching a bullet in the back. Like a coward, Frost remained in place with the knife and lanyard in either hand, while the rest of the bad guys advanced in a semi-circle around him. Though Parker had his gun out, he was charging instead of shooting. The lanky guy on his left cleared a Glock and brought it up. In a half-second Jake mapped out his movements.

As Parker closed, Jake chopped Parker's gun arm and brought an elbow to the man's jaw, a direct hit stopping his momentum cold. Jake spun to his left, dropping his mass low and bringing his Sig up as Lanky's shot went high and right. Jake took aim and squeezed three shots, hitting Lanky in the gut and leg with two of them. Screams erupted from the club behind him. Jake continued to turn and fired two more at Frost's figure as it dove behind the couch. Jake hit the ground and rolled, firing low and hitting Stocky in the knee and shin. The man dropped his gun and crashed to the ground holding his leg.

Parker jumped on top of Jake, his compressed ribs screaming in protest. Jake turned his head and caught sight of Frost's back busting through the emergency exit, the alarm wailing over the music. Parker grabbed Jake's wrist with one hand and slid his other arm under Jake's. It took a millisecond before Jake realized the guy was trying to execute an Americana Armlock, a basic Brazilian Jiu-Jitsu submission move. Unfortunately for Parker, Jake spent a couple months training with one of Keats's lackeys who had a black belt in Jiu-Jitsu. Parker held Jake's arm too high, and as he applied pressure for the armlock, Jake was able to roll him over and free his arm.

Conover was already on the move chasing Frost out the back door as Parker grunted and struggled to get free of Jake. Jake cracked a knee into Parker's midsection and relished the woof of air Parker released. He pinned Parker down with one arm and crushed him with his body weight while reaching out for the Sig laying nearby. His fingers gripped the handle and Jake jerked the barrel under Parker's chin.

"Jesus, don't shoot," Parker groaned. "I'm a federal agent. I'm a fucking FBI agent, don't shoot me."

Jake pressed the barrel harder under the man's chin as his brain processed the sentence. A fed? What kind of bullshit was this?

Shots rang out from the back of the building and Conover dove back through the open door. An engine roared, tires kicked up gravel. Motley Crüe's "Kickstart My Heart" wound down and screams and commotion from the club pierced the VIP area before Metallica's "Nothing Else Matters" seeped through the air.

Jake twisted Parker's shirt around his throat. "Federal agent, my ass."

"I swear to God," he moaned. "Jesus, can you get off me?"

Jake kept the gun jammed into the soft tissue under Parker's jaw but let up on the body weight. He glanced to Conover. "Go get Bear." When Conover darted out the VIP room, he growled at Parker. "You better start making some sense."

Parker spoke low, eyes darting to the man writhing on the ground nearby. "I've been working the Triad undercover for two goddamn years."

"You saying it doesn't prove anything."

"I've been coordinating with Snell the past few weeks. You can ask her yourself."

Now Jake did let up, but kept the gun trained on Parker. "She's alive?"

"Last time I checked."

"Where?"

"Basement of my house in town."

Jake jumped up and yanked Parker to his feet, jerking him across the room and away from the club music and what remained of Frost's crew, though the men were now either dead or passed out. Shoving his forearm against Parker's chest, Jake pinned him to the wall. "Start talking."

Parker raised his hands. "Listen, I'm with the FBI out of Dallas. We were tracking a drug pipeline coming out of Lansdale, Texas, up here."

Lansdale. Jake knew from a previous adventure the cartel running that pipeline brought up more than drugs.

"La Familia," Jake said.

Parker's eyes widened. "Yeah, La Familia. I've been gathering evidence for two years on the cartel, Frost, the Triad. Everything. We were close to moving in before you showed and screwed it up."

"How is Snell involved?"

Parker's eyes shot around the room. "We've gotta get out of here. If the Kearney PD gets here, I get taken in—"

"If you really are with the FBI, that shouldn't worry you."

"But the time it takes to sort it out will kill Victoria. Frost knows where she is. La Familia has people in town, and blood is going to flow if they don't get the money the Triad owes. Seriously, let's get the hell out of here."

Jake was torn. This could be an elaborate, bullshit story, but it rang true. Parker didn't engage in the fight at the Dome. At the trailer park, he made the point of telling Jake they didn't do the drive-by. He didn't shoot Jake moments ago when he had the chance but lowered his gun and charged. The armlock he attempted could be a defense tactic taught at the FBI Academy in Quantico. Your average schmuck off the street wouldn't know it. Still, there were questions.

Parker read the disbelief in Jake's eyes. "I get it, you're not convinced. How about this? You're Jake Caldwell and two years ago you saved Victoria's daughter Beth at some lab in Kansas City. You took out some Russian spies, got married not long ago, have a daughter...shit, I can't remember anything else. She said you're one of the bravest men she ever met."

Jake drew back and released the pressure. "When did she tell you this?"

"Two days ago. If you want to see her again, we gotta go. Once the cops get here, it'll be too late to save her."

Bear and Conover burst in the room. Bear surveyed the carnage and ran over as Jake tugged Parker toward the rear exit.

Jake turned to Bear. "This guy's a fed working undercover with Snell. He knows where she is."

Bear's eyes shot wide. "What the—"

"I'll explain on the way. We gotta move before Airy shows up."

Bear led the way out the back door. "Probably a good idea. She looked like she wanted to take a bite out of your ass at the trailer park."

Parker stumbled along, wiping blood from his nose. "That and she's on Xavier Frost's payroll."

They ran around the back of the building toward Bear's Expedition. By the time they reached the front, sirens wailed in the distance, and the cars of the Clam's patrons fled the scene like cockroaches when the lights flipped on.

Bear started the engine and turned to Parker who slumped in the backseat with Conover. "Where to?"

"My house. Take 2nd Avenue north until I tell you to turn."

Bear jammed the pedal down, kicking gravel against the steel sides of the Fuzzy Clam. The Expedition gained traction and screeched onto the asphalt of the highway. A half mile later, a stream of squad cars blared south toward the club.

Bear turned to Jake. "Why can't you ever go to a strip joint without shooting someone?"

"Why didn't you come up with a better safe word than pineapple?"

Parker grinned in the back. "Ahhh. I wondered why the hell you kept yelling that."

CHAPTER FORTY

Darius Frost swerved through the puttering traffic moving up 2nd Avenue toward Tyson Storage. The pit stop he made on the way cost him too much time. He pumped the brakes and slowed as a line of screaming Kearney police cars tore south toward the Fuzzy Clam.

His cell buzzed and his ass clenched when he checked the display. His father. "Yes, sir?"

"Where the hell are you? The cartel guys are pacing around the house like caged tigers at supper time. Tell me you have something to feed them."

Darius jammed the accelerator, minutes away from the storage building. "I will in a few minutes. Got the key to the storage unit where Juan hid the money."

"And Juan?"

Darius's brain sped to the shallow grave they buried Juan in. "That's a problem we're not solvin' in the next hour."

"Did you kill him?"

"Let's say he won't be walkin' through the front door."

Xavier rumbled, "Goddamn it, Darius. Diaz is expecting the money and his man."

Darius turned into the Tyson Storage parking lot and screeched to a halt in front of the door. "Maybe he'll be satisfied with just the money. We admit we killed Juan and he'll kill us all."

"He might kill us anyway. If we can't produce Juan, we'll need to give him something else. Bring the woman with you."

"You know what the cartel would do to an FBI agent?"

"Better her than us. Get the money, the woman, and your ass over here now."

Darius clicked off and hopped from the truck. This was Juan Hidalgo's fault. If the little shit hadn't stolen the money, the cartel wouldn't be here demanding payment, because Darius would've replenished the money he borrowed for his own little venture. If Juan hadn't stolen the money, he wouldn't be dead and the Triad machine would keep rolling. And he couldn't forget Jake Caldwell. The man would go through a world of hurt if Darius squirmed out of this alive.

Throwing open the door, Darius stormed past the man reading at the front desk toward the storage area. He jerked on the handle before noticing the keypad.

"You gotta enter your code," the man at the desk said.

"I don't remember it. I have my key," Darius said, holding it up.

"No code, no entry. Why is this simple concept so hard for people to understand tonight?"

Darius stomped toward the desk. The ass kickings, the missing money, the cartel killing his crew, Caldwell taking out the rest. The last thing he needed was this pencil dick giving him lip. He grabbed the man by the shirt and jerked him off the stool, dragging him toward the door.

He threw the screaming man against the wall. "Open the fucking door before I squash your greasy head like a watermelon."

The man's eyes shot wide, blood trickling down his chin. His fingers trembled but managed to punch in a four-digit code and the lock clicked open. Darius realized he didn't know which unit was Juan's. He didn't have time to try them all.

He spun back to the manager. "Which one of these was Juan Hidalgo's?"

"I don't know who he is—"

Darius grabbed the man and threw him across the polished concrete floor. He slid and smacked into the door of one of the units.

"You'd better figure out which one was his."

The man cowered on the ground, hands raised in surrender. "Try unit twenty-eight."

Darius advanced, fist clenched. "Thought you didn't know who Juan Hidalgo was."

"I don't, but some other guys pulled the same strong-arm tactic you're pulling and made me tell them."

Darius stopped, his heart thundering. "What other guys?"

"His cousins. At least that's what they said."

Darius jerked the man to his feet and cracked him against the door. "What did they take out of the unit?"

The man crunched his eyes closed, as if that would make the nightmare go away. "J-j-j-just a duffel bag. That's all that was in there anyway. I s-s-swear, that's it."

"Show me."

The manager stumbled down the row and stopped in front of unit twenty-eight. Darius's stomach flipped and he was on the verge of throwing up. He tossed the key to the manager who took several attempts to jab the key into the lock with trembling hands. He opened the lock and raised the screeching door. Darius stared at the emptiness of the unit, mouth ajar, red flecks of rage peppering his vision. He needed to break something, someone.

The manager backed away as if sensing the danger. "They were here like an hour ago. Maybe you can still catch them."

Darius's nails bit into his palms, his teeth grinding. "What'd they look like?"

But he already knew the answer.

CHAPTER FORTY-ONE

"Turn right here." Parker pointed east down 39th Street. "You know, you guys are going to have some explaining to do to my superiors."

Bear snorted. "For what?"

"For blowing two years of undercover work in just a few days."

Jake gunned the Expedition down the hill. "Like I give a damn what your superiors have to say."

"That's what Snell said. You help us take down the Triad, and it'll go a long way to smoothing things over. Turn right up here on Avenue E."

"How did you get in so deep with Frost's crew?" Jake asked.

"Started off drinking at the same bar. Let Frost win some money off me playing pool while I dropped breadcrumbs about my fake background. After a few weeks of that, we staged an incident where someone tried to stab Darius in the bar, and I jumped in and prevented it from happening. Darius was drunker than shit, so I volunteered to take care of the guy."

"What did you do with him?"

"The agent took some licks to make it seem real. Lucky for the agent Darius could barely stand, or he probably would've beat the guy to death. I drove the agent to the edge of town where we doctored up a gunshot wound to the head and I snapped a picture on my phone. Once the agent was safely on his way back to Dallas, I went back to the bar and showed Darius the picture to demonstrate the asset I could be to his organization. He bought it hook, line, and sinker. After that, I was in with the crew. It still took a year before he let me in on what was really going on with the Triad."

Conover asked, "Can you tell me what happened to Juan Hidalgo?"

Jake watched Parker's head drop in the rearview mirror.

"You sure you want to know?"

"My client will."

"He's dead," Parker said. "Darius killed him. Gathered everyone in a circle around Juan in a field. Whipped him bloody and shot him in the face with a shotgun."

"Where's his body?" Conover asked.

"Buried in that field outside of town."

"Why'd he kill him?"

"Juan stole money from us, and Darius made sure he paid the price."

"Us?" Bear asked. "Which side are you on?"

Parker's eyebrow cocked. "Did I say us? Sorry, old habit."

"Where were you when this shit happened?"

"Making sure Snell didn't get killed."

"Frost shot Juan right in front of you?" Conover asked.

"Dude is crazy. I didn't know he would do it. But, Snell's alive because of me. Make no mistake. There's the house on the corner."

The way Parker described everything struck Jake as odd. Jake didn't know anything about what it was like to work undercover, and he had no doubts feelings and loyalties could get mixed up. But his tone was the wrong kind of emotion. Almost annoyance. Parker described the murder the same way he'd tell the tale of getting a speeding ticket.

Jake pulled into the driveway next to Parker's truck. "You have any ID that shows you're really a Fed?"

Parker blinked. "You don't believe me?"

"I've always operated on the credo of trust but verify."

"How would I know all that shit about you and Snell if I wasn't on the level?"

"Dude, being evasive isn't helping your cause."

Parker rolled his eyes. "In my truck. Hidden compartment on the driver's side door."

"Lead the way."

They climbed out and walked to the driver's door. Parker opened it and Jake slid his Sig out, holding it down at his side. Parker noticed and made slow, deliberate movements. He reached under the frame, and a door panel popped open, revealing a gun and billfold. Jake's hand tightened on his gun as Parker reached for the stash. He plucked the billfold and passed it over to Jake, moving clear from the door.

Jake flipped open the billfold. The badge was small and gold, Federal Bureau of Investigation in full at the top. The gold wasn't chipped or dull, everything on the badge was embossed, not engraved. The bald eagle and blindfolded Lady Justice flanked by the letters U and S were right where they should be. The picture was a cleaner cut version of Parker with the name Milton Banks. Jake had seen fake identifications before and this one was legit.

Jake handed the billfold back to Parker/Banks. "Weren't you worried Frost and his crew might find it?"

Parker put the wallet back into the side door stash and clicked the secret compartment closed. "Nah, those dumbasses never would've found it. Thought I might need it handy in case I got in a jam."

"Any of the local PD know who you are?"

"Not a one. The Triad has some friends on the inside of the department, and my bosses didn't want to take a chance."

Between the details about him and Snell and the legit ID, Jake believed him. "Let's go get Snell."

Parker opened the garage door by punching in a code on a keypad. Other than a few screw drivers and a hammer, the wood shelves lining the wall were barren. The only things in the garage were a green trash can and blue recycling bin. Parker strode across the oil-stained concrete, pushing open the door to the house. He led the way down a threadbare carpeted hall, Jake, Bear, and Conover following close.

Parker opened a door leading to the basement, holding up his cell phone. "Listen, La Familia is in town at Xavier's house on Husker Road. I gotta make arrangements to get a team together, because we won't have another chance like this again. You go get Victoria. She's in a backroom through the green door at the far end of the basement. Bring her up and we'll coordinate next steps."

Parker punched a number on the phone and talked to some guy named Justin about getting some firepower together.

Jake turned to Conover and whispered, "Stay with him. Badge or no badge, I don't trust him yet."

Jake and Bear headed down the creaky stairs. The stairs opened into a thirty by fifty expanse enclosed by cinderblock walls showing signs of buckling in any day now. Like the garage, the basement was empty save a few boxes and matching avocado green washer and dryer units from the seventies. Something itched Jake's brain, but scrambled away when he tried to scratch it.

At the end of the basement was a green door set in mudded and unpainted drywall. He jogged across the floor and opened the door. The ammonia smell of urine hit him first, emanating from a bucket in the corner. A nineteen-inch television sat on a beat-up coffee table. The one other item in the ten by ten room was an empty chair with ropes hanging from scarred arms. No Victoria Snell.

Behind them, a truck roared in the distance followed by screeching tires. The elusive tickle in his brain jumped to the forefront. Jake spun and darted across the basement floor, thundering up the stairs into the house. He ran down the hall, into the empty garage and stopped. Parker's truck was gone.

"Goddamn it," Jake muttered.

Bear filed out behind him. "Where'd he go? Parker...I mean Banks or whatever name we're calling him?"

"Your guess is as good as mine," Jake said. "I don't know what to think or what to call him."

"I'm calling him Parker until I'm sure otherwise."

Jake turned to check on Conover, when the man came through the garage rubbing the back of his head. "You okay?"

"Son of a bitch knocked the shit outta me. If he's really a Fed, what would he run for?"

Jake thought it was a great question. "That badge seemed legit, didn't it?"

Bear nodded. "If that was a fake, it was a fucking masterpiece."

"I walked around a bit while he talked on the phone," Conover said. "The house is empty, not a lick of furniture. Don't think anyone has lived here for a while."

That explained it. The most empty garage he'd ever seen should have been clue number one. The way Parker held the basement door open in the hall which blocked the view of the rest of the house. Parker told them he had to hang back and make a call. Which left them back at square one with the question "Where was Snell?"

Bear started for the Expedition. "Let's chase Parker's scrawny ass down. I'm going to use his FBI head as a piñata. If he even is a Fed. Hell, at this point I don't care."

Jake held out his arm stopping him, pointing to the front tire which lay flat against the pitted concrete. A three-inch long gash marred the tire's sidewall. Parker had slashed it before escaping in his truck. Plus, they'd already used the spare tire after the shootout in Gibbon. "We aren't chasing after anybody."

CHAPTER FORTY-TWO

Perspiration dotted Darius's forehead, palms clammy as his finger hovered over the dial button. The night wind gusts rocked the truck as he parked at the entrance to Husker Road. He racked his brain trying to think of a way out of this massive chasm he'd dug himself, but the effort induced fewer ideas and more panic.

At first, it'd been a few thousand dollars here, a few thousand there. With the amount of money flowing through the Triad, it wasn't hard to hide. The longer he got away with it, the bolder he got, taking larger chunks. His original plan was to start his own operation with his own crew, out from under the sadistic thumb of his father. A combination of bad deals with the wrong people and even worse cards at the Horseshoe Casino in Omaha turned the walk down the wrong path into an all-out sprint.

He knew the shell game of moving incoming funds into payments owed to La Familia was nothing but a band-aid on a gaping wound. The money train would have fixed everything. Now Juan and Jake Caldwell ruined it all.

He steeled himself and hit the speed dial.

"Tell me you're on your way with the cash," Xavier said, his voice as taunt as wire.

"You standing near Diaz?"

"Yes. Why?"

"You'd better move to somewhere you can talk."

Xavier waited a beat. "Yes, I have those codes in my office. Give me second."

His father's boot heels clicked on the hardwood floor. Darius remembered a short period of time when he loved hearing that sound coming toward him. When he was a child, it meant his favorite person in the entire universe was approaching. When was the last time he looked forward to hearing those boots?

A door closed and his father whisper shouted. "What's going on, Darius? Where the hell are you and where's the goddamn money?"

"It's gone, Dad. I found the place where Juan hid it, but it's gone. I'd tell you I'm sorry, but you told me not to."

"I told you to stop getting in the position where you'd have to tell me. Do you realize what this means? You've just signed our death warrants."

A picture flashed of Wendall and Ronnie with their brains splattered on the fireplace mantel. Darius doubted Diaz would go any less easy on them.

"You stole two million dollars from one of the most ruthless drug cartels in the world, killed their man, and now you're telling me you have nothing?"

Darius shrank in his seat. He didn't have an answer. He should run. Fly back home, grab the meager stash of cash hidden in his house and run. They'd kill Xavier for sure, he couldn't stop it from happening. Would Twila go with him? Maybe escape to Canada together? He batted the thought away. The cartel would find him eventually, and he'd spend his remaining days on the planet looking over his shoulder. If he'd found the key sooner before…before Caldwell found it.

Darius sat upright in the truck. "I know how we can get the money."

"How?"

"Jake Caldwell has it. He raided the storage locker before me so he must have it."

"And you think he'll hand it over to you?"

Darius turned to the whimpering lump lying along the cold floor boards in the back seat. "If he wants his FBI bitch back alive, I think he will."

"Bring her here and tell Diaz the plan. Their trigger fingers are getting mighty itchy. Knowing the plan might buy us some time."

"I'll be there in a few."

Darius hung up, thankful his first stop after the shootout at the Clam had been to grab the agent. He pulled out Conover's phone and hit redial on the number for Caldwell who answered on the second ring. This plan better work or La Familia would dice him into pieces.

CHAPTER FORTY-THREE

"Listen up, asshole," Darius said.

Jake stood at the side of the Expedition watching Bear and Conover figure out if there was a way to patch the tire. "I'm listening."

"I'll make this simple. Bring the money you swiped from the storage locker to my dad's place. Right now."

"You figured that out, eh? Maybe you do have more than two brain cells to rub together. Why should I rush over there?"

"Because the money belongs to some important out-of-town guests. And these are people you don't want to be on the wrong side of."

"I know about La Familia, Frost. If they're even here."

Darius sighed. "Oh they're here, alright. Trust me."

"Sounds like your problem, not mine."

Darius clucked his tongue. "It is your problem. Because if you don't show up with the money, I'll turn your bitch FBI friend over to Diaz, and I've seen his handiwork up close."

Jake stiffened. Scenarios flew through his head.

Had Parker known she was already gone from his house when he brought them here? Did he think she was here and Jake would at least rescue her so he could get away? What if Frost told the truth and he had her? If Jake failed to show up, Snell gets handed to the cartel. If he showed up, the cartel kills them all including Snell. A frontal assault with Jake, an overweight county sheriff, and a geriatric PI against Xavier's forces and a Mexican cartel entourage was an unworkable scenario as well.

"How do I know you have her?"

Jake listened, sounds of muffled screams emanating through the speaker. Whoever was doing the screaming was gagged. It could be anyone.

A female voice screamed. "Let me go, you hillbilly motherfu—"

Definitely Snell. Jake's face burned and his jaw ached from the tension.

"Satisfied?" Darius asked.

"You hurt her and I'll fucking kill you, Frost. Slow and painful. You'll be begging for me to end it."

"You think you can do anything to me the cartel won't? You got one hour to get to my dad's place on Husker Road with the money. All of it. And you come alone. I see a hint of a cop and I'll slit her throat and take my chances with the cartel."

The call ended, leaving Jake with the urge to punch something. He tried to think of a way out of this. He filled in Bear and Conover as they mulled over options to obtain wheels.

Bear stroked his beard. "La Familia. Keats know these guys?"

"I think they're one of his suppliers," Jake said.

"Goddamn it. Can't believe I'm actually going to

say this, but maybe you should call him."

"Seriously? Bet that hurt to say."

"You have no idea. But, if it could save Snell, it might be worth a shot."

Jake had his doubts. Keats operated ninety-nine percent of the time on the premise of "What's in it for me?" He would have to stick his neck out and call in a favor with one of his suppliers, a ruthless Mexican drug cartel, over an FBI agent whom he hated and who'd done everything in her power to make his life as miserable as possible. Jake couldn't conjure an upside for it, and whatever Keats wanted in return for the favor would be astronomical.

The bag of money for Snell's life, and even that was doubtful. It'd be even more doubtful if the whole one point five million wasn't in the bag. Juan hid it and could've taken some for himself. The question was how much? Time to find out.

Jake opened the back and pulled the duffel bag toward him. He yanked the zipper back and spread the edges wide to reveal the jumbled stacks of banded hundred-dollar bills. He ran a thumb over the edges of the first few stacks on top. Ten thousand each. The problem became apparent the deeper into the bag he went.

"Oh oh," he said, leaning around the back of the Expedition. "Houston, we have a problem."

Bear and Conover slid around to the back, and Jake tossed them each a banded stack from the bottom of the bag. They both thumbed the edges of the stack and wore matching jaw-dropped expressions of disbelief. Jake rooted through the rest of the stack. The top of each stack was, indeed, a c-note. The rest of the stack was nothing but blank paper.

Jake pulled the stacks out and did a quick mental calculation.

"How much is actually there?" Bear asked.

Jake threw the last bundle back in the duffel bag. "Maybe twenty grand."

"Where the hell is the rest of it?"

"Frost doesn't have it or he wouldn't be calling," Conover said. "Juan must've stashed it somewhere else."

"Which does us no good. We can't exchange Snell for twenty grand when they're expecting one point five million."

"Unless we—"

A car door slammed behind them. Raasch stalked up the driveway, popping the strap to the holster holding his Glock.

Jake closed the hatch as Raasch drew closer. A rapid deadline approaching with no plan of attack, and the last person they wanted was coming toward them.

"Jake," Raasch said. "You're under arrest for the murders of Ronnie Pitts and Wendall Roberts."

CHAPTER FORTY-FOUR

"Murder?" Bear asked. "Who the hell are those guys?"

Raasch pulled within a few feet and stopped. "Two guys in Frost's crew. Both shot in the head and bodies dumped in a nearby field."

"Why am I a suspect?" Jake asked.

"Anonymous tip," Raasch said. He pointed to Bear and Conover. "You two are coming in as well. Material witnesses."

Jake's shoulders dropped. Airy. If she was on Xavier Frost's payroll, Xavier must have made the call the three of them were screwing up his plans. The only question was if Raasch was on the take as well. "I didn't murder anyone. I don't even know who they are."

"We have a dozen witnesses who saw you fight them at the Dome."

"But nobody to press charges."

"Plus, there's your presence at the shootout at the Clam."

Jake folded his arms. "We don't know anything about a shootout at the Clam."

Raasch's face reddened. "You guys were there. We have witnesses coming out of our asses giving your descriptions and the make, model, and plate of your Expedition fleeing the scene. I'll bet the security cameras will verify it, too."

"You going to trust a bunch of strippers?"

"Yeah, for now. They also said Darius Frost was there, and given the crap going down between you and his gang, it adds up. You were warned to get your asses out of town."

Jake softened. "Raasch, come on, man. We didn't murder anyone. You know it because you're here alone and haven't pulled your piece on a double murder suspect."

Bear stormed forward. "If you think your crooked Sheriff is going to—"

Jake stepped in front of Bear to cut him off. "We didn't have a choice but to go to the Clam. Frost kidnapped Conover."

"You did have a choice," Raasch spat. "You coulda called me."

"Why? So you could rat us out to the Triad?"

Raasch's features softened. "What are you talking about?"

Jake crowded him. "You were the one person who knew about the key. Thirty minutes after we left you in Gibbon, Frost shows up demanding it. Even Airy brought up the key when she showed up at Juan's trailer."

"Jake, I swear, the only person I told about the key was Airy. Chain of command. I didn't say anything to anyone in Frost's crew. I swear. If someone let Frost in on the existence of the key, it had to be Airy."

"You didn't call it in on your radio?"

"Jesus, no. I called her on my cell phone from Gibbon."

Jake glanced to Bear and Conover, both with their eyes locked on Raasch, assessing the veracity of what the deputy said.

Conover stepped up. "One question, how'd you know where we were?"

"Got an anonymous call a few minutes ago into the switchboard," Raasch said. "Caller gave an exact address and a description of your vehicle. I was on my way to the Clam."

A distant wail of sirens broke the quiet of the neighborhood. Parker must have made the call to buy himself time to get away.

Raasch clicked his radio. "Dispatch, this is Raasch. That's a negative on the subject vehicle at the Parker residence. Nobody here. Call off the dogs."

They turned toward the wailing, Jake wanting to bail, but starting to believe Raasch. Thirty seconds later, the sirens silenced.

"Now," Raasch said. "I know you didn't murder anyone, but Airy is applying the screws. Someone please tell me what's going on."

Jake looked at Bear who gave him an assenting nod. He was reluctant, but they needed all kinds of help to get Snell back. "It's going to be the Readers' Digest version. We don't have much time."

Jake told Raasch everything. The money train robbery. Juan stealing the money from Frost. Snell's kidnapping. Finding the storage unit with the bag full of worthless paper. Conover getting nabbed. La Familia in town. The shootout at the Clam and Parker being a Fed. Darius calling him with Snell in his possession and demanding the money be delivered to Husker

Road.

Raasch took it in, eyes probing the ground as he processed the information, his breath clouding the cold Nebraska air under the street lights. "Why didn't you tell me everything sooner?"

"Bear trusted you, I didn't."

"Where's Parker?"

"I don't know, but we gotta go. The clock is ticking hard against us. Think you could keep Airy off our asses for an hour?"

"Screw that, I'm coming with you."

"Can't let you do that, man. They see a cop and Snell's dead."

Raasch's lips pressed together. "You three cowboys are going to take on the Triad and a Mexican drug cartel by yourselves?"

"I'm pretty sure it's not the whole cartel," Jake offered.

"Take them on with what? Three pistols?"

"It's what we got, man."

Raasch scratched his head for a beat. He pulled out his cell phone and punched a number. "Daryl, it's me. Your Xavier dream's going to come true. Get your gear and meet me behind the highway department building on Antelope. Bring Carl with you." He paused and listened. "Yeah, but we can't do anything about it unless you want to bounce cross country or build another road. Ten minutes."

Raasch clicked off.

"Cross country?" Conover asked.

"There's one way into the highway department property and that's from Antelope Avenue. We're going to be within spitting distance of Xavier's place."

"Another place we can stage?"

"Not if you want eyes on the target."

Bear slipped a wad of chew in his mouth. "Who the hell are Daryl and Carl?"

"Couple of good old boys I know. Xavier Frost screwed Daryl out of a hundred acres of land a couple of years ago, and he's been scheming for a way to get back at him. They'll come loaded for bear, no pun intended."

"Can we trust them?"

Raasch see-sawed his hand. "They're both a lot right of center, but they'll be down for the cause. Let me get some stuff from my car. Can't take mine because they might spot it."

Bear pointed to his tire. "Can't take ours, either. Jake and Conover's cars are too far away unless you wanna go back across town."

Raasch spit. "All right, climb in."

Raasch opened the doors and dropped behind the wheel. Bear grabbed the money bag from the Expedition and dropped it on the floorboard.

"What's that?" Raasch asked.

"One point five million dollars."

"No shit?"

"As far as Frost is concerned it is. Let's go."

Raasch sped back down Avenue E. Bear took the front with him, while Jake and Conover sat in the back.

"You don't have to do this, man," Bear said. "If you don't get killed in the shootout, you lose your job."

Raasch said, "Maybe, but I never liked Airy anyway. Plus, you said you'd hire me. I do miss the Ozark waters."

CHAPTER FORTY-FIVE

Raasch drove them into the blackness of the Nebraska countryside. The headlights of the squad car beat back the night, gravel pinging against the body of the vehicle. Ten minutes later, they hit asphalt and wheeled toward Husker Road. As they rolled north on Antelope, a bank of lights in the distance glowed against a large building on a hill on the west side of the road and the Frost ranch on the east.

"Hope they don't have eyes on the road," Raasch said, rumbling over washboard ruts.

The highway department's maintenance building sat atop a hill a hundred yards from Antelope Avenue. The building sprawled a hundred and fifty feet by eighty, angled southeast to northwest. A bank of trees split the area between the building and the access road. To their right, a large lot held piles of stored piping laid out in neat rows.

Raasch maneuvered the car around the trees and parked at the back of the building, out of sight of the Frost compound.

Jake waited for Raasch to open his door, climbed

out, and shrank against the bitter cold of the night. Up on the hill, the wind sliced through them, drawing them toward the certain warmth inside. Headlights spilled across the group as a dark pickup rolled into the lot. It pulled even to Raasch's squad car, and the truck engine rattled to a stop. Two guys in matching tan Carhartt jackets hopped from the cab, closed the distance, and shook hands with Raasch. One held a bulky black case and the other a two-foot-long roll of paper.

Raasch flipped a hand toward the newcomers. "This is Daryl Findlay and Carl Cole."

The men exchanged handshakes in a complicated cross-over ritual. Jake didn't know if Daryl served in the armed forces, but he was a poster child for any one of the branches—six foot two, buzz cut, iron jaw, steely eyes measuring up the trio in front of him. Carl was a few inches shorter, beer gut pushing out the fabric of the jacket and a salt and pepper Brillo pad head of hair.

"Heard you boys might require a little assistance," Carl said, slipping a can of Coors original from his pocket and popping the top.

"We heard you have a beef with the Frosts," Jake said.

Carl took a long pull and drew an arm across his mouth. "Hell, everyone in town has a beef with those untouchable jackoffs. If Raasch vouches for you, what's ours is yours."

"What'd you bring?"

Daryl pointed to the truck. "AR-15s, a mix of Glocks, Berettas and CZs. Some smoke grenades, tactical vests. Even got a new MK13 Mod 7 sniper rifle."

Raasch scanned the arsenal, eyes wide. "That's

it?"

Daryl shrugged. "You said come quick. Only had time to grab a few things."

"It'll do. You have the drone?"

Carl held up the black plastic case. "Got Tracy right here."

"Now I know where to come when the zombie apocalypse hits," Jake said.

Raasch pulled open the door to the building. "Let's get outta this cold and put our plan together."

Conover, Bear, and Daryl followed Raasch inside. Jake walked alongside Carl and pointed toward the case. "Tracy? Kinda an unusual name for a drone."

"Named it after my ex-wife," Carl said, his nostrils flaring. "Used the drone to catch her banging the guy down the street. They left the shades up. Idiots."

"Sorry to hear that."

"I'm not. A thousand-dollar drone saved my bank account when I insinuated the footage might make its way on-line."

"What'd you do to the guy?"

Carl's face crimped. "Not much I could do. It was Darius Frost. Why the hell do you think I'm out here?"

They followed Raasch through a high-ceilinged maintenance shop, like a mini hangar. Heavy duty road trucks in various states of repair scattered across the concrete floor. Shelves and workbenches lined the walls on either side. A black guy in grease-stained coveralls sat in the corner, smoking and reading a copy of a book called *Dead Man's Badge*. Raasch said Woodrow wouldn't say anything. Two minutes later they huddled around a conference table in the break room off the maintenance area.

Daryl spread the rolled-up paper across the table,

weighting down the ends with various bolts and parts available. It was an aerial map of the area showing the maintenance building, nearby subdivisions, the golf course and, of course, the Frost compound across the road.

"Xavier Frost has been buying up the surrounding land for years," Daryl said. He waved a finger over a large tract of land to the north of the compound. "This was mine until two years ago, when Xavier screwed me out of it."

"What'd he do?" Bear asked.

"I run a bar and grill downtown. It's a nice place, clean, good food and cold beer. When I wouldn't sell the land, Xavier squeezed the liquor distributors, the health inspectors, and spread the word it would be unhealthy to frequent my establishment. Those who did found themselves in the crosshairs of Darius's crew. Business plummeted and I was on the verge of bankruptcy. Xavier swooped in and offered to talk to the town on my behalf."

Jake had seen this extortion racket before. "If you sold him the land he wanted."

"Exactly. I didn't have a choice."

"How much did he buy it for?"

Daryl's lip curled. "A thousand bucks."

"A thousand an acre?"

"A thousand for the whole hundred acres. It was a serious kick in the nuts. The land was in my family for generations. That son of a bitch has a mountain of bad karma waitin' to fall on his evil head. We'll help you out any way we can."

"What are we lookin' at doing?" Carl asked.

Jake gave them the two-minute version of events, highlighting the potential presence of Snell and the

La Familia cartel inside Xavier's house.

Daryl sucked in his cheeks. "With that many people in there, a frontal assault's out." He pointed to a line of trees south of the house. "Best bet would be to come in from the south from this tree line."

"Let's get eyes on the house first and find out what we're dealing with," Jake said. "Can you fire Tracy up and get her over there? Can you even fly the thing at night?"

Carl grinned. "How you think I caught my ex? Let me get her going."

A few minutes later, Carl launched the midnight black drone in the air and directed it east. They huddled around him, watching the action unfold on the controller's screen. He sent Tracy up high, the lights from the Frost compound like a beacon.

"How long can you keep this thing in the air?" Conover asked.

"It's a Phantom 4 Pro," Carl said. "Thirty minutes of flight time."

Jake watched him breach the Frost property, dropping in altitude as he loomed in on a driveway littered with vehicles. The front windows of the house were dark. Carl held the drone in place when a guy emerged through the front door and lit a cigarette.

Conover whistled. "Helluva camera on it. The clarity is amazing."

"4K videos and twenty megapixels," Carl said. "There's better drones out there for photography, but I had a finite budget, and this baby's been great to me."

"Might have to get me one."

"Got a guy who could make you a deal if you—"

Jake interrupted the tech fest. "Swing it around the backside of the house, Carl."

Carl swooped the drone to the backside of the house. A spacious patio with large pavers, an outdoor fireplace surrounded by deck chairs, a hot tub and an outdoor bar. Large bay windows cased either side of a fireplace. Further down the house, a door led into what looked like the kitchen.

"Go back to the bay windows. Let's see who's home."

"Better hurry, Jake," Bear said, tapping on his watch. "Time's almost up."

Carl moved the drone back to the south, closing in on the nearest bay window. Through it, Jake made out Darius, Stumpy, and one other guy from the trailer park fight pacing the floor. How the hell did Stumpy get out of jail? Then he remembered Xavier owned the town. A couple of Hispanic heavies against the wall. No Parker.

"There's that asshole Darius," Carl said. "I wanna shoot his dick off."

"Before you do that," Jake said. "Move over to the other window."

Carl slipped the drone to the left, the camera aimed through the other bay window. Two more Hispanic guys in dark suits milling in the background and a third lounging in a high back chair talking on a cell phone.

"Must be the cartel guys," Conover said. "I count five in the room."

"And the smoking guy from out front," Daryl said. "Plus Frost and his two goons. I'm assuming Xavier is in there somewhere as well."

"There he is," Raasch piped in, pointing at the screen.

Jake spotted the old man, crossing the room and handing the seated guy a drink. He walked stiff, like someone shoved a ramrod through the top of his head and out his ass. He withered a stare across the room, probably toward his son.

"No sign of Snell. Damn. We're looking at ten guys in there?" Jake asked. "Six of us, but we have the element of surprise."

Carl and Daryl exchanged looks.

"Actually, four of you," Daryl said, eyes dropping to the ground.

"Wait, I thought you said you wanted to help," Raasch said.

"We do and that's why we brought all that gear with us. You guys are welcome to it. I hope you take these assholes down."

"But you're not storming the gates with us," Jake said.

Daryl ran a tongue over his lips. "No offense, and I'm not tryin' to douse the mission with bad mojo, but if you don't succeed, Carl and I still have to live here. Xavier and the Triad have enough pull in town to crush both of us without breaking a sweat."

"No problem, man. I understand. Will you stay here and be our eyes in the sky?"

"Abso-fuckin'-lutely."

"We have a plan?" Bear asked.

Jake swept his eyes over the aerial map one last time. "I really don't want to do anything until we confirm Snell's in there."

Carl spoke up. "Is she a blonde? Hell, what am I sayin'? She's the only woman in the place, so I gotta assume it's her. They just brought her in the living room."

They turned back to the screen. Darius manhandled Snell across the room, her hands bound behind her back. He shoved her onto the couch near the fireplace.

"Can you move the drone closer?"

"I don't wanna get too close," Carl said. "They might hear the rotors spinning."

"That's her, Jake," Bear said. "What's your plan?"

Jake grimaced. "I don't think you're going to like it."

CHAPTER FORTY-SIX

"Are you crazy?" Bear exclaimed, bearded jaw set. "You're just going to walk through the front door with the money?"

"I'm with Bear, man," Raasch said. "With the shit you've caused, Darius will shoot you on the spot if the cartel guys don't do it first."

Jake had laid out the plan of attack. Bear, Conover, and Raasch would arm to the teeth and enter the property from the south through the tree line. Jake would draw attention by calling Darius and announcing he was coming up the drive. Once they were in place and Jake entered the house, Daryl would call Raasch and they'd breach the house through the door on the east side. Once Jake verified Snell was safe, he'd give the signal word.

"What signal word?" Bear asked.

Jake grinned. "Pineapple?"

Bear rolled his eyes. "It worked out so well last time."

Conover stepped to the table. "I'll take the money in."

"What? Why?" Bear asked.

"Raasch is right," Conover said. "Darius seeing Jake could light the spark to an already flammable powder keg. Darius already nabbed me once, and he'll feel safer with me than you. Besides, whoever brings the money in is going to have to do it unarmed. I've seen Jake in action, and he'd be better in a surprise attack with a gun in hand."

"Don't be crazy," Jake said. "It's my plan, I should take the risk."

"Is your plan going to work?" Conover asked.

"I hope so. But, you'd be safer with the rear entry group."

"With all due respect, Jake," Conover said. "This is going to be a shit show any way you slice it. I like our chances better with you tramping around in the dark than me."

Raasch swept his eyes across the room's occupants. "We really going to do this?"

Jake clapped him on the back. "Yup. What could possibly go wrong?"

"A lot. This Snell worth it?"

"She saved my life. I owe her."

"Good enough for me," Raasch said. "I've had to eat enough shit from the Frost clan to last me a lifetime. Let's suit up."

They headed back out to the bitter cold and grabbed the gear from Daryl's truck. They donned tactical vests, slipped in extra magazines for their nine-millimeters along with an AR-15.

Carl stood by the door watching the drone screen. "Smoking dude just went inside. You guys are clear."

"I'll drive you boys to the tree line in my truck," Daryl said. "Your cop car might just draw unwanted attention."

"What am I supposed to drive to the house?" Conover asked.

Raasch disappeared inside and came back out dangling a set of keys. "Woodrow loaned us his wife's Taurus. He asked that you bring it back unharmed or she'll kill him."

Conover snatched the keys. "I'll do my best, but no promises."

Jake handed Conover the money bag. "They'll pat you down which is fine, because you won't be carrying anything on you. I duct taped a loaded Glock to the bottom of the bag. Try to keep the bag low and whatever you do, don't set it down on the floor too hard."

Bear said, "Once they realize the money's fake, you yell the signal word and we'll bust in. Hug the goddamn floor because bullets will be flyin'. Get to the Glock and shoot the bad guys."

Conover dipped his chin down and up. "Got it. We still going with pineapple?"

"Why the hell not? Seemed to throw them off last time," Jake said. "Be careful. We'll call you when we're in place."

"See you on the other side," Conover said.

Jake, Bear and Raasch piled into Daryl's truck which smelled of wintergreen and dust. Daryl fired up the truck, swung down the access road, and turned south on Antelope Avenue. The Frost ranch loomed to their left, and Jake tracked the lights as they passed. The butterflies kicked up in his stomach, and the adrenaline valve seeped open. Nobody said a word all the way to the tree line. Jake assumed they were busy praying like him.

CHAPTER FORTY-SEVEN

Darius paced the hardwood floors of his father's study, walking heel to toe along a single board. Thirty paces from the bookcase to the hallway feeding the kitchen. Thirty paces back. He checked his cell phone at the end of each trip. With each passing minute, the La Familia cartel crew grew more anxious, shifting in place, peering out windows, checking the guns in their shoulder holsters.

Darius dialed Parker's number again. Voicemail. Where the hell was he? Was he dead? Nabbed by Caldwell or the Kearney PD? If it was the police, they would've heard by now. Unless it was Raasch. The uncertainty of it knotted the muscles in his back and neck. He wanted nothing more than to hit something to relieve the pressure, but he had to play it cool which made things worse.

Diaz lounged in a high back chair by the fireplace, smoking a cigar and talking on his cell phone. He spoke in Spanish, of course, so nobody knew what the hell he said. Darius wished he'd paid more attention to Ms. Rodriguez in high school. Puta was about all he came away with, and she hadn't been the one to teach him that.

Stumpy camped out by the bar, sipping on a beer, eyes darting around the room, jaw set with nervous energy. It hit Darius that Stumpy was the last surviving member in his crew, and even he had an assault charge pending from knocking around the bitch in the trailer. He wondered how many chips Xavier had to cash in to spring him. Who knew where Parker was. He pressed his lips tight, pissed he didn't take the money train funds and disappear the second he had them at the rest stop. They could've killed the FBI agent or at least tied her up and blew south away from Kearney. Of course, Juan would've been with them and ratted them out to the cartel. Even in his last-minute fantasy scenarios, Darius lost.

Xavier went to the bar and Darius sidled up. "What about Browers and Roth? Can they help us?"

Xavier's head turned slow. He gritted his teeth, eyes ablaze. "And how exactly are they going to help, Darius? Order us a truck made out of money? Find us a shipping route out of here?"

"I thought since they were part of the Triad, they could—"

Xavier slammed the glass on the bar top, his voice low but fierce. "I am the Triad. Me." He turned from the stares from the La Familia members, smoothing his wispy hair and pouring Scotch into the glass. "Browers and Roth bark but have no bite. They're as useless as you are. This is on you, son. Even if we make it out of here alive I might fucking kill you myself."

Xavier spun from the bar and handed the glass to Diaz. He took a sip, savored it, and offered a raised eyebrow, indicating his approval of the quality of the beverage.

"D," Stumpy whispered. "We should get the fuck outta here. I got a bad feelin' about this."

"You think? Pray Caldwell shows up with the money."

"But, if we—"

"Chill, Stump. Have a drink. It might be your last."

Darius resumed his walk along the board. He made it to the bookcase, when Diaz ended his call and slipped the cell phone in his jacket pocket. He puffed a cigar, letting the broad cloud waft to the ceiling, rolling the tobacco tube between his fingers, eyes locked on Darius.

"Time is almost up, Darius," Diaz said. "Where is my money?"

"It'll be here any minute. I swear."

"That's what you said ten minutes ago. I'm a patient man, but my employer isn't."

Darius's gut clenched, the stench of the cigar smoke blending with overwrought nerves and the prospect of impending death made him want to puke. "They'll bring the money for the girl. She's important to them."

Diaz squinted, tongue licking at his peppered goatee. "Let's see just how important. Bring her to me."

Darius tromped down the hall to his old bedroom. Outside the door, he tried Parker again. Straight to voicemail.

Snell lay on the bed, handcuffed to the iron rail of the headboard, bandana wrapped around her mouth. Her eyes glowered as he entered. Darius walked past his trophy case lined with football awards, wrestling medals, and framed newspaper clippings. He dropped a hand to her throat and squeezed, not enough to stop her from breathing, but enough to hurt. This trophy might be the one to save his life.

"The man in charge wants to talk to you. I suggest you play it cool. You let your mouth go wild, and he'll make you wish you were dead. Got it?"

When she nodded, Darius slipped the gag down from her mouth.

"Listen, Darius. I can get you out. The FBI is after La Familia, not you. Get me out of here, and I'll get you a deal."

Darius pulled the handcuff keys from his pocket. "There ain't a deal on the planet that's gonna get you out of this. You better hope and pray your boy Caldwell gets here with the money."

"Jake?" she asked, eyes flying wide. "He's here?"

"He's coming so shut up."

With the cuffs unlocked, he jerked Snell from the bed, crushing her wrist in his hand. She tried to squirm free, but Darius jerked her arm behind her back and pressed her into the wall.

"Don't you worry about Caldwell," he said. "You try anything and these Mexican boys will carve you up in front of us for entertainment. You getting this?"

Snell jerked her head up and down, panting in pain as Darius cranked her arm up behind her back. He secured the cuffs, grabbed a wad of her hair in one hand and the cuffs in the other, and drove her out the bedroom door. She stumbled but kept her feet.

Once in the study, he shoved her to the couch where she toppled over, face biting into the cushion. Diaz shook his head in disgust, like Darius pissed on the floor in his living room.

"Treat others the way you want to be treated,

Darius. Isn't that how the saying goes?"

Darius thought Ronnie and Wendall's brain matter on the fireplace might beg to differ with Diaz's sentiments, but nodded his head in agreement.

"Remove the handcuffs and give Ms. Snell something to drink while we talk. Would you like some water?"

Once Darius removed the cuffs, Snell straightened, rubbing her raw wrists. Her jade eyes darting around the room at the muscle. She swept her tangled blonde hair from her face, trying to smooth it back. "Since it might be my last drink, I'll take a Scotch. Neat."

Diaz eyed Darius. "You heard the lady."

Darius fought the urge to throw the drink in her face as he handed it to her, instead crossing back to the bookcase and sulking against the mahogany.

"Now, Ms. Snell," Diaz said. "Tell me everything the FBI knows about my employer."

Darius checked his watch. Time was up. The cartel wasn't going to wait much longer before bullets started meeting heads. Where the hell was Caldwell?

CHAPTER FORTY-EIGHT

Daryl killed the lights of the truck as he turned east along a rutted dirt path running parallel to the tree line bordering the south side of the Frost property. The truck bounced and groaned as he maneuvered by the scarce light shining from a sliver of moon.

"Sorry for the bumpy ride," Daryl said. "But we can't let the bad guys see you. You got enough of an uphill climb ahead."

"Whose property are we on?" Jake asked. "Any chance some farmer is going to roust us?"

"That would be me. Xavier screwed me out of buying the land, but he pays me to farm it."

"Who'll pay you if he goes away?"

"I'll pay myself. If the crooked old fart goes down, I'm buying the land back. Win win for everyone."

Daryl let the truck coast to a stop. He pointed through the thick line of pine trees. A handful of lights from the Frost compound managed to work their way through the branches.

"Run to the south side of the house. Lights are scarce and there's no windows. Work your way around to the back of the house. There's a rock wall you can stay low behind. Keep your heads down at the bay windows."

"You seem to know the layout well," Jake said.

Daryl's jaw set. "I spend a lot of time behind the wheel of a tractor. Gives me plenty of time to think. Anyway, make your way around the wall. There's a door leading into a mudroom with a hallway feeding the living room and study area where they're gathered."

Jake eyed him for a moment. "There's a fine line between thinking and casing the joint."

"A boy can dream, can't he?"

After Daryl disappeared down the path, Jake, Bear, and Raasch waded through the pine trees, bundled in thick coats and camo hats.

"Jesus Pete," Bear said. "It's colder than a witch's tit out here."

Raasch shivered. "It's a bad one. Even for Kearney."

"You have to welcome the cold," Jake said. "Trick your brain into thinking you like it, and it won't be as bad."

Bear cocked his head. "That's the stupidest fucking thing I've heard of in my life. What dumbass told you that?"

"You did. At football practice in high school."

"You gonna believe something a stupid teenager said?"

Jake gripped the AR-15. "Seems to work for me. Let's go. Stay tight and watch your footing up the slope."

They broke through the tree line and were welcomed by a manure infused Nebraska wind in their faces. The smell of money some rancher told Jake once. Jake led the way, ginger stepping up the snowy incline, footsteps crunching through the frozen layer. Thinking about the guy coming out front for a smoke, he listened for sounds from the house. Hopefully, the wind would carry their noisy steps away.

"You go any slower and we'll be popsicles," Bear whispered.

Jake hushed him but picked up the pace a bit. Bear was right. The bitter cold seeped through the coat and into his limbs. Cold people moved slow and their margin of error on this little mission was slim to none.

The south side of the house was bordered with a sidewalk holding back a sea of dead plants drooping away from the brick. They crept east toward the back patio, the stone wall Daryl mentioned looming ahead. Jake held up as they reached the corner of the house as a coyote wailed in the distance. The faint buzz of the drone's whirring blades told him Carl had eyes on them up above.

"Bad news for the fat guy," Bear whispered, pointing to the wall.

Jake saw what he meant. The wall was less than three feet high. It started at the corner of the patio and curved to the north, hugging the side of the back patio. Spotlights bright enough to send the Bat Signal all the way to Gotham City drenched the stonework.

"No way I can hide behind that," Bear continued. "It'd be like an elephant trying to hide behind a band-aid. Maybe I can circle around front and meet you on the other side?"

Jake considered the idea. "What if they have cameras out front?"

"What if they have cameras out back?" Raasch countered.

Jake said, "They could have one of those video

doorbells, or one of them could come out front for a cigarette."

"One of them could go out back for a smoke, too," Raasch said. "We can 'what if' this to death. I say you and I crawl behind the wall like Daryl said. Bear can go around front. There's a string of cars he can move behind."

Jake didn't like splitting up, but they didn't have much of a choice. "Fine. Be careful."

"I'll tiptoe if it'll make you happy," Bear said. "Keep your asses down."

As Bear moved toward the front of the house, Jake and Raasch crouched at the back corner. Jake peeked around the edge of the house. The patio was still. Nothing but furniture, a hot tub with steam leaking around the cover, and a barbecue grill encased by the same stonework as the wall. The patio itself was twenty-five feet deep and ran along the backside of the house. There was a six-foot gap between the house and the wall where they'd be exposed if someone looked out the back window.

"You ready?" Jake whispered to Raasch.

"Not in the slightest, but let's do it anyway."

Jake dropped to his knees and eased his body away from the safety of the house, his eyes locked on the back bay window. A large body stood with his back to them, mere feet from Jake as he scurried past and dropped to his stomach behind the wall. He held out a hand for Raasch to wait, bear-crawling toward the bend in the wall. Once there, he sucked in a lungful of the frigid air and snuck a peek over the top of the wall.

Through the window he spotted Darius, Xavier, and a handful of mean ass looking Mexicans. His stomach clenched when he caught sight of Snell, perched on the edge of the couch, drink in hand, but eyes wide with worry. She looked like a trapped animal, wild-eyed and scared, not something he'd seen in their firefights together. The last time he saw that look was when her daughter was kidnapped a couple years back. A man in a high-backed leather chair dipped forward, elbows on his knees talking to her. Jake dropped again and waved Raasch forward.

It took Jake and Raasch a couple of minutes to crawl their way out of sight of the bay window. The wet and cold worked their way through his pants and gloved hands. As the wall bent back toward the house, Jake rose from his knees and duck-walked to the back of the house by the door. He pressed his back into the cold wood to the door's side and was about to wave Raasch forward, when the door handle turned and out stepped one of the Mexicans.

CHAPTER FORTY-NINE

The Mexican was sturdy, like a rain barrel resting on two tree trunks. Thick black hair swooped back, and a fashionable amount of stubble graced his dark face. He gazed at the abundance of stars and slid a pack of cigarettes from his jacket pocket as the door closed behind him. If Jake exhaled too hard, he'd tickle the black hairs on the back of the guy's neck.

Jake held his breath as options whirred through his brain. If he did nothing, the guy would eventually turn and spot him, or Bear would come crashing around the corner and sound the alarm. If he tried to slide away, the guy would hear him and sound the alarm. The potential of no contact was out the window. Jake hoped even Maggie would understand the need for brute force.

Which left two physical options—knock the bejesus out of the guy with the butt of the AR-15 and hope he could end it quick or take him down silently. Given the guy's build, it would have to be silent or as close to it as Jake could manage. One move came to mind. He thought it would work, because Jake had been on the receiving end of it years ago with a great degree of success.

The man lit the cigarette as Jake steeled himself. As the Mexican sucked in a lungful of carcinogens, Jake pounced. He jumped in the air and kicked both booted feet into the back of the thug's legs, right behind the knees. At the same time, he jammed the ridge of his hand to the side of the neck and slid it around until his thick bicep and forearm wrapped around the man's throat and jerked back. The opposite action dropped the man toward the ground. Jake managed to twist them both to the side lest the man's body weight land on top of Jake. They thumped to the flagstone patio, and Jake tightened his grip around the man's neck by grabbing his own bicep and using his opposite hand to shove the man's head forward. He squeezed on the neck and pulled his shoulders back, fortifying his control by wrapping his legs around the man's waist and locking his ankles. The Mexican beat at Jake's arms, tried prying them loose, attempted to throw pointed elbows into Jake's side, but it was too late. The pressure on both the man's carotid arteries and the two arteries in the back of the neck cut off the blood supply to the brain, and seconds later he was out.

Raasch scrambled forward, handcuffs in hand. "You've got a future in mixed martial arts if you want to go that route."

Jake let the man flop to the cold stone. Raasch hooked the cuffs around the Mexican's limp wrists as Bear rounded the corner.

"Bear, help me drag this bastard away," Jake whispered. "Raasch, cover the door. Gimme your cuff key."

Jake and Bear hooked the Mexican under his armpits and dragged him to the side of the house.

"I miss all the fun," Bear grunted. "What are we supposed to do when this guy wakes up?"

Jake scanned his surroundings. The only thing to secure the guy to was a drainpipe, but he could beat on the house and cause a ruckus. On the opposite side of the driveway was a basketball pole set in the ground near a pickup.

"Basketball pole," Jake said. "I'll secure him. See if there's anything in the truck to tie his feet with."

The Mexican stirred, moaning as Jake unlocked the cuffs and wrapped his thick arms around the pole before securing the cuffs again.

Jake cocked his fist and threw a hard punch across the man's jaw.

Bear returned with the rope. "This is takin' too long."

"Too late to stop now. Tie the rope to his feet."

Jake undid the man's necktie and gagged him with it. He took the other end of the rope Bear tied to his feet and slid it through the bumper of the truck. He pulled the rope tight, the Mexican stretched until the cuffs strained against the pole.

Jake secured the rope and patted Bear on the shoulder. "That's good enough. He gets out of this before we're done then we deserve to get our asses kicked."

They darted back around the corner where Raasch waited, gun drawn and aimed toward the door.

"You ready?" Jake asked.

"Let's break up the party."

Jake grimaced. "That sounded like a bad line from an eighties action movie."

Raasch smiled. "Yippee ki-yay, motherfucker."

Jake drew his gun, depressed the handle, and eased the door open. He slipped into the mud room. A basin sink with cabinets on his left and a built-in stack of cubby holes and coat hooks on his right. Muffled voices echoed down the darkened hallway, along with the scents of the wood-burning fireplace and cigar smoke.

Jake moved fifteen feet ahead to the hallway, the barrel of the AR-15 raised. He panned to his right and picked up nothing but closed doors and darkness. To his left, moving shadows threw themselves against the wall thirty feet away down a hallway wallpapered in a muted floral pattern. He waited as Bear and Raasch made their way into the mudroom, easing the outside door shut behind them.

Jake pulled out his cell and texted Conover. *We're ready.*

Then he texted Maggie. *I love you.*

One was his whole truth. He hoped the other wasn't a lie.

CHAPTER FIFTY

Darius Frost was at the desperate mental tipping point of pulling out the gun Xavier hid under the bar and shooting the members of La Familia in the room. He couldn't figure any other way he'd come out of this alive. He'd stolen money from the cartel and killed their man on the inside. They had to suspect Juan was dead. How much intel had Juan fed back to them? The grandfather clock in the corner of the study ticked away the seconds, like a metronome, each click a maddening countdown to his inevitable demise.

His eyes swept over the La Familia members in the room. Diaz lounged in the high back chair questioning Snell. Four more members stationed at the corners of the room. He sucked his lips in tight. No way he could take them all out before they gunned him down, even if he was a dead-eye shot, which he wasn't. He resolved himself to one thing, he'd eat his own bullet before he let these killers take him anywhere.

His ringing cell phone yanked him away from the gloomy thoughts. He answered as every eye in the room focused on him.

"It's Conover," the voice from the other end said.

Darius scowled. "Why the fuck are you calling me? Where's Caldwell?"

"I'm bringing the money in. It's better this way. Trust me. I'm at the bottom of your driveway ready to come up."

"Where's Caldwell?" Darius demanded.

Conover paused. "You want the money or not, Darius?"

Conover hung up. All eyes in the room locked on Darius. "Money's on its way. That private investigator Conover is bringing it in now."

Headlights spilled through the front of the house, sweeping across the main hallway. Diaz ticked his head toward his men and two of them filed out the front door. A minute later, they returned with Conover marching in front of them carrying a duffel bag low to the floor.

Diaz stood. "Mr. Conover, thank you for bringing the money."

Darius's vision swam with relief at the presence of the bag. His slim chance of escaping alive went up a few points. People could be replaced. Maybe they would consider Juan's disappearance a cost of doing business.

"We have a problem, though," Conover said.

Darius's relief flipped the switch to panic.

"And what is that?" Diaz asked.

"There's no money in the bag," Conover offered, cutting his eyes to Darius. "It's almost all fake."

Darius's mouth went dry. He walked across the room, knees weak, yanking the bag from Conover's feet. It thunked on the granite. He jerked back the zipper and pawed through the contents. A few c-notes, but most of it was blank paper. His gut ached as if punched, heart thudding in his ears.

"And one more thing," Conover said, stepping toward Diaz. He dropped his voice as he spoke. Diaz's eyes widened a bit, focusing on Darius. The stare made Darius take a step back. What would Conover need to say to Diaz much less do it secretively? Whatever it was, it was bad for Darius.

Diaz motioned two of his guys to him and whispered. Darius edged behind the bar, pretending to get a drink, but instead reached under the bar where Xavier kept a pistol.

The two Mexicans stomped toward Darius as his hand wrapped around the butt of the gun. If he was going to die, they were coming with him. He started to pull out the pistol, but they walked past him toward the living room. Darius maintained his grip on the gun and drew a deep breath. He had almost started a gunfight. Something was going down, and he didn't think it would be good for anyone involved.

CHAPTER FIFTY-ONE

Jake crouched, head peeking around the corner and ear tuning into the conversation in the study. The dim lighting in the mudroom provided them some measure of cover, but he didn't like them being bunched together in such a confined space. However, being unfamiliar with the layout of the house made him reticent to spread out.

A closed door sat across from them, but he had no idea where it led, and they'd risk being spotted if they crossed the hallway. He glanced again to his right. Nothing but a darkened hall turning away after two doors and twenty feet. No telling where it went, either.

He turned his attention back to the voices from the study, their echoes faint but audible.

"What are they saying?" Bear whispered, shifting his weight and causing the floorboards to creak. "I can't hear a thing."

Jake shushed him with a wave of the hand and risked another peek around the corner.

Conover entered the picture carrying the money bag. He flicked his eyes to Jake and turned back to the group in the study. He set the bag on the floor at his feet.

One of the guys thanked Conover for bringing the money. Jake tightened his grip on his rifle. Behind him, Bear or Raasch stepped again, causing another creak. He turned back to Bear and Raasch and whispered, "Stop moving around."

Craning his head back around the corner, he heard Conover say there was no money in the bag. Jake's face crunched in confusion. What the hell was Conover doing? That wasn't the plan. Maybe Conover had to call an audible.

Darius jerked the bag from the floor and threw it on the bar top. Jake flinched as he heard the Glock thunk against the bar top. He couldn't see the bag but could imagine Darius rifling through the nearly worthless stacks of bills.

Jake held up a hand behind him. Wait for it. He inhaled through his nose, letting the oxygen seep from his lungs to slow his increasing heartrate. The beautiful faces of Maggie and Halle dashed across his mind.

Conover said, "One more thing." He stepped forward in the study and out of Jake's view. Darius moved around the end of the bar and disappeared from sight. Seconds later, two of the Mexicans strode across the hall toward the front of the house. Where were they going? Had Carl or Daryl come up the drive? Something spooked them toward the front of the house.

The voices were faint, like whispers in the wind, and Jake leaned further out to hear them. He shifted his weight toward his toes, hands tingling with adrenaline, waiting for the signal word. A board creaked, and he was about to shush Bear and Raasch again when his brain registered the sound was not directly behind him, but to his right. He didn't even have time to turn his head when the pistol barrel pressed into his temple hard enough to force his head against the wall. Flicking his eyes to his right, he spotted a pair of shiny, black shoes.

"Drop your guns," the voice above him said, a thick Hispanic accent enunciating each word carefully. The man shouted toward the living room. "I have them."

Jake thought of knocking the gun away and getting physical, but he was off balance and pinned to the wall. The option was crushed when another pair of shoes emerged from the shadows. Bear and Raasch's guns thumped to the floor.

"Shit," Bear said.

The man holding the gun to Jake's head stepped back, and the black maw of an HK MP7 machine pistol barrel touched his forehead. One twitch of the guy's finger and Jake would be pumped full of lead at nine hundred and fifty rounds per minute. Jake scanned to the guy's right and noted his counterpart had another one trained on Bear and Raasch. The men emerged from the shadows, and Jake cursed himself for allowing them to get close. There must have been a hallway from the front leading to this one.

"Muèvelo," the man said, jerking the barrel of the pistol toward the study. "Move it."

Jake raised his hands in the air as he stood, assessing the two men holding them at gunpoint. The chances of controlling either one of those HK's without casualty was close to zero, then dropped to zero as two more men filled the hallway from the study, both armed with handguns trained on them. The men searched them and confiscated their weapons.

Bear uttered, "We couldn't see anything back there."

Jake stepped down the hall. "We're not dead yet."

Bear thumped behind him. "Feels like the grim reaper is pounding on the fucking door pretty loud."

"Don't answer."

"Shut up," one of the men said, shoving Jake in the back.

They emerged into the study. The first thing Jake spotted was Darius Frost behind the bar. The second was Snell's crestfallen face as she sat on the couch. Her hair was disheveled, clothes rumpled, a bruise adorning one cheek. They locked eyes and Jake mouthed "It's okay" though he was pretty damn sure it wasn't.

The pepper-haired man in the middle of the room slipped on a politician's smile. "Gentlemen, welcome. You could have simply knocked."

Jake swept the room with his eyes, taking inventory. The two Mexicans who caught them in the mud room blocked the doorway behind them. The two other ones blocked the exit route through the front of the house. All guns were unholstered and ready. Jake spotted another one barring the door to the patio. Darius and Stumpy stood behind the bar, but they looked more like targets than threats. Conover stood behind the armchair by the fireplace near Diaz.

All five of the Mexican henchmen had guns aimed at Jake, Bear, and Raasch. It took Jake a second to realize nobody guarded Conover.

Conover, who didn't raise his eyes to meet Jake's.

There's no money in the bag.

One more thing.

Conover drifting out of sight.

The men appearing exactly where they needed in order to sneak up on Jake and his crew.

"Jesus, Conover," Jake breathed. "You're with them?"

Conover looked up at last, his lips tight. "Sorry, Jake."

"When did you flip?"

"Five years ago." Conover's voice was wooden and distant. "I've worked for the cartel for years. I didn't have a choice. They'll kill my entire family."

If there was a period in his life when Jake misread people so utterly wrong, he couldn't think of it. First Parker and now Conover. His mistake could very well kill all of them.

CHAPTER FIFTY-TWO

"I'd invite you to sit and have a drink," the pepper-haired man said. "But I don't think this will take long."

"Who are you?" Jake asked.

"Armando Diaz," the man said. "You will forgive me if I keep my distance."

"Probably a good idea on your part."

Diaz cocked a bushy eyebrow. "I like you. You have a great spirit inside. Too bad we have to extinguish it."

Jake's brain scrambled to come up with a plan. If Diaz was smart, he'd execute the three of them on the spot. The longer Jake could keep him talking, the more options might present themselves.

"Why do you have to extinguish anybody? We didn't do anything to you."

Diaz pointed to the bag. "Ahhh, but you did. You stole two million dollars from my employer."

"We didn't steal a dime. Darius did."

"Oh, we will deal with the Frosts. Trust me. But you had it most recently and sent Conover here with nothing but worthless paper."

Jake detected an opening and put on his best

surprised face. "What are you talking about? That's not true."

"Come now, Mr. Caldwell. Do not insult my intelligence."

"I'm serious. Worthless paper? There was one point five million dollars in the bag when I handed it to Conover."

"He's lying," Conover said. "It was that way when he found it in the storage locker."

The first spark of uncertainty flickered on Diaz's face. It was brief but it was there.

"Shut up, Conover," Jake said. "You traitor. What did you do? Stash the real cash by the side of the road? Hide it in the trunk? I swear on my mother's life, Diaz. The bag was full of cash when I handed it to Conover."

Since Jake's mother was dead for twenty-five years, he didn't think she'd mind using her to get out of a jam such as this. Besides, he thought he might be nominated for an Oscar with his indignant performance.

"He's right," Bear said. "I was there. One hundred and fifty bundles, ten thousand each."

Diaz said, "Desperate men will say anything to save their own lives. Do you believe me to be a fool?"

Jake pumped his shoulders. "I believe you are a man who cares about the truth. We don't give a damn about the money. We just want Victoria."

On the couch, Snell offered a tight-lipped smile. Jake was surprised he was still being allowed to talk. But this grace period would end in seconds, not minutes if he didn't deflect the action from himself and his team.

Jake continued. "If you're going to shoot anyone,

it should be Darius. Didn't he tell you what he did to Juan Hidalgo?"

Diaz's face clouded. "What about Juan?"

"Darius shot him in the face in a cornfield," Jake said. "In cold blood. And Darius has been stealing from you for a long time. He robbed the money train of a mobster to get it back. But, Juan stole it from Darius, and Darius killed him for it."

"He's full of shit," Darius shouted, coming around the bar and raising a Glock toward Jake. One of Diaz's men darted forward and knocked the gun free, placing the barrel of his own against Frost's head.

Jake saw in Diaz's eyes that Juan meant something to him. If Jake could turn Diaz's attention away from the three of them onto Frost and his crew, it might buy them an opening.

"Parker told me everything," Jake said. "How you gathered in a circle and whipped Juan bloody. How he begged you not to. How he warned you what would happen if you did. But you didn't care. All you cared about is getting back the money you stole from the most feared cartel on the planet. You blasted the poor kid in the face with a shotgun and buried his body in a field, leaving it for the animals and worms to feed on his carcass."

"Parker?" Darius asked. "How did you—"

"He's an FBI agent, numb nuts. Did you know that, Diaz? Your idiot errand boy had a fed in his crew for the last two years. No telling what kind of intel they have on La Familia. He killed your inside man and probably fed enough dirt on the cartel to the U.S. government to cause your boss all kinds of headaches. Far more expensive headaches than two million bucks."

"It's true," Snell said. "Parker is an agent out of the Dallas office."

Diaz shot a glance to Snell, then back to Frost, his mouth tightening to a stubborn line.

"Mr. Diaz," Darius stammered. "He's lying. I'm telling you that—"

Diaz dipped his chin to the man holding the gun on Darius. The man squeezed the trigger and blew Darius's brains across the bar top, splattering the worthless money bag in a mist of red. Darius collapsed to the floor, his gun falling to Jake's feet as Xavier's cries mixed with the echoed gunshot.

Darting forward, Xavier grabbed Snell by the neck and jerked her off the couch. He grabbed a nearby Scotch bottle, smashed the end, and pressed the jagged edge to her throat. His voice trembled. "You son of a bitch. You killed my boy. And all because of these lies."

Annoyance crossed Diaz's dark complexion. "Xavier, do not be stupid. Your son was too much of a liability and made far too many mistakes. Even you must recognize that."

"He was my son," Xavier raged, his balding head red under shaking white hair.

Jake tensed. Snell's eyes were wide, a single tear rolling down the side of her bruised cheek, a line of crimson trickling down her neck. While goading Diaz achieved the intended effect of taking out Darius, it had the unintended consequence of placing Snell in the crosshairs and amping up the tension. Jake slid his foot to the side, measuring where Darius's gun was. The question was how he would get it without the bad guys blowing a thousand holes into him.

"What are you going to do, Xavier?" Diaz asked,

crossing his arms as if addressing a toddler throwing a temper tantrum.

The La Familia men shifted, cutting their eyes between Diaz and Xavier. The barrels of their guns drifted toward Xavier.

The room seemed hotter, like someone added more wood to the fire. Beads of sweat dotted Jake's forehead as his eyes swept the room for something, anything to get the shattered bottle off Snell.

Xavier pressed the jagged glass against Snell's throat. "I'm going to cut the head off your little prize if you don't get out of here."

Diaz flipped his hand. "Do with her what you will. We have our own people within the FBI. We have no need for her."

Xavier's face glowed with an anguished rage. He was going to cut Snell's throat and there wasn't a damn thing Jake could do.

"I'll do it," Xavier said, teeth gritted.

"Go ahead."

Xavier's head exploded. Everyone in the room froze, trying to comprehend the moment. Jake was already in motion, dropping to the floor to grab Darius's gun. As he wrapped his hand around the butt, his brain registered the sound of the glass in the bay window shattering and the distant crack of a rifle. As Xavier's body fell to the floor, Jake spun and trained the sight on the Mexican who shot Darius.

Jake squeezed the trigger twice and caught the Mexican in the chest and throat.

By the time Xavier's body thumped to the ground, the study was filled with the deafening roar of gunfire, a haze of smoke, and the acrid smell of blood.

CHAPTER FIFTY-THREE

Jake loved Star Wars. The original trilogy was the best but the last three to wrap up the series were great as well. Nobody thought the prequels were any good, and anyone who did was full of shit. Saying you liked Jar Jar Binks was worthy of a punch in the mouth. Jake thought he'd make a good Jedi because, if nothing else, he could follow Obi Wan Kenobi's advice—*Let go of your conscience self and act on instinct.*

It was sad to say he was somewhat accustomed to fire fights in close quarters. Time slowed. To the point where Jake could count off the milliseconds on his fingers. The shouts of those in the room sounded like someone screaming in a fully-enclosed motorcycle helmet while underwater. His targets lit up as if by spotlight on a dark background. He moved and fired, rolled and blasted non-stop until the bad guys were dead. The rest could be sorted out later.

By the time the Mexican hit the floor, Jake was already squeezing the trigger of Frost's Glock 19, sweeping to his right, his bullets flying over the diving form of Diaz and slamming into the henchman by the window. He'd put two shots into one guy and three more shots into the other. The standard magazine of the Glock 19 held fifteen rounds, but he had no idea how many Frost would have loaded his with and didn't have the time to stop and count. He squeezed off two more shots, then nothing. Empty.

Bullets ripped through the sofa next to Jake as the Mexican in the far corner let loose with the MP7. Jake dove to the floor and rolled to his right, taking cover behind the bar. Shells crashed into the thick wood and took out the bottles and shelves above him as the muzzle of the machine pistol climbed. Glass shards rained down, slicing into his face. Three shots sounded and the machine pistol stopped, followed by a crash of glass which he envisioned as one of the bay windows shattering.

Jake jumped at movement. Stumpy crouched behind the bar, hands covering his head, eyes wide. Jake had no gun and no ammo. An unfortunate place to be in the middle of a fire fight.

Snell yelled to Bear to watch out. More gunfire. Bear cursing. Furniture breaking. Three more shots.

Jake slipped up and jerked the money bag from the bar, ripping the Glock loose.

"Move and I'll kill you," Jake said.

Stumpy's terrified eyes blinked rapidly. Jake considered shooting him to be safe, but an unarmed Stumpy wasn't his biggest problem at the moment.

With the lack of shots in the last few seconds in his direction, Jake raised the barrel over the countertop and rose, ready to drop back down if he spotted a muzzle aimed in his direction. Diaz dragged Snell by the hair back toward the blasted-out bay window.

She cursed and scratched at his hands, but couldn't seem to get her feet under her. Raasch dove to the floor to grab the MP7 the Mexican dropped when he went down. Jake couldn't see Bear, but his cursing meant he was still alive. Jake ducked as more bullets whizzed by his head and slammed into the wood paneling. Jake caught a glimpse of another Mexican henchman by the bookcase on the far side of the room. How many of these guys were left?

Jake edged forward, staying below the cover of the bar, emerging at the end and cranking out four shots, hitting the shooter with two of them, chest and leg. The man crashed back into the bookcase, bringing shelves of books and knickknacks down on his head as he dropped to the hardwood.

Snell. Jake swung his muzzle toward the shattered bay windows in time to spot Diaz wrestling Snell to the back patio, gun pressed to her head. Jake took aim.

"Jake," she screamed. "Shoot this asshole."

Jake's finger tightened on the trigger but hesitated. It wasn't a stationary target he was shooting at. If it was, he'd hit the bullseye nine times out of ten. But this was Snell and ninety percent wasn't good enough.

Grunts sounded from around the corner. Jake came around the end of the bar where Bear wrestled with the Mexican who had surprised them earlier in the mudroom. Bear was on the bottom but had control of a gun, fighting to bring it up. The Mexican pinned Bear's wrist to the ground and threw an elbow into Bear's jaw. As Jake ran over, Bear braced his feet, bucked his hips, and threw the Mexican off balance. When the Mexican released his hand, Bear jerked the gun to the henchman's midsection and fired three rounds into his belly. The Mexican woofed and rolled off to the side, going limp as Bear scrambled free.

"You good?" Jake asked.

Bear's face was bloody and his hair wild. His chest heaved but he nodded.

Jake spun back to the living room, sweeping the gun to all four corners. Nothing.

He turned toward the bay window to find Raasch on the ground, his shoulder bloody, hand wrapped around the MP7.

"Raasch," Jake shouted over the ringing in his ears.

"Get Snell," Raasch moaned.

Jake did a quick mental calculation of the time since Diaz disappeared. He turned toward the front of the house, leaping over bodies, boot slipping in a pool of blood. He wobbled but kept his footing. Out of the corner of his eye, he spotted Conover lying face down atop an ornamental rug. He wasn't moving. He half-hoped the man stayed that way.

"Bear, check Conover. I'm going after Snell."

Jake darted down the hall and threw open the front door as a car started. The frigid night air blasted his face, like a welcoming slap to clear his head. Two cars ahead, taillights blinked, gravel churned, and the dark SUV tore forward, spinning to the left of the circle drive. Jake scampered around the back end of the twin SUV in front of him, Glock trained on the car, but knowing he couldn't shoot. He might hit Snell. The SUV slipped to the left as it hit Husker Road and blasted into the night.

Jake's heart dropped as he watched Snell disappear, calculating how to give chase when a cough sounded to his right. Jake raised his gun and swung around the front of the SUV and found Snell sitting up, the glow from the spotlights on the house flooding her face revealing cuts and bruises and her jaw hanging open in shock.

"Jesus, Victoria," Jake said as he dropped to a knee.

Her eyes crawled from the driveway to his face. She raised her hands, angry red rings around her wrists. "Help me up. This gravel is biting my ass."

Jake slipped behind her and pulled her up by her armpits. She nearly collapsed as she put weight on her right ankle. "You okay?"

"I kicked at Diaz while he was dragging me and clipped a fencepost."

"How'd you get away?"

"The second he took the gun off my head to try and shove me in the car, I clocked him and ran. Get these goddamn cuffs off me, and let's go get the son of a bitch."

"You're not going anywhere on that ankle."

Jake's eyes shot over her shoulder as the red taillights from the SUV disappeared south down Antelope Avenue. By the time he found keys to one of these vehicles, Diaz would be long gone. It would probably be better to get Sheriff Airy's folks to mobilize and track him down. With the head of the Triad dead, maybe she'd do her job. He didn't look forward to the conversation.

Bear stumbled out the front door, supporting Raasch. "We okay?"

"We're good," Jake said. "Conover?"

A pair of headlights flew up Husker Road toward them. Jake's hand tightened on the Glock, relaxing as the shape of Daryl's truck took form.

Raasch shook his head. "Dead. What about Diaz?"

"Get on the horn. He's gone."

Daryl slid to a stop and jumped out, face tight with concern. "We get 'em all? It was like watching a disco strobe fest."

"All but one. Raasch is calling in reinforcements, but Diaz will be long gone before they get here."

Daryl swept his arm toward his truck. "Let's go get him."

"We don't know where he went."

Daryl pointed to the sky with one hand and tapped his earpiece with the other. "We do. Carl's tracking him with the drone. At least until it runs out of range."

"How long is that?"

Daryl rolled his eyes to the sky and pursed his lips, thinking. "A red ball hair under four and a half miles. Probably not much longer. Let's go."

"Let us handle it, Caldwell," Raasch said, raising his cell to his ear.

Jake put a hand on the truck, throwing on his best wide-eyed innocent look. "Oh, we will. We're just going to track him for you."

Raasch rolled his eyes. "Yeah, right. Pull my dick and it plays Jingle Bells." Raasch winced and turned his attention to the phone. "No, not you, Sheriff."

Jake slid into the truck.

CHAPTER FIFTY-FOUR

Carl directed them south on Antelope and then west on Highway 10. The headlights from Daryl's truck sliced through the frigid darkness. Rather than cram in the front seat again with Bear, Jake shoved tools and papers to the side and jammed himself in the backseat. When he plopped onto the seat, a puff of dirt rose up and made him sneeze.

"Sorry for the mess," Daryl said as he slammed his door shut. "Maid's on vacation this week."

As the dust settled, the smell of wintergreen chew and grease wafted around Jake. Ralph Lauren should bottle the scent and call it Redneck Wonderland.

Daryl tore down the driveway as Bear yanked the door closed. He gunned the engine and fishtailed down the gravel of Husker Road, Bear fighting to put on a seatbelt and Jake hanging on for dear life in the back after discovering the seatbelts were buried.

"You doin' all right back there?" Bear asked as Daryl turned down Antelope. A smoother ride.

"You're going on a diet this week," Jake said, wiping his hands on his jeans. Something greasy coated his palms. "No way I should have to take the backseat because you're too goddamn fat to fit."

"I'm not fat. I'm festively plump."

"Your arteries are plump."

Bear shouted over his shoulder. "Keep quiet back there or I'll turn this car around and we'll go straight home."

"Promise?"

Daryl grinned. "I'm really starting to like you guys."

Carl belted out over Daryl's cell phone. "He's still headed west toward Glenwood Corners. I lost my range on the drone."

"Hope Tracy flies home to you this time," Daryl said.

"Raasch better hope she does, or he owes me a grand. Keep me on the line. I wanna hear what happens."

Jake called Raasch's cell and put him on speaker. "We're heading west on...what's this road?"

"Highway 10, just past Buffalo Ridge," Daryl called out.

"How far ahead of you is Diaz?" Raasch asked.

"A few miles. Assuming he's still heading west. He could've turned up any one of these side roads."

Bear swung his head with each road they passed. "I've been lookin' but no sign of taillights or dust. I don't know that he'd want to risk some random road."

"And he can't know for sure we're this close on his ass."

"Keep heading west," Raasch said. "We've got a guy at Glenwood with his eyes peeled."

"What's Glenwood?" Bear asked.

"Gas station slash convenience store," Carl said through the speaker. "Daryl, grab me some Coors on your way back, would you?"

Raasch popped back on, excited. "Got him. Black SUV just went through the roundabout and heading south on Second Avenue toward town. Was moving fast until he saw the patrol car."

"Tail him, but don't light him up," Jake said.

"This ain't my first rodeo, Caldwell. I found some keys on one of the dead guys and am heading your way."

"Anybody else with a heartbeat at Frost's house?"

"Stumpy," Raasch said. "But I cuffed him to the bar. He ain't goin' anywhere."

"At least he'll have something to drink," Bear said.

They swung through the roundabout, Glenwood Corners zipping by on their right.

Daryl gunned the truck south and said, "Don't let me forget about Carl's beer. I owe him."

"What for?"

"I bet him you'd get your asses shot off at the house. I was wrong."

Jake reached forward and patted Daryl on the shoulder. "I'm assuming you took out Xavier?"

"Hell of a shot, wasn't it?" Daryl asked. "In fact, Carl bet me I couldn't make it. Maybe we're even on the beers."

CHAPTER FIFTY-FIVE

"You guys have eyes on him?" Raasch asked through the phone.

Daryl managed to close the distance between them and Diaz, now trailing fifty yards back with the Kearney PD car in between them. They'd made it to the mall, the 39th Street intersection looming ahead.

"We got him," Jake said. "He's playing it cool."

"My guy says Diaz is checking his mirrors like he's gettin' nervous."

"He's speeding up a bit," Daryl said.

Raasch said, "I'll tell my guy to peel off and you stay on him. Let me know if he changes course. We've got a unit coming up from the south."

The Kearney PD car turned east. Daryl closed the distance to thirty yards. As they passed 39th Street, the cop car turned around and headed back their way. Diaz increased his speed.

"Where the hell is this guy going?" Daryl asked.

"Maybe he has another car or more cartel members stashed somewhere?" Bear offered.

Raasch's voice crackled over the speaker. "Keep

following him. Airy has units ready to pounce."

What was Diaz doing? He'd been involved in a shootout, tried to kidnap a federal agent, and now cruised through town a few miles an hour above the speed limit. It didn't make sense. Bear could be right. He had another car stashed somewhere, maybe their hotel. But why would they have another car? There was like six of them in a couple of SUVs.

"Maybe he's lost," Daryl offered. "Navigation sent him this way?"

"Or he's headed toward the hotels," Jake offered. "Maybe to pick up someone or something before he heads out."

"Makes sense," Bear said. "I can't think of any other reason. But where is he heading out to? Assuming he's not driving back to Mexico."

Raasch spoke up. "Got units heading out of downtown coming your way. I'm closing in."

"Don't make it a goddamn parade of lights and sirens," Jake said. "We don't want to spook him."

As if on cue, a Kearney patrol car approached from the other side of the road. The cop behind the wheel craned his neck as he tracked the SUV as it passed. By the time he passed Daryl's truck, the lights and sirens lit up the night and he spun around to the southbound lane and tore toward them. Ahead, Diaz's SUV shot forward.

"Son of a bitch," Jake said. "Raasch, one of your cops just blew the tail."

"I see you guys ahead. Bet it was that asshole Curtis."

Daryl's pickup roared as he chased after Diaz. The Kearney patrol car gained ground and passed them on the right, just missing the back of an elderly couple in a sedan. He avoided it by cutting off Daryl's truck.

"It's Curtis, alright," Daryl spat, teeth grinding together. "The testosterone ridden prick always was wound too tight."

Diaz wove through the traffic, crossing to the wrong side a couple of times, causing cars to swerve out of the way. An old, blue Camaro and a rusted pickup truck slammed head-on in a twisted thunk of metal and broken glass. A small red SUV jerked left, hopped the curb, and took out a light pole. Curtis weaved around the carnage, but Daryl wasn't as lucky. His front bumper clipped one of the cars and the truck spun, sending Jake crashing against the door. Raasch whipped around them in the bad guy's other SUV as Daryl revved the truck back south.

Ahead, Diaz accelerated then pumped the brakes. The car drifted sideways and came to a rest blocking both southbound lanes. Curtis's squad car closed in. Though fifty yards back, Jake spotted the driver's side window drop and Diaz raising a gun. Sparks spit into the night, bullets shattering the bar lights on Curtis's patrol car. It careened to the right, taking Raasch's car out with it into a thankfully empty parking lot. Stray bullets peppered the front frame and windshield of Daryl's truck. Daryl slammed on the brakes, hard enough to shoot Jake's upper half through the bench seat opening and carve a seat belt strap mark on Bear's chest. By the time Jake sat up, Diaz was already southbound in the SUV.

"Go," Bear yelled. "Get that asshole."

Daryl pressed the gas pedal to the floor and the truck rocked forward. "I just got this thing painted, too."

At 25th Street, Diaz ran a red light. Two pickups

swerved to miss him and crashed into each other, one coming to a stop in the middle of the street, the other careening into a light pole that toppled across the street.

Daryl whipped around the red-faced drivers who stood in the street screaming obscenities in Diaz's direction. Daryl's truck lurched as an unhealthy rattling emanated from under the hood. Diaz started to stretch the distance between them.

"There any hotels this way?" Bear asked.

"None. I don't know where he's going," Daryl said. "But if he's ruined my truck, I'm gonna beat his ass."

Jake called out their location to Raasch, an array of blue and whites flashing through the back window. It looked like the whole police force was en route. The question was where were they going? If Diaz had another car stashed or was picking up someone or something at one of the hotels, his plan was shot. He was going to Plan B—escape.

"Daryl," Jake said. "Where would someone land in a private plane?"

The knocking sound under the hood grew louder. Jake thought he smelled smoke as they zoomed past N. Avenue.

"Kearney Regional Airport. You think that's where he's headin'?"

"Where is it?"

"Straight down this road. Less than three miles."

That was it. The cartel would have their own jet. Jake hoped Daryl's truck wouldn't fall apart before they got there.

CHAPTER FIFTY-SIX

The distance between Daryl's bullet-ridden truck and Diaz's SUV grew. Twenty-five yards, fifty, a hundred. By the time Jake and crew swung left on Airport Road, Daryl's truck shuddered, and wisps of smoke snaked their way up the hood. Ahead, they spotted the terminal building, a single level beige structure with vertical windows and a funky slanted awning over the entrance.

"If he's catching a private plane, how would he get to it?" Jake asked.

"I've flown on a few out of here," Daryl said. "There's a few access gates with an individual entry code south of the airline terminal, but it doesn't look like he's heading for it."

"Won't he have to get clearance from the tower or something?"

"No air traffic control tower here. Pilots communicate with each other over a common frequency."

A pickup truck meandering through the entrance lane in front of the Kearney Regional Airport Terminal sign slowed Diaz's SUV, giving Daryl enough time to close the distance a bit. Out the back of the truck, a wave of flashing lights from the Kearney PD posse lit up the horizon, but they were still a ways back. This thing could be over before they arrived.

Jake checked the Glock he'd taken from the money bag. Popping out the magazine, he counted four rounds, plus the one in the chamber.

"You have any magazines for a Glock 19?" Jake asked.

Daryl locked both hands on the shaking wheel, the smoke from the hood wafting across the windshield. "I don't think so. Check the box behind my seat."

Jake groped in the dark, his hands landing on a square plastic case with a touch pad. "What's the code?"

"2-1-1-2," Daryl said. "I'm a big Rush fan."

Jake punched in the code and the box sprung open. He pulled out a black finished Springfield 1911 .45 caliber with a four-inch barrel. A good gun. He'd shot one at a range before he'd bought his Sig. Also in the box were two loaded magazines, seven bullets in each. Jake slammed a magazine in and racked in the round. He left the Glock behind.

Daryl's truck jerked forward, something under the hood popped, and smoke bellowed as they rolled into the parking lot. Jake threw open the side door and hit the pavement, running toward the terminal building.

Diaz's SUV screeched around the parking lot, hopping a curb and narrowly missing an elderly couple trying to cross to the terminal. He straightened the wheel and headed for the fence. Past the car, Jake saw a sleek, white jet rolling toward the terminal building. The getaway plane, he presumed, but a ten-foot, black perimeter chain-link fence bordered the tarmac with three strands of barbed wire running along the top. He was going to bust through it.

Diaz crossed the half-empty parking lot, thirty yards from the fence. Out of nowhere, a white Chevy pickup flew into view. Even from this distance, Jake could see the driver's head tilted down to the cell phone in his hand. The pickup clipped Diaz's SUV, crumpling the passenger side rear quarter panel. Diaz's SUV swerved, zig zagging toward the gate as he fought for control

Jake ran past the white pickup, the driver with a dazed look on his face, pulling bloodied fingertips from his forehead.

Diaz fought for control of the SUV, the right rear tire in shreds. He careened toward the fencing as sparks spit into the night from the rim biting the asphalt. The SUV slammed into the fencing pole, dead center in the grill. The fence toppled over, catching under the tires, and the SUV skid to a stop. Diaz's door flung open and the man jumped from the driver's seat. He turned toward the parking lot, raised the pistol, and released a torrent of bullets in Jake's direction.

Jake dove behind an empty minivan, letting the car take the brunt of the shots. He leaned around the end and returned fire, expending a magazine. He thought he saw Diaz spin with one of the shots. Did he hit him? Diaz answered with another spray of bullets before turning and sprinting toward the private jet which had stopped a hundred yards away, the door opening. A man emerged and waved Diaz on.

Jake hopped the downed fence and bolted toward the tarmac, slamming a second magazine into the Springfield. He squeezed off several more shots, but Diaz seemed unaffected. Ahead, the plane waited.

It was white with a thin orange stripe curling toward the engines, the tips of the wings angling to the sky. Learjet 75 Liberty was stenciled on the tail. Diaz limped badly, he was maybe thirty yards from the plane and thirty yards ahead of Jake. Maybe Jake caught him with one of his shots, because he was closing the gap between them.

Diaz still had the HK in his hand, but Jake figured Diaz couldn't have many rounds left after the fire fight. Then again, it only took one to make Maggie a widow. Jake realized he couldn't have many left himself. He'd already dipped into the second magazine, and he had maybe two or three shots left at most.

His legs burned as he closed the gap on Diaz, the Springfield pumping by his side. An ache radiated from his bad knee, and a stitch jabbed under his ribcage. Even with Diaz impaired, Jake wasn't going to catch him before he reached the open door of the Learjet.

Though he didn't have many shots left, he had to slow Diaz down, either by shooting him or making Diaz think he was closer than he really was. Jake didn't think he could stop or hit him from this distance. He leveled the Springfield ahead, the barrel bobbing up and down with each stride and squeezed off a round in Diaz's direction. He had no idea how close the bullet came to its target, but the thundering boom caused Diaz to turn his head. His eyes widened at Jake's proximity and he half-turned while running, bringing the MP7 up to fire.

The pistol spewed rounds which flew nowhere near Jake, but the threat distracted Diaz, causing his feet to tangle, and he crashed to the tarmac. He rolled a couple of times and landed on his back but maintained his grip on the gun. If Jake kept going, he would run right into a hail of gunfire.

Twenty yards away, his lungs burning as he sucked in the cold night air, Jake dropped to a crouch, gripping the Springfield with both hands and drawing a bead on Diaz's form on the ground. He shouted over the whine of the jet engines. "Give it up, Diaz. You got nowhere to go."

Diaz sat up and brought the HK level in Jake's direction. Jake emptied the Springfield into the man, the bullets slamming Diaz in the chest and head. Diaz collapsed to the ground, his arms splayed to the sides of his body.

Jake's heart thundered, his mouth dry. Over Diaz's body, the door to the Learjet slammed shut and seconds later, the engine noise rose and the jet edged toward the runway. There was nothing Jake could do to stop it.

He kept the Springfield trained on Diaz as he walked forward, though all he could do if Diaz somehow managed to survive the gunshots was throw the thing at him. Footsteps pounded from behind, reaching him as Jake pulled even to Diaz's body. The tarmac lights revealed the cartel man's chest was soaked red, his dead eyes gazing at the clear Nebraska sky.

"You. Okay. Man?" Bear asked, a full second between each word as he sucked in oxygen.

"Think so," Jake said, kicking the HK clear of Diaz's dead hand. They tracked the jet as it tore down the runway and disappeared into the night. "Plane got away, though."

Bear clapped him on the shoulder before bending over, hands on his knees. "You're good, Caldwell, but you're not Superman. Close, though."

A wave of police lights and sirens descended upon them. Dozens of doors opened and shut. Exhaustion settled in and Jake wanted nothing more than to sit, preferably with a stiff drink in hand. Bear clutched his side, chest still heaving from the run.

Raasch reached them first. He studied Diaz's body. "Well, this will be fun to explain."

"Have fun with that," Bear said. "I think I'm going to go sit down and have a heart attack."

"Don't die," Raasch said, hand pressed to his bloody shoulder. "I think I'm gonna need a job when this is over."

CHAPTER FIFTY-SEVEN

The aftermath of the firefight at Husker Road and the ensuing shootout at the airport made for a sleepless night and intense day of questioning at the Kearney police station from Sheriff Airy and the FBI who swarmed Kearney. A couple of stiff-necked agents from Washington even joined the circus. Foster arrived the next morning with her boss and a thick folder Jake recognized from Snell's apartment.

She pulled Jake to the side. "You should've called me."

"And let you get your ass in a sling?"

She jutted out a pouty lip. "I miss all the fun."

"Trust me, there was nothing fun about it. Is Snell good?"

"I think so. Once word of the whole Triad/La Familia fiasco reached Omaha, I packaged up Snell's work and delivered it to her boss. She'll get her ass chewed for going lone wolf, but what she gathered will be key to going after the bad guys."

"Snell owes you one."

"Thanks." A spindly man in a wrinkled navy suit

yelled her name from down the hall and waved her over. "Beer next time you're in KC?"

"You got it. I'm buying. Thanks, Foster."

The authorities questioned Jake, Bear and Raasch separately, but the men agreed while standing on the tarmac over Diaz's body to tell the same basic fact pattern. Jake searched for Snell via some funds stolen by the man Conover wanted. The converging paths led to Darius Frost, his father, and the Triad. They worried about leaks in the Kearney PD given the pull the Triad held in town and worked with Raasch to continue the investigation. Once they found out Snell was in mortal danger with the Triad and La Familia, they made the questionable move to rescue her which resulted in a lot of unfortunate dead bodies at Husker Road.

Jake called Maggie and gave her a sanitized version of what happened, doing his best to minimize his role and participation in the bloodshed and focusing on the fact Snell was alive and well.

Maggie was quiet for a beat. "You expect me to believe that bullshit story, Caldwell?"

"That's what happened, babe."

"You know I'll just get Bear drunk and he'll tell me everything."

"Let's focus on the fact that everyone important is alive. I'll be home in a day or two."

"You're not getting off that easy. See you when you get here."

"Ten four." Jake crossed his fingers. "Love you."

She sighed. "I love you, too."

Jake hung up and rubbed his stubbled face. It wasn't going to be a fun conversation when he went back to Warsaw.

Daryl and Carl escaped most of the scrutiny as Jake and crew claimed they flagged Daryl down for a ride. The guns in Daryl's truck were legal and registered. There wasn't a person in law enforcement who believed the tale, but they had bigger issues to deal with and let them go.

***

"Did Daryl remember to get Carl's beer?" Jake asked.

Jake, Bear, and Raasch sat around a conference table drinking their millionth cup of coffee while the Feds and Sheriff's Department buzzed around.

Raasch shrugged. "I forgot to ask. He's pretty pissed about his truck. I have a feeling I'm going to have to buy him drinks for life."

"Did we figure out where Diaz was going before he diverted to the airport?"

Raasch twirled a pen in his fingers. "We think so. They stayed at the Hampton. Had four rooms. Hotel security footage shows a young Hispanic woman who arrived with Diaz leaving in a hurry. She hopped into a late model sedan and disappeared. We still don't know where they got the cars from. Might have arranged to have them delivered to the airport when they arrived."

"And the plane?"

"They tracked it to Kansas City, but the pilot was nowhere to be found. They're tracking papers on the plane but haven't figured anything out yet."

Did Keats have anything to do with helping the pilot disappear? Given his connection with La Familia, it wouldn't surprise Jake.

They chatted for a few more minutes. Bear left to

use the bathroom and Sheriff Airy pulled Raasch from the room. Snell entered, freshly scrubbed in a pair of tan slacks and a navy blouse Foster brought from her apartment in Omaha. She'd managed to conceal most of the cuts and bruises on her face.

"Guess I owe you…again," she said after hugging Jake, nearly squeezing the life out of him.

"You don't owe me a damn thing. What are friends for?"

She rested against the conference table. "I think this goes beyond the call of duty for a friend. Storming the house? That was a seriously stupid plan."

"It worked out, didn't it?"

"You should buy a lottery ticket," she said.

"Maybe. Any news on Parker?"

"It's Agent Milton Banks, actually."

"So he was telling the truth," Jake said. "He showed me his ID, but I couldn't be sure."

"Randall Parker was the alias the Dallas office gave him. Came complete with a criminal history in case the Triad did a background check on him, which they did."

"How long did you know about him?"

She took a drink from Jake's cold coffee and shuddered. "Jesus, that's bad. I read in the file that they were trying to get someone on the inside of the Triad, but I didn't know about him until they strapped me to a chair in that basement. Once we were alone, he identified himself, and we worked on a plan to take down the Triad and get me out. Darius Frost got to me first."

"Where's Parker…I mean Banks now?"

"Nobody knows," Snell said. "He's gone, but nobody has been able to find him."

"Is that a good thing?"

She see-sawed her hand. "Yes and no. He did keep Frost from killing me, but if they find him, he's going to have to answer for what he did."

"So, the money trail disappeared when Juan died?"

"Maybe we'll stumble on it someday."

"You going to survive?"

She pressed her lips together. "I think so. If I get out of this mess with the Bureau, I think I'm going to transfer somewhere far from here. I gotta let Keats go. The crooked son of a bitch is going to be the end of me one way or the other if I don't. Better to let it go on my terms than let him win by losing my job."

"Sounds like a good idea."

She ran her hand along the conference table, the bruises on her wrists jumping out. "I have one more loose end to tie up concerning Banks. You want to help?"

Jake jumped to his feet. "I'd shoot the Pope if it'd get me out of here."

CHAPTER FIFTY-EIGHT

After prying Bear loose from a pair of overzealous FBI agents named Wilson and Packer, Snell drove them to the house where Frost and Parker held her captive. Bear's shot up Expedition still sat in the driveway as she pulled in.

"I see nobody fixed my flat tire," Bear grumbled. "Snell, you have any pull to get those douchebags Wilson and Packer to do it?"

"Any pull I had is gone. Sorry," she said. "If it's any consolation, nobody in the Bureau likes Wilson and Packer, either."

As they entered the house, Bear called Daryl and asked if he knew anyone who could deliver and change his tire. Jake and Snell continued down the hall, dropping down the stairs into the basement. Snell strode toward the green door room where she was kept, standing in front of the chair and the bonds which held her to it.

"What are we doing here?" Jake asked.

She broke her gaze from the chair. "I'm not sure, exactly. Banks treated me well when Darius wasn't around, shielded me from Darius when Darius wanted to beat the shit out of me. He volunteered to be the one to keep an eye on me, and we formulated a plan on how to bring down the Triad. He kept me fed, made sure my restraints were loose enough so I could wriggle my way out if I needed to while they were gone."

"Why didn't you just escape? I don't get it."

She pressed against the doorjamb. "Frost was tied into Keats. Trying to establish a relationship to set up his own network, somewhere far away from his father."

"Darius tell you that?"

"Banks did. Darius stole for years from his father, and he panicked once he learned La Familia was on the scent of the missing money. He knew Keats's bag man was coming up with a load to launder through the Omaha casino. I'd been tracking Keats and the connection with the Triad—"

"I know. We saw the files in your apartment. You did some good work there."

Her face crunched and cleared. "Ahh, Foster. The other angel on my other shoulder."

"She might be an angel, but I'm not," Jake said.

She smiled. "You're close enough."

"How'd you get caught at the money train robbery?"

Her smile melted. "Stupidity. I picked up Vinny's van forty miles south of Omaha and followed at a distance. Once he pulled into the rest stop, I killed the lights and parked at the far end of the lot. He sat there for quite a while, and I worked my way in the dark to get a good vantage point. Frost shows up, they argued, and then Frost shot him. When they dragged Vinny into the bathroom, I made my move. Thought

I could get the drop on them and contain them in the bathroom until I could get help there. What I didn't know was there was a fourth guy in the back of the van. The bastard snuck up behind me while I was containing the three guys coming out of the bathroom. Like I said, stupid."

"Why didn't they kill you then and there?"

"Banks. Once they got hold of my badge and figured out who I was, he talked Frost out of killing me. He might've crossed the line, but he saved my ass. Anyway, I didn't escape because I thought I could wrap this whole mess into a neat little box with Keats inside and tie it together with a pretty red bow. I stuck with Banks because he thought he could help make it happen. Then he disappears. I want to know where and why. That's why we're back here. Thought there might be some clue somewhere."

Jake understood. She needed closure with Banks. He didn't rule out the thought she hoped for some kind of file he left behind which would give her ammunition against Keats. She said she had to let her Keats vendetta go, but it'd be hard to snap your fingers and let go of a quest that consumed over a decade of your life.

"Let's start looking," Jake offered.

It didn't take long as there wasn't much left in the house. It was one pickup load of material and a sweep of the broom away from being shown by a realtor to prospective buyers. While Snell rummaged through the few boxes left, Jake and Bear rummaged through closets and cubby holes. Jake found pay dirt in the master bedroom. Using the shelves as a ladder, he popped a false ceiling tile leading to the attic and found a Nike shoebox stashed away. He climbed down the shelves and called out to Bear and Snell. They entered the room as he blew a thin layer of dust from the top of the shoebox and handed it to Snell.

"You can do the honors."

Snell opened up the box. Inside was a Beretta, a banded wad of cash, a couple of watches, and a folded piece of paper. Snell unfolded the paper.

"What the hell?" she whispered.

Jake and Bear swung around to her back and read over her shoulder. It was a marriage license for Randall Patrick Parker and Lucinda Ramirez dated six months earlier. Witnesses were Juan Hidalgo and Maria Almodavar. Jake thought back to Lucinda at the house in Gibbon.

Lucinda wanting to wait for her husband who would protect her.

Maria hiding out at the house.

The panic on Parker's face and the immediate phone call when Jake told Darius about the drive-by shooting in Gibbon at the trailer park fight.

Parker making a point of telling Jake they didn't do the shooting.

Bear whistled. "He fell in love and married a local. Does it count when it's under a false name?"

"It explains why this place is empty," Snell said. "He wasn't living here anymore. The Bureau set up the house for him as a part of the undercover operation, so he kept it."

"He never said anything about being married?"

"Not a word. You guys know where this Lucinda lives?"

"As a matter of fact, we do."

***

Twenty minutes later, they pulled to the curb of the house in Gibbon. Snowflakes spun to the earth as they crossed the lawn. Plywood covered the shattered front windows and yellow police tape crisscrossed the locked door. Jake found an unlocked window at the back of the house and crawled through, moving to the living room to unlock the door. Snell and Bear dipped under the tape and came inside.

"Do we need to let anyone know we're in here?" Jake asked.

"Nah," Snell said, waving the thought away. "I'm in enough trouble as it is. Let's see what we can find."

They split up and combed through the house. Jake found the master bedroom. Empty dresser drawers hung open, and the closet door was pulled back revealing nothing but empty hangers. The suitcases he thought he remembered along the back of the closet were gone.

"Anything?" Bear asked. "Bathroom cabinets are cleaned out."

"So's the closet," Jake said. "They're gone."

Snell called out from the kitchen. Jake and Bear found her standing with a handwritten note she passed to them. "It was on the table in an envelope addressed to me."

Snell – If you're reading this, you've probably figured out what's going on. When I started this operation, the last thing I expected to do was fall in love. I've seen things I can't unsee and done things I wish to God I hadn't. I had justified so many of the wrongs I did as part of Frost's crew as building a case against them, but it took Juan's brutal death where I did nothing to stop it to realize I crossed a line I can't come back from. At least I was able to save you. The funds from the money train is going to help Lucinda, our daughter and I disappear. Maybe we can do some good with it to make up for all the shit I did wrong. I'm sorry you got caught in the middle of this mess. Don't bother looking for us. By the time you get this, we'll be long gone from the country under new names. Take care of yourself. Banks.

Jake handed the note back to Snell. "How'd he switch out the money bag from the storage unit?"

"You'll have to ask him."

"Maybe he had it all along, and Juan took the fall for it. You going to try and find him?"

She turned her head back and forth slowly. "No. He saved my life. I owe him that much. If not for him, for their daughter."

Bear said, "His letter could put the nail in his coffin if you hand it over to your bosses and they find him."

Snell grabbed a lighter from the kitchen table and walked to the sink. She flicked on a flame and touched it to the base of the note. The flame caught and the paper burned quickly. She dropped the remnants in the sink. "They won't find it. Let's get out of here."

Jake followed her out the door. If Banks made off with the money, what the hell was he going to tell Keats?

CHAPTER FIFTY-NINE

A few months later, Jake lounged on the couch, the spring time air blowing the earthy smell of the Ozark woods through the open window. His head was heavy and foggy. He wasn't a big daytime napper, but sleep these days was a precious commodity, as rare as a unicorn sighting. The remnants of another Stony and Nicky dream melted to the ethos. No blood and no stag tattoos this time, but perhaps a reminder he needed to go to the Turkey Creek Cemetery and pay his family a visit. It would be just like Stony to haunt his dreams with the worst images possible.

His cell phone vibrated with a message. He groped at the coffee table and pulled the phone to him. Text from an unknown number. *Check your front porch.*

He lumbered to his feet and opened the front door. A black backpack rested on the weathered wood. Grabbing it, he carried the bag to the kitchen table and unzipped it with one hand. He dropped back half a step at the contents. Inside were stacks of bills, c-notes banded together with rubber bands. A Post-It note was stapled to a newspaper article.

For your troubles.

The newspaper article was short. Three quick paragraphs from Aruba Today with a picture. An unknown man was found shot and killed in an alley behind a bar in Eagle Beach. Police suspect robbery as a motive as the man had no cash or credit cards. The only defining feature was a large tattoo of a stag on the man's left hand. Anyone with information was supposed to call the Aruba police.

Jake pawed with one hand through the money – forty thousand. He was surprised Keats gave him anything at all. All he did was tell Keats that Banks disappeared with his money and left it at that. After Jake turned down an offer to track Banks down, Keats must have found his own guy.

The tracker wasn't Franco Lunetti. Lunetti was locked up and, given the charges against him, wouldn't breathe free air for at least fifteen years. Jake broke his promise to Lunetti by failing to put in a good word for him with Keats for getting them into the storage unit. No matter what Jake told him at the time, Lunetti did try to gun him down, and Jake wasn't going to forgive his indiscretion. The two lackies who tried to kick Jake's ass in the Glenwood Corners parking lot faced several weapons charges in Buffalo County, at least according to Amanda Hunter, the cop who helped him out.

Jake's swaddled son fussed under the blanket, cradled in Jake's right arm. Ten pounds of insomnia producing infant became surprisingly heavy after a while. He stroked Connor's cheek, Maggie's piercing eyes gazing back at him. Jake planted a kiss on the baby's forehead as Maggie entered the room, hair mussed and mouth thrown wide in a yawn.

"What's in the backpack?" she asked as she crossed to the kitchen to get a drink of water.

Jake crammed the news article in his jeans pocket and held up one of the bundles. It was a coin flip how his wife would react. Since he held their baby, he was pretty sure she wouldn't throw anything at him. "Payment for the money train deal."

It took four weeks to thaw her out when she learned what happened in Nebraska. The heavy contractions during the birthing process seemed to have knocked the last remnants of ice free. He was terrified another glacier was about to come between them.

She set the glass on the table and walked over, grabbing the bills and thumbing through them. "How much?"

"Forty grand. Pays for a couple of years of school for Halle."

He gritted his teeth and waited.

She dropped the wad back in the backpack and plucked the baby from Jake's arms, cooing and kissing him. "At least I know you didn't do anything to collect it. Put it someplace safe. I'm going to give Connor a bath."

She kissed Jake on the cheek and disappeared down the hall, singing about the wheels on the bus going round and round. Jake let out a sigh of relief as his cell phone rang. It was Raasch. They exchanged pleasantries before Raasch spilled the news.

"Farmer found Juan's body," he said. "Buried in a field a few miles northeast of town."

"At least he'll get a decent burial now."

"He won't be alone. Airy is going down. The FBI linked her to the Triad."

"She going to jail?"

"Quietly retiring. The links were pretty skimpy, but there. With the other two Triad guys going away for a few years, I guess there is some measure of justice."

Jake supposed it was better than nothing. "What are you gonna do? Come work for Bear?"

Raasch laughed. "Are you kidding? I'm the local cop who broke up a major gun and drug running ring. I'm a lock for Airy's replacement."

"Sheriff Raasch? Lord help Kearney."

They chatted for a few more minutes about Bear and the baby before ending the call. Jake took the backpack toward the bedroom, stacking the bills in the floor safe. On his way back to the front of the house, he stopped to watch Maggie drizzling water over Connor. His heart swelled full at the sight of the two of them together. He had to admit, he loved every minute of being the father of a baby, even those screaming bouts in the middle of the night and cleaning crap off the backs of chubby little legs. The quiet moments, when it was just him and Connor rocking in the chair as they gazed out to the trees swaying in the Ozark night were the most peaceful he'd ever felt.

"What are you doing?" Maggie asked.

Jake pulled focus to her smiling face. "Watching you two. I love you, you know."

"I know. Love you too."

The front door burst open, and a shrieking Halle pounded down the hall, clutching a piece of paper in her hand. She thrust the letter in Jake's hands, jumping up and down.

A giant red N adorned the upper right corner of the letter. He scanned to the text, and his heart leapt at the word "Congratulations."

His eyes misted. "You did it. I'm so proud of you,

baby girl."

"I'm a Husker," Halle exclaimed.

Maggie wrapped Connor in a towel and the four of them shared a tight hug in the hallway. Jake sighed. Life was good.

ACKNOWLEDGMENTS

There were many fine folks who had a hand in shaping Husker Road, and I'd like to take a moment to acknowledge them. If I left anyone off the list, my humblest of apologies.

Writer, friend and fellow Kansas Citian Barry Brakeville was a great help in shaping the storyline, offering suggestions to ratchet up the tension and holding my feet to the fire when the story started to lag. Thanks, Barry! Next lunch at Jose Pepper's is on me.

Jim McKernan has been one of my beta readers for a long time and I so appreciate his input! I now feel bad for allowing his character to be shot in the throat a couple of books back. Looking forward to sharing some Tito's in the near future.

Uber talented author Jodi Gallegos provided fantastic insights and suggestions. Our Facebook and Twitter exchanges never fail to put a smile on my face. You should absolutely check out her work.

Kate Foster, publisher, editor, writer and friend. I don't know if Jake Caldwell would exist without you so thank you for your continued input and support.

Rebecca Carpenter, writer and editor extraordinaire for her input and continuing to school me on how to properly use a comma. I promise, I'll get it figured out one of these days. Can't wait to read your next book.

For my in-laws Randy and Jere Sue Schroer for grabbing Kearney pics and local information when my memory failed and for Angie Schroer for beta reading the book and making sure I didn't screw up any of the local Kearney references. Love you guys.

Steven Cole at the Kearney Regional Airport for providing me logistical information I needed to complete the book. I hope I got the operational aspects of the airport relatively close!

Finally, to the folks at Wolfpack Publishing for picking up the Jake Caldwell torch and running with it. Appreciate your help!

A LOOK AT: ANARCH ROAD (A JAKE CALDWELL THRILLER)

When former mob leg-breaker turned PI, Jake Caldwell leaves a rock concert with his daughter, they fall victim to a bombing by a mad man with a depraved vision. Jake quickly discovers they weren't the first victims and, if he doesn't do something fast, they won't be the last.

While his daughter Halle fights for her life, Jake and his best friend Sheriff Bear Parley follow the bloody clues and uncover an evil plot to pit the polarized sides of the nation against each other to shred the fragile remains of the social fabric holding the country together.

If Jake, Bear and their friends with the FBI fail, more people will die, and the country will plummet into chaos and a point of no return.

This sixth installment of the action-packed Jake Caldwell thrillers will have you on the edge of your seat begging you never make the wrong turn onto Anarchy Road.

COMING JULY 2021

ABOUT THE AUTHOR

James L Weaver is the Kansas City author of the Jake Caldwell series. He makes his home in Olathe, Kansas with his wife and two children. His previous publishing credits include a six-part story called "The Nuts" and his 5-star rated debut novel Jack & Diane, which is available on Amazon.com and has been optioned.

His limited free time is spent writing into the wee hours of the morning, working out, golfing, running, and binge-watching Netflix, Amazon Prime or Hulu - he's not picky.

You can read his blog at www.jameslweaver.net and follow him on Twitter @jlweaverbooks.